I0667609

THE WARLORD'S CONCUBINE

BOOK TWO

By

PAUL BLADES

Dark Visions Publications
darkvisionspub@gmail.com

All characters and events portrayed in this work are fictitious

Other books by Paul Blades:

   * Available as a paperback at Amazon.com and an ebook at bdsmbooks.com
   ** Available as a paperback and an ebook at pinkflamingo.com

军阀 外家

CHAPTER ONE

While the 3rd floor of General Wang Ku's fortress was reserved for his private accommodations, the second floor was devoted to more public uses. There was a large dining room, a smaller one for more intimate use, a meeting hall, where he held court, a salon, where he met privately with the various visitors to the 13th century, stone structure, a large kitchen, a library and a number of guest rooms. There was even a billiards room where Wang could show off to European visitors the skills he learned while attending the British school back in Shanghai. The guest rooms ranged from the simple to the sumptuous. Your importance to the warlord determined in which room you stayed.

Violet was lying on the luxurious, king sized bed in the most sumptuous of the guestrooms. She was blindfolded and her wrists, bound behind her with a soft, silken cord, were connected to her crossed and similarly bound ankles. The cord that connected them was about a foot long and the position itself caused the British concubine no particular stress. In fact, it was quite comfortable. She had been lying there for about an hour, having been escorted down from the concubines' chambers on the third floor by Li Pao, General Wang's eunuch, the man who ruled the seraglio like a hawk watching chickens. Violet didn't know who she was waiting for. And when he finally did arrive and was done fucking her, she probably still wouldn't.

It was part of her duties as General Wang's 'Whore Number Four', as he had named her, to entertain his guests, not to know who she was entertaining. The other concubines did it too, but she seemed to be the one picked most often. She knew that there was a general animosity towards all things British in some parts of China, dating back to the Opium Wars and the unfair treaties that had been foisted on the Middle Kingdom by the European powers, Britain in the lead. So, she assumed that many of the native men who visited her lord and master took special pleasure in fucking, and sometimes beating, a subservient, English whore. In fact, when she was compelled to attend various of Wang's parties, to display her breasts for the salacious entertainment of his guests or to service her master on her knees while the other diners gleefully watched, that's how he referred to her in Chinese, as, "*My English whore.*"

Violet had been assiduously trying to learn Chinese ever since her induction as one of Wang's concubines. It was a difficult language to learn, especially since she had to learn it from Wang's other concubines, the maids or one of the older Chinese women who acted as the concubines' chaperones. None of them spoke English. Violet had to learn mostly from pantomime. After she had heard Wang use the same Chinese expression a few times when he introduced her, she had tried to find out what it meant. She knew the Chinese word for whore. It was the common word he used when he addressed not only her, but also *Whore Number One*, *Whore Number Two* and *Whore Number Three*. But what did the first part mean?

One day while playing gin rummy with Me Ling and Pu Wei, Wang's young, pretty, Chinese concubines, in the community room of the seraglio, a game that she had taught them to help fight the boredom of sitting around all day waiting for the master's call, she had asked them. She said the words she had repeatedly heard and the expression she had learned which she understood translated roughly as, "What does that mean?" Me Ling and Pu Wei giggled. It was Pu Wei, the older of the two by one year, she was 22 now, having rolled over a year during the winter, who answered. She pointed to Violet, "*You are English Whore,*" she said in Chinese.

That didn't make much sense to Violet. She knew that the phrase pertained to her, but it still could mean a hundred different things. When Me Ling and Pu stopped giggling, Pu pointed to herself saying, "*Chinese whore.*" Then she pointed to Me and repeated, "*Chinese Whore.*" Seeing that Violet still looked perplexed, she pointed to Tatiana, known as *Whore Number Three*, and said, "*Russian whore.*" Then she went around fast, pointing to each of them in turn, "*Chinese whore, Chinese whore, Russian whore, English whore.*" That was when Violet finally got it.

Taking into consideration the general resentment of Britain, and adding to that Wang's particular emphasis on her nationality again and again when he introduced her, Violet came to realize that her popularity with Wang's friends was, partly, at least, based on her heritage.

So, at least three or four times a month Violet found herself being led down to the guest rooms, a golden chain connected to a ring in the black collar that all the concubines wore, after a party at which her charms had been brazenly displayed, or, like tonight, having been selected in advance of the party, lying on one of the beds in the guest bedrooms, bound as she was now, waiting for whoever it was she was to serve. They never bothered to introduce themselves formally, even though a few of them were regular visitors. Sometimes the man Wang was honoring through her use stayed for several days, in which case she was kept in his room in a little cage for his convenience. Sometimes it was a just for one night and she never saw the man again.

Rarely was she assigned to please a European. On those nights, Wang normally brought either Me or Pu or both down to the dining hall. There had been a few. Notable among them was Robert Preston, the prominent, 40ish, English trader from Shanghai, and Wang's partner in the opium business. Serving him was particularly onerous to

Violet since he was the one who had sold her into slavery in the first place.

They were to have been married after a short, long distance, courtship. Violet had sailed out from England a little over a year ago. When she arrived, she found out that Robert had been living with a Chinese tart in the mansion which was to have been their family home. Her boat had arrived a day early and when she had taken a taxi to Robert's house, she found Robert still trying to get her out. Violet broke the engagement and decided to return to England. Robert, not wanting a scandal, no one yet knew of the termination of their engagement, convinced Wang to kidnap her and make her his slave.

Robert garnered the sympathy of every hostess in the International Settlement. He was comforted especially by Antonia Hoover, Lord Hoover's 21 year old daughter. The last time Robert visited, he had announced to Violet their engagement. Robert's father, the Earl of Wilford, was now satisfied that Robert would buckle down and have a family, so Robert's succession to the title was secured, and, Lord Hoover was to settle an income of some 5,000 pounds a year on Robert as a wedding present. All in all, he had done much better than he would have had he married the penurious, 27 year old Violet, and he was very happy the way things turned out, something he told her each time he came to Wang's domain.

He had come to Wang's fortress three times since her kidnapping to discuss business with Wang and to enjoy his hospitality and he always made sure to spend at least a few nights with Violet. The first time, he brought with him Qua Li, the very same, young tart Violet had seen him moving out of his house that fateful day. The pair of them abused Violet savagely for a week, Robert, as part of his revenge against her for throwing him over, and Qua Li, in retribution of having been the cause of her forced removal from Robert's mansion.

Qua Li's satisfaction was to be short lived. At Robert's request, after that first week, she was thrown into General Wang's dungeon to be trained as one of his whores, something that she actually had been when Robert first met her. It seems that Robert was taking no chances on spoiling his budding romance with Antonia Hoover. According to one of the maids, the woman was now serving as one of the attractions in the general's high class whore house in Yeuyang, the teeming port on the Yangtze River that served Wang's domain, and less than a mile from Wang's castle fortress. Robert would have had Qua Li thrown into the dungeon on their arrival, but the thought of having her torment and humiliate the woman who had refused his proffer of marriage was too satisfying to forgo.

As she lay on the bed in the guestroom, awaiting her assailant for the night, Violet was ruminating about how quickly the year had gone. It was a time of great reflection. She didn't know the exact date. Wang's concubines were kept in ignorance of most things in the outside world. There were no calendars in the seraglio. But there were tell tale signs of the imminence of one of Wang's quarterly visits to Shanghai, where he had a number of legitimate and illegitimate interests. The principal sign was the incessant bickering and fighting between Wang's wives, Li Hua and Yu Jie. Wang only took one of his wives with him on the trip. The last two times, Wife Number One, Li Hua, had had the privilege of accompanying him. The time before, the first trip that the warlord made after Violet had become his sex slave, Wife Number Two, Yu, had gone.

So, besides the fact that the winter had passed and signs of spring were everywhere, Wang was going on his fourth quarterly trip since Violet's enslavement. That made it April,

1923, or thereabouts, one year since her abduction and brutal conversion into one of his whores.

Although she had surrendered herself to the warlord in an official ceremony before a crowd of Wang's subjects, she had not been prepared for the reality of being his concubine. Starting on the evening of the ceremony, Wang used her almost continuously for five days in a row. The first night included a brutal whipping to remind her that she was his slave to do with as he saw fit. She had had several more since.

He used all of her gateways to pleasure that first night, but he did not spill himself into her womb. Violet, while not objecting, thought that rather odd. She found her answer on the fourth night of her slavery.

Each time before she was taken to Wang's plush, sumptuous bedroom on the third floor of the fortress, Li, the eunuch, had her make a stop at the chambers of a wizened old, Chinese woman. She had pure, grey hair and dissolved, red teeth from chewing the betel nut. Each time, she had Violet strip and ran her hands over the new concubine's belly and between her thighs. She used her hand to excite her and, when she was loose and lubricated, delved her bony fingers inside like she was looking for something. Afterwards, she painted Violet's love mound red.

Violet thought that this was some bizarre ritual, until, on the fourth night, the old woman emerged from her pussy and gave her a lugubrious smile. She gave a nod to the eunuch who had stood and watched each time. Li smiled as well. It was then that Violet understood that the old lady was in charge of determining if she were in her fecund time of the month. Red meant stop. No red meant go.

Later, as she awaited her master's pleasure, hogtied on his bed, she was trembling with unhappy anticipation that this night Wang would make up for his earlier discipline in not discharging himself in her lush canal. She was right.

When he came into his room, she was blindfolded so she did not see his reaction as he took in her unpainted mound. She knew that he had taken cognizance of it when, after he had stripped and sat down on the bed next to her, he stroked her smooth, hairless quim and uttered a self satisfied phrase in Chinese.

Violet counted that night as the night that she really became Wang's whore. The first three nights, he had used her either with her hands bound to a ring in the headboard of his bed, or affixed behind her back. This night, after he had finished his ritualistic caressing of her helpless, bound body, stoking the flames of her lust, he removed her blindfold and untied her hands completely.

He threw open her legs while she lay on her back and insinuated his hips between her thighs. Violet detected on his face the look of a hunter who has cornered his prey. He had fucked her pussy every night, and in two afternoon sessions that she had had with him, but he had not discharged himself in her quim and he certainly had not looked like this. Violet cringed when she felt his thick manhood nudge against her inner labia. She tried to pull away, but there was nowhere to go. He had her leaning back against one of his oversized pillows and the way her torso was propped up, she had a bird's eye view of her ravishment.

There was something about having Wang flood her belly with his cum that was especially offensive to her. She had only made love to one man before she had been transformed into a whore and that had been a little more than seven years before, when she was just about to turn 20. It was a summer affair that ended abruptly when the young boy's, unbeknownst to Violet, fiancé returned from a summer holiday in France. He had spilled himself in her quite a few times during their 8 or 9 trysts. Although she spent many a worried night, she had been overjoyed to accept the seed of her lover. It was like she had admitted his essence to her inner being, formed a biological bond with him.

She did not look forward to the prospect of receiving her new master's spunk in her now. She detested the general with every ounce of her being. Each time he put a hand or his lips on her or thrust his manhood within her body, her mind revolted. She tried to hide these feeling of enmity from her lord, fearful of another beating, but she knew that she had not been completely successful. To her surprise, Wang seemed to enjoy the fact that he could produce such a strong, emotional response in her. She knew, though, that her revulsion at being his whore could never, ever, spill over into disobedience, reluctance to open herself to him at his whim, or lack of enthusiasm at her ravishing.

While her mind rebelled at her forcible possession by the callous general, unfortunately, her body did not. It was Li Pao, the eunuch, who had broken her in during the week she had spent in the general's dungeon below the castle. He varied long periods of cruel confinement with long, patient sessions of drawing out her lusts. Bound and gagged, her legs forcibly spread, she had succumbed almost right away to the agile skill of the seducer's tongue. She realized later that his campaign to debase her had been assisted by an herbal remedy brewed by the same old lady who had tested her for her ripeness. As one of Wang's concubines, she now received a dose of the concoction every morning, and heaven help her if Li saw that she hadn't drunk the whole thing, and, usually, another dose before she was actually brought to service the master or his guests, either in the afternoon or at night.

As a result, Violet had not been able to resist the lust driving caresses of her lord. She knew her pussy was moist and flush, poised to receive him. Her breath had already begun to become labored and she could feel that her heavy, plump breasts had become taut with blood. She looked down and watched with revulsion as Wang inched his piece forwards slowly inside her, pushing her soft, hairless, outer labia aside. His cock advanced by inches and she felt its heat and bulk invading her love channel. Her hands were free on either side of her and she had to fight off the urge to use them to defend herself, to try and push the heavyset, well built, fit man off of her. It would certainly have been in vain and resulted in a long session with a whip.

As the thick, sleek, uncut cock disappeared inside her, Violet began to whine. She looked up at the smiling face of her tormentor. He was clearly aware of the significance of this night to his new slave. Dog owners no longer consider pure bitches who have been mounted by a dog outside their breed. Violet was feeling something similar. She knew that she would never think of herself as pure again once the Chinese warlord's seed crept up her flush canal to mingle with her blood.

Although she reviled swallowing the warlord's spunk or receiving his discharge in her rear portal, these were not the same thing to her. Pouring his cum into her womb would be like poisoning her essence, coating her innards. She knew that she would never feel the same afterwards.

On that night, when her master's cock had sunk to its hilt, he began a slow, rhythmic motion inside her. He was in no hurry and he clearly wanted Violet to be at the height of passion when she received her first vaginal delivery of his creamy, white, viscous fluids. Violet's hands were clenched by her sides. Her lips were sealed tightly together. A wave of nausea passed through her. It was soon overwhelmed by the disdained and unwanted, pleasurable sensations of the sawing meat inside her. She tried to lay motionless as he fucked her, a sin that was a whipping offense under different circumstances, which Violet later found out to her dismay. Wang liked his whores pumping back at him, squeezing their pussy's muscles to accentuate his enjoyment, a skill Violet was yet to learn. For tonight, however, he was content to see the shame and humiliation on her face as she considered the inevitability of the event which so revolted her.

Wang's strong hips kept up their relentless assault. His pace had picked up and his traverses along her fevered canal were driving Violet further and further along the road to completion. Her body was sweating with excitement. Her pussy trilled, her breathing had become heavy. And then, her master slowed his thrusts. She moaned reactively at the postponement of her pleasure. Wang waited until she had calmed and her body had cooled before increasing his pace once more. It was the look that signaled him to continue, the look on Violet's face that betrayed her renewed realization that the event which she so dreaded was still to come.

He went on and on, starting, stopping, starting and then stopping again. Wang was an experienced cocksman and he could go on almost indefinitely if he wanted. Violet was crying; her torment was almost too much to bear.

Then she saw a look of determination arise in her owner's face. He was done playing games with her. She would receive his spunk whether she liked it or not. His pace accelerated. Violet's crisis immediately loomed. Her hands started weakly pushing at the callous man's strong torso as if she could somehow hold back his desires. Then, her orgasm struck her. Her hips bucked and her mouth opened. The throbs of her pussy's walls sent wave after wave of pleasure through her. Her hands, with a mind of their own, clutched desperately at the beast that was possessing her. When her second orgasm began, she circled her thin, graceful arms around his shoulders and drew him into her while she moaned her pleasure ecstatically into the luxurious room.

It was on the verge of her third cascade of pleasure that she knew she was lost. Her legs had crossed behind Wang's thighs, seeking to drive him deeper within her. Her arms and hands clasped at his body as if she were in danger of being flung across the room. His head had been buried in her shoulder as he pumped relentlessly away at her quim. He slowed his thrusts for just a moment, just enough time for him to draw back and capture her eyes with his own. Her mind had been lost in the throes of pleasure and she had tossed aside her horror at her prospective despoilment. When she saw his piercing stare, she recalled the significance of the moment and moaned in despair.

He resumed his powerful, rapid thrusts, keeping her eyes locked into his until the very moment that her third climax tore through her. It was the signal he was waiting for. He groaned with energized pleasure as he felt his cock spasming within her puss. She felt it too, and she moaned and cried, all the while rocking her hips back at him desperately, clutching at his body needfullly, trying to bring the center of their beings together. His hot juice filled her canal, shot back deep inside her, mingled with her core.

When his cock's tremors had dwindled to feint echoes, Wang finally brought his motions to a cessation. Violet was crying and moaning in her shame. He let her go on for a few minutes. Then he forced her to her knees, bent her over and entered her from behind. Within a few minutes, she was panting and moaning in forced pleasure once more. He waited until she came before dumping another load into her.

He toyed with her body for the rest of the night, bringing her up and down the scales of lust at his command, suckling her ample breasts, dragging his tongue between her throbbing labia, washing the stiff, electrified nubbin at their apex. When he had supped at her flesh to his heart's content, he brought her to her back, ran his arms under her thighs, forcing them back until her knees touched her breasts, and plunged himself into her soaking crevasse. Violet felt his cock pierce her deeper than she had ever felt a manhood descend. She groaned with pleasure and remorse. She came when she felt his spewm flooding into her.

Afterwards, as he sipped a snifter of 50 year old, French cognac, he rang for the eunuch to come and get her and take her back to the seraglio. On prior nights, after he had abused her, she had held back her tears stoically, even when she lay down on the double sized, plush mattress in her new room. On this night, however, once her maids had laid her down and dutifully tied off her ankles to her wrists behind her with soft, silken cords, she wept inconsolably.

军阀 外家

CHAPTER TWO

After that night, Violet considered her blood debased and poisoned. Her royal blood, actually.

When Robert had told Wang that Violet's family was within three degrees of relation to the royal family, the warlord had laughed with glee. It was during Robert's first stay. Violet had been on her knees, naked, and servicing her lord's cock with her mouth.

It was the day of Robert's arrival and he and the Chinese tart were in Wang's second floor salon when Violet was delivered there by Li Pao. She had been startled and chagrined to see Robert and his mistress. She had known that they were coming, but somehow thought the dread day still weeks away. Time had lost meaning for her as it was filled with exciting, delirious moments of sexual enthrallment, interspersed with long, laconic periods of lassitude in the seraglio.

"Hello, Violet," Robert said when she entered. "It's so good to see you."

Violet's heart skipped a beat. A void opened in her belly. She fought off the urge to run from the room.

Although Wang had said that he would never speak English to Violet again, he had never said that he wouldn't use it in her presence. The opportunity to humiliate her was too exquisite to hide his comments from her, even though Robert spoke fluent Chinese.

"She's not permitted to speak English," he told Robert. "She would be whipped severely if she did."

"Oh, I see," Robert answered. "That's okay. She was a bit of a chatterbox anyway when we spent the week together in Shanghai. It pained me to tolerate it. I had to, though, because she had me over a barrel. It's too bad for her that the tide turned so decisively."

Violet was standing with her head bowed down, her delicate hands by her sides. She was wearing a silken, red and yellow robe that wrapped around her body and showed off her graceful curves. It just covered the bracelets on her ankles and the 18" long chain that went between them. Li always required the occidental concubines to wear a chain whenever they were escorted through the palatial fortress so that they would maintain the proper gait of a subservient Chinese woman. Also, it added to the hopelessness of any idea of escape since it was hard to run with a chain between your feet.

Her face was made up with a light, white power that made her pale mien even paler. She was adorned with bright red lipstick and her eyebrows had been tweaked until they were just a fine line above her starry, green eyes. Her fingernails, which her maids had let grow, were also painted red as were her toenails. Her eyelids were shaded a tranquil blue. Her dark brown hair was tied loosely behind her. It had not yet grown as long as Li Pao wanted it, coming just a few inches below her shoulders.

She was trembling. Violet had been trying to "bear up" to her new status, as Robert had mockingly urged her in a letter in which he had revealed his perfidy. The letter had been read to her at the induction ceremony by Wang and the revelation of Robert's betrayal had crushed her brief rebellion against her fate. Robert's presence was an unwelcome reminder of her past, all that she had lost, how low she had sunk.

Wang's salon sat 15 people comfortably. He was sitting in a dark green overstuffed chair with large, carved arm rests that looked like dragons. Robert and Qua Li were sitting opposite him in smaller, but similarly decorated chairs. Small tables stood at their sides and Violet had noticed three refreshing looking glasses of what appeared to be gin and tonics, bright green limes floating in them. She stood to Wang's right and to Robert's left. The Chinese floozy was sitting directly ahead of her and staring at her uncomfortably.

"How is she working out as one of your whores," Robert asked the warlord as he lit a Pall Mall and then issued forth a cloud of grayish blue smoke.

"It is still too early to tell," Wang replied. He was smoking too, a Chesterfield. "She is sufficiently passionate. You will enjoy hearing her scream and yell when she climaxes. And her cocksucking is coming up to speed, although she has a long way to go. Perhaps your friend, Qua Li can give her some pointers."

Robert laughed. "I'll bet she could. Qua Li has a couple of things she would like to teach her." He took a long swallow from his drink. "I would like to see her naked," he said when he put his glass back down on the table. "I have been wondering what her tits looked like from the first time I saw them. Of course, they were covered by her blouse then."

Wang smiled. He turned to Violet. "*Strip!*" he ordered her harshly in Chinese.

Violet quailed at the order. She looked forlornly at the powerful man who held supreme authority over her. The smoke from his Chesterfield swirled around his head, making him appear god-like. Her hands went to move to untie the sash around her waist, but when she took hold of the ends to pull the knot loose, she hesitated. She just couldn't do it.

She felt immediately the sensation of a viciously swung whippy stick across her back. "Owwwwwwww!" she yelled unhappily. The pain was startling, pervasive. It was deeply humiliating for Robert to witness how she was treated.

Li Pao had remained in the room to see how the English whore behaved. He had known that something like this would happen.

Tearfully afraid of another blow, the distraught concubine quickly undid the knot at her waist and opened the robe. She knew fully well that if she hesitated any further she could expect more later when he got her back to the seraglio. She swiftly pulled her luxurious robe free of her shoulders and let it fall to the ground behind her.

Violet's charms were revealed for all to see. Her breasts were heavy, her hips sweetly narrow, but wide enough to give her torso a nice hourglass shape. Her belly was slightly plumper than it had been in Shanghai, approximating a different standard of beauty. Her denuded pudendum stood out prominently. Its lips had been shaded with red, accentuating the divide between them, as were her wide areolas and nipples. Her thighs tapered gracefully to her knees.

She wore only the black collar that adorned all of Wang's concubines' necks and the leather bracelets around her ankles. On the collar was embossed in gold four Chinese ideograms announcing her as "General Wang's Concubine." There was a large, golden ring dangling in the front.

For a few moments there was silence in the room as her nudity was contemplated. What had become natural for her to display to her lord and master, although still wrenchingly distasteful, was grossly humiliating in front of her former fiancé and his trollop. An ache developed in her belly and her eyes watered.

"I must say, she's beautiful," Robert stated finally with genuine astonishment. "I had no idea. Now, if she had sent me a picture of her naked before she came to Shanghai, I'm sure we wouldn't have had any problems. Qua Li or no Qua Li, I would have not have given her any chance of getting away."

"Yes, I'm grateful, Robert," Wang responded, laughing. "She does not have the body of a woman one would normally associate with an arranged marriage. It's my fortune that no such picture was ever sent."

The men laughed together.

Violet could see Qua Li begin to steam. Robert had just reminded her of the humiliation she had felt when he had kicked her out of his mansion. Here, right in front of her, soon to be subject to her whip, was the woman responsible. Violet was sure that she couldn't wait to lay a whip across her plump breasts. The girl made a complaint to Robert in Chinese. He ignored her.

"Turn around, Violet," Robert said casually as he crushed out his cigarette. "I want to see your ass."

"*Turn around!*" Li yelled in Chinese, not taking any chances on further disobedience. He gave her a fierce blow of his whippy stick on her rear cheeks to emphasize the mandatory nature of the command. Violet screeched in pain, executing a little jump in the air as she was struck. She quickly shuffled her feet until her posterior was presented to her betrayer. There was a long red line across it. She was on the verge of breakdown. She looked at Li forlornly. He returned only a stern stare.

"Oh, my, you've got quite an ass, Violet," Robert exclaimed. He turned to Wang. "I'm sure that you've already made good use of it," he said.

"Of course," Wang replied. "She still squeals a bit when she's penetrated, but if you get her good and excited before you do, she'll give you a wonderful ride."

"I'm happy to hear it," Robert said. "Qua Li won't let me do it to her. I'm sure I'll enjoy it immensely."

There was a pause in the conversation while all three looked at Violet's long, graceful back and her plump, but firm rear. Violet shuddered as she anticipated Robert's upcoming use of her and what he would make her do with the vengeful, Chinese strumpet. She trembled at the thought. She could only hope and pray that Robert's stay would be a short one. But since he came via Wang's steamboat, there would be no return trip for eight days, the time it took for the paddle boat to make it to Shanghai and back. Violet knew because she had often watched it come and go from the window of the seraglio that overlooked Yeuyang where it docked. That meant he would be here for at least that time. She felt ashamed as she harbored the hope that his interest would shift to one of the other concubines.

She heard Robert's voice behind her. "I was wondering, General, if you would satisfy a whim of mine."

"If I can, certainly," Wang replied in his Oxford accented English.

"Ever since I handed her over to you, I have had a happy picture in my mind of her on her knees sucking your cock. I can't get it out of my head. I'm betting that the reality of seeing it in person would be even more satisfying. It's an exquisite image and would make my revenge against her piquant. And, if you could have her hands bound behind her while she does it," Robert added, "it will complete my mental picture of a slut pleasing her master."

Violet suppressed a sob when she heard Robert's request. Her stomach sank. Her lips were drawn tightly together in an effort not to cry.

"I would be delighted to fulfill your fantasy, Robert," the warlord replied, stamping his cigarette out in the porcelain ashtray on the finely carved table next to him. "Later, you can fulfill some of mine with her as well," he continued. "I would love to watch while your companion lays some strokes into her. I anticipate that Whore Number Four will present a satisfying picture of humiliation and distress."

Robert laughed. "I'm sure that she will," he sad.

Wang nodded to his eunuch who immediately produced the needed strap for Violet's wrists. He ordered the English whore to turn around, tied them off tightly behind her and then instructed her loudly and emphatically in Chinese, "*Suck Master's cock!*"

Her lips trembling, Violet shuffled slowly up to her lord and master and sank to her knees. She had already done this probably two dozen or more times since she had been enslaved a few weeks ago; she knew what to do.

Wang pulled his still soft weapon from his trousers. Violet leaned over and took it between her lips. Tears running down her face, she swirled her tongue around it and slowly moved her head back and forth in order to bring it to life. Her efforts were soon rewarded as she felt the thick meat begin to harden in her mouth.

Robert had gotten up from his chair and was standing by her side so that he could get a clear view of the workings of her lips and jaw. She felt him towering over her and she began to whine with unhappiness. This was a side of Robert she hadn't seen during the week they spent together in Shanghai. Ironically, it confirmed in her the rightness of her judgment to reject him even though her decision had proved catastrophic.

"Look, Qua Li," Robert said. "She's crying. Doesn't it make you feel sorry for her?"

Qua Li spat something out in Chinese as if she disdained the use of English. It made Robert laugh.

He crouched down and brought his face level with Violet's. "How do you like sucking General Wang's cock?" he asked her tauntingly. "When he has his meat in your mouth, do you think about how you rejected me and what a mistake you made? You could be sitting on the veranda of my mansion right now, sipping tea and eating crumpets with the best of Shanghai society," he continued. "Instead of being naked and on your knees with a Chinaman's cock in your mouth, you could be eating biscuits and jam. But maybe you like the taste

of Chinese cock better? I hope you get to like it because I'll
bet that before General Wang is through with you, you will
have sucked him off a thousand times. And each time that he
jets his cream down your throat, I want you to think of me.
Will you do that for me, Whore Number Four?" He rendered
her slavish appellation with undisguised venom. His voice had
become virtually demonic as he progressed through his tirade.
His hatred of her was like a poisonous snake within him.

Violet cringed at the spiteful words, but did not break her
attentions to her master's pleasure. She wanted him to come
quickly so that her humiliating ordeal could come to an end,
but she knew better than that. Her master liked his blow jobs
long and slow. He would determine when to discharge
himself, not her. And she was sure that he was enjoying her
degradation sufficiently to want to make it last.

The hard meat filled her mouth as she brought it to the
edge of her throat on each downward stroke. She tried to
think about other things, about her maids who treated her like
a sacred jewel, Tatiana, who she had come to love, the
beautiful sunsets that could be seen from the veranda of the
communal room in the seraglio, anything than what she was
doing and who was watching her. Soon, she realized, she
would have Robert's cock in her mouth. The Chinese girl
would beat her. Her Golgotha would probably last a week.
She needed to steel herself against the shame and humiliation,
treat Robert and his devilish companion as if they were people
she did not know and would never see again. It was the only
way to get through it.

Having her hands bound reminded her of the first time
they had been tied together, within seconds of her capture.
She had been a prisoner ever since. It made her nauseous then
and was making her nauseous now. She hated the feeling of
helplessness, of powerlessness, that it brought her.

Wang had put his hand on her head and was urging her to produce faster strokes on his iron rod. Violet complied dutifully. She heard him moan and her hopes rose that she would soon be done. Robert snuck his hand in underneath her chest and took hold of one of her breasts. He squeezed her stiffened nipple harshly, making her moan. A new cascade of tears poured down her face.

"When your master comes in your mouth, Whore Number Four," he said, "I want you to hold his spewm until you've shown it to me. Then you can swallow it. I want to see what a relative of the royal family looks like when she has cum on her tongue."

Wang had been lost in his reverie at the hot and energetic mouth pleasuring his prick. Robert's statement jolted him out of it.

"W,what did you say?" he asked Robert. "Royal family?"

Robert laughed. "Didn't you know? Your Whore Number Four would become Queen of England if about sixty people all died at once."

Wang gave a hearty laugh. It would be a good story to tell at his parties while the whore showed off her tits. "You've given me something to think about whenever she has my cock in her mouth," he said mirthfully. "Now she can count on me emptying myself in her mouth two thousand times before I tire of her." He and Robert both laughed.

Wang took hold of the sides of Violet's head and began to forcibly accelerate her attentions to his needy tool. He pumped it back and forth and thrust his hips at her lips. Violet made an anguished gagging sound whenever the tip of his pole struck at the back of her mouth. Her bound hands writhed behind her. Her heart ached at the humiliating picture that she knew she was making. "Oh, God, please help me," she thought miserably.

Then Wang's cock began to dance and throb. Normally, she would have absorbed his viscous emissions directly into her belly, but she knew that Robert would have his whore beat her even more severely if she did not obey his command. She cringed at the thought of showing the white, gooey discharge to him as it lay at the bottom of her mouth. She would do it nonetheless.

The warlord groaned his pleasure as his cock spasmed again and again. His grip on her head had become as tight as a vice. His eyes rolled back and his body shuddered.

Once his cock's aftershocks were done, he slowly eased Violet's head from his lap. Violet kept her lips tightly adhered to the long shaft as it withdrew, afraid that some of his spewm would leak out over them. She didn't want to give Robert any more reason to be cruel to her. The unfairness of all of this, the spitefulness of the men who had power over her, absolute, unrestrained power, made her heart ache and her stomach quail. When her mouth was free, she turned her head to her former fiancé and, lips trembling, tears flowing down her face, opened it. She could feel the pooled emissions lying on her tongue and she shivered with disgust. "I should let them kill me", she thought. "I should make them whip me to death. Anything would be better than this shame!"

Robert looked at the mess in her mouth and smiled. "Very good, Whore Number Four," he said. "Now show it to Qua Li. She has a more than an academic interest in seeing you disgraced and subservient."

Violet gave a little sob as she turned and displayed her open mouth to the Chinese strumpet. Her heavy breasts swayed as she shifted herself on her knees. When she saw the glee on the Chinese girl's face she cringed. She then turned back to Robert, her eyes begging for permission to swallow the spunk. He waited a moment and then said, "Okay, Whore Number Four. You can swallow it now."

Soon afterwards, foregoing the formality of having her redon her gown, Robert reaffixed the golden chain to her collar and led her to his room where, over the next seven days, he and his Chinese whore abused her abysmally.

* * * * * * * * * * * * *

Violet stirred on the soft mattress of the guest room as she recalled that day. Reflexively, her hands tested her bonds. It was a disturbing memory.

Over her year as the warlord's slave, he had used her mouth, as Robert had predicted, many, many times. It seemed, though, that the general took especial enjoyment in using her pussy. How many times had he used her there by now, she wondered, a hundred, a hundred and fifty, two hundred? She would never be able to count them. It was more than five times a week, for on most nights that she was assigned to service him, he used her there more than once. And, then there were the occasional afternoon or morning sessions, forcing her to bend over an ottoman in his salon or library, or even on the rug in the private dining room. Most of the time, except for those few days that she was fertile and those few that her diminishing monthly flow made her taboo, a side effect of the old lady's potion, she assumed, he emptied himself inside her there. He seemed to have a preferred path with all of his whores and for her that was it.

Although he owned her totally, it was his ownership of her pussy that was the most stark and degrading to her. When not in his presence, her other body parts, even her lips and small entrance, which he ravaged almost as much as her quim, seemed to revert back to her. After all, they had other functions unrelated to her sexual slavery. Not so with the sexual organ between her thighs. Whenever she thought of it, and that was often due to the old lady's elixir, she thought of it not as hers, but as his. He had taken total control of it. In essence, she just carried it around for him and made it perform when he desired it.

The rules of her embondment, and there seemed to be many of them, most of which she discovered when she transgressed them and received either a sharp blow from the eunuch's 3' long whippy stick, or, if the offense was more serious, an actual thrashing, only emphasized that title to her purse and other sexual parts had shifted from her to him.

It had actually taken her a little time to understand that fully. Ever since she had been delivered to the warlord's castle, she had been attended by the same, three, pretty, young Chinese maids. They had given her first bath, an event that had helped restore her sanity after a ten day trip upriver spent mostly cruelly bound, alone and in darkness in the hold of a Chinese junk. When Li Pao, the eunuch, had forced her to begin her initiation into Sapphic sex, they had been her instructors. They had bathed and prepared her body with a sweet smelling oil, and manicured and adorned her with makeup the day of her initiation into her present duties.

They had been her constant companions ever since, one or more of the three present with her at all times. They had been waiting in the seraglio, ready to comfort her, the night of her first whipping by the master, covering her raw, red flesh with a soothing salve, stroking and petting her lovingly until she was able finally to fall asleep. Since then, they seemed to maintain a round robin of sexual excitement of her, caressing her body, making love to her, proffering their soft, welcoming bodies for her enjoyment. One of them even held watch over her as she slept in her bed.

During her sojourn on the boat to Wang's fortress, and while a prisoner in his dungeon, Violet had been unable to perform the most elementary human functions without assistance. She would be instructed to relieve herself in a bowl or a bucket and the person attending her would take care of the necessary hygienic functions since Violet's hands were kept continuously bound behind her. This pattern continued after her official induction as one of Wang's whores. There were no running toilets in the house, and necessary functions were released into chamber pots for the maids to remove and dispose of. Whenever Violet had need of the chamber pot, one of the maids would assist her, wiping her clean with a cloth. Even when she ate, her hands bound behind her with a silken cord, one of the maids would feed her with chopsticks or a wooden spoon.

Violet's first clue that her pussy was off bounds to her was when, on her third or fourth day, she had reached for the cloth to dry her sex after releasing her liquids. The maid, the one who called herself Jinjing, the tallest and most voluptuous of her trio of caretakers, quickly stole the cloth from her hand. The chamber pot was located behind a 6' high rice paper screen elegantly hand painted with a bucolic scene. There was no door. Jinjing had been kneeling, watching Violet perform, as one of the maids always did. She shook her head and wagged a finger at Violet, issuing a gentle admonition in Chinese.

It disconcerted Violet not to have control of her basic needs, but the maids were so seemingly happy to take care of her, she let it slide. She had more pressing things on her mind, like how she was going to cope with being a sex slave for the next ten or fifteen years until she was too old to justify her carrying expense, and what would happen to her then.

The full meaning of Jinjing's admonition became abundantly clear after Violet had experienced her first pussy whipping. It was a week after Robert had returned to Shanghai, about six weeks after her enslavement. This night, she was led to the warlord's bedroom by Li and left naked and bound on his bed prefatory to his use of her when he retired for the evening. His use of her had, more or less, settled into the routine of the seraglio with each of the concubines taking their sequential turn as his plaything for the night. This was Violet's scheduled night.

When Wang came into his bedroom, Violet felt that there was something wrong. He usually spent some time admiring her body when he came through the door, but this time the interregnum between his entrance and doffing his clothes and then coming to the bed was longer. She sensed that he was coming to a decision of some sort.

After a full two minutes or so, she heard him move again. She heard the sounds of him disrobing and then felt the mattress depress when he sat on it. He pushed her to her back and began to stroke her bare belly. Because of her bound legs, her pussy was squeezed between her thighs. He was able to just insinuate a finger on its apex. His other hand was on one of her breasts, caressing it. The contact of his flesh with hers was electric. He had fucked her dozens of times by now and all Violet wanted to do was to get the maximum pleasure she could extract from a bad situation. That, and to make every effort to please the cruel man so as to avoid his whip.

Wang was uttering something in Chinese. His voice was low and menacing, like he was taunting her. He reached behind her and freed her ankles from her wrists and then from each other. He pushed her legs apart, exposing her moistening crux to his whims. His hand pinched her denuded, outer labia and squeezed them together harshly. Violet issued a moan of discomfort, and then pain, as he squeezed the plump lips harder. A pit began to form in her stomach, as the man seemed to be in one of his violent moods.

Suddenly, as if he had finally come to a decision, he slid off of the bed and stepped away from it. Violet heard him going into the closet where he kept his instruments of torture and her heart began to pound in her chest. She bit her lower lip and squeezed her bound hands together into little fists. Her mouth went dry and her throat constricted.

When her master returned, he took hold of an ankle and pulled her to the side of the bed. She felt him tying one end of a strap to her left ankle and then, a moment later, she felt it rising into the air. When he did her other ankle, her legs were splayed widely and her rear end was lifted from the bed.

Violet shivered when she felt the man drag his hands along the exposed insides of her thighs. He placed his hand over her sex and began to massage it gently, until, despite her fear, Violet felt her tunnel begin to moisten and dilate. He knelt forwards and his lips replaced his hand. She felt his tongue drifting up her slit until it reached the top. It worried her little, stiffening nubbin and than came back down.

He did that several times. Violet was beginning to get quite aroused.

"Maybe," she thought hopefully, "this is all he wants to do." That was, under the circumstances, all right with her. After she allowed a moan of pleasure to escape her lips, he rose from his task. There was a pause. Violet thought that he was getting ready to fuck her.

Instead, she felt the point of something dragging across her taut, electrified belly. It slid across her breasts and traced a line between them, descending to her defenseless quim. Her stomach pulled in reflexively. When he began to softly tap it on her love button, Violet knew what it was. It was a whip! He was going to whip her! And not on her back, or her ass, or even her breasts. He was going to attack those parts of her that he had exposed, her sensitive, soft, inner thighs and her vulnerable pussy!

Violet issued a moan of dismay. Tears started to well in her eyes, tears soaked up by the soft, black cloth that rendered her into darkness. She whined pitifully as the point of the whip dragged up her inner, left thigh, back down and along the length of her right one. She squirmed and her hands struggled beneath her. She could feel her lips trembling.

Wang said something to her. His tone was challenging, ironic. When he had whipped her that one, prior time, she had mustered all of her resources to prevent herself from screeching in pain or to beg for desistance almost until the very end. Finally, her defenses collapsed and she pleaded and begged for mercy to no avail. Violet sensed that he was reminding her of her prior mental resistance and challenging her to try it again.

It was when the cruel warlord stopped teasing her with the tip of the whip that she started to sob. Her whole body felt sickened in anticipation of what she knew she would have to endure. She knew what was coming and knew that she would not be able to hold back her wails of pain or her pleas for mercy. It was doubly cruel since she would have no warning of when the blows would fall.

The sound of the long, thin whip zizzing through the air and the paralyzing line of fire that erupted across her left, inner thigh seemed to take place simultaneously.

"Ohhhhhhhhhhh!" Violet moaned. The pain was exquisite. Her body jumped, her wounded thigh stiffened. "Oh, god! Oh, god!" she called out in her mind. "I'll never be able to stand it!"

There was a pause and another zizzing sound and the long, thin wand of leather covered steel struck the inside of her right thigh, a few inches from her knee.

Her defenses were crushed. "Ohhhhhh! Pleeeeease! Pleeeease don't!" she begged the cruel warlord as the pain coursed through her. She knew that her pleas would do nothing but add to her abuser's enjoyment, but she couldn't help herself. The pain made her body shake. She tugged futilely against the bonds that held her ankles high.

She trembled as she awaited the next blow. She did not have to wait long. She heard the general shout angrily in Chinese, *"No talking!"* and the fire renewed itself on her left thigh, just below the first laceration, and much, much fiercer.

"Aaaahhhhhhhhh!" she cried out. "Ahhhhhhhhh! Ahhh-hhhhhhh!"

She yearned to beg him to stop, wanted to promise him anything he desired of her, but he had shown her that that would only prolong and intensify her suffering. *Zzzzzzzz!* The whip sang again. This was back on her right thigh. Violet screeched in pain.

The warlord worked himself slowly, but surely, down her thighs, alternating between them, towards what Violet knew would be his ultimate target. By the time strokes were laid just inside the crease between her thighs and her loins, she was blubbering and moaning without relent.

"Please don't let him do it! Please don't let him do it!" she begged her deity in her mind.

He made her wait for the blow. Violet whined and moaned, her hips twisted grotesquely. She was biting down on her lower lip. Her thighs were vibrating wildly. She felt the tip of the wand tap lightly on her crevasse.

"Ooooooooooommmmmm!" she moaned plaintively as her whole body cringed. "Get it over with! Get it over with! Please!" her mind screamed.

Then there was the zizzy sound, and a pain sprung up from her delicate sex so fierce it left her breathless. Her body leapt up from the bed. When her breath returned, she roared a piteous wail. "Ooooooooooooouuuuu! Oooooooooooo-oouuuuuu! Ooooooooooooooouuuuuu!" All the previous insults to her body paled before this one. And then he struck her mons again, a little to the left, just atop her outer labial lip.

"Oooooooooouuuuu!   Ooooooooooouuuuuuuu!" she screamed. "Please! No more! Please, for god's sake! Please!"

she shouted. The warlord's response was another blow to the center of her being.

"*No talking!*" he shouted back at her angrily. He hit the center of her being again, as if for emphasis, and repeated, in a loud fearsome voice, "*No talking!*"

Violet's voice was now in a continuous wail. Her breath whooshed out of her. For a moment, it seemed that she would asphyxiate. When she regained her breath, she resumed her violent moans.

Wang did not wait for her to find equillibrium. Her pussy lacked symmetry. There was a vicious red wound on her right labial lip, but none on her left. He let the whip descend one, last time. Violet's body writhed and twisted on the bed. She moaned deeply, the only response that she had the energy left to emit.

While she continued to moan and whine, Wang went to get himself a glass of scotch. He had enjoyed the experience immensely, but was almost sad that the poor Englishwoman had to suffer so. It was important, though, aside from the satisfaction that it gave him, that the slut realize that he could impose virulently painful experiences on her body at will. Just as important was for her to understand that he could erupt into violence at any time, without warning. She needed to be on tenterhooks whenever she was in the same room with him, or when the door to the seraglio opened and there existed the possibility that it might be him. All of his whores had suffered a similar travail. Some more than once.

While the general enjoyed his smoky liquor, Violet was struggling to resume control over herself. Her pussy burned like it was afire, a fire that would never go out. She was limp and energyless when she felt her ankles being lowered from the top of the bed frame. When they were free, she turned to her side and slumped to the floor. She wanted to crawl from the room to the relative safety of the seraglio. But the warlord was not done with her.

He let her lay there moaning and crying her unhappiness for a while. When he felt that she had had enough of a respite, he prodded her with his foot and ordered, "*On knees!*"

Violet heard the order and, panicked that he should have an excuse to resume her torture, obeyed as quickly as she could. She sensed him stepping near her. He took hold of a clump of hair on the top of her head and churlishly commanded her to "*Open mouth!*"

A well of self pity and sorrow rose up in her, but she meekly followed her lord's order. She felt the soft, but rigid flesh of his manly weapon cross over her lips. She started to suck it assiduously. She had no thought but to please her tormentor. The thought of having to bear his whip again terrorized her. She licked her tongue along the shaft each time that her mouth ascended and descended along it. She kept her lips pursed solidly against it.

The man took his time within her. He rocked his hips back and forth slowly in rhythm with the strokes of her lips. He had her hair gripped tightly in his fist, but he did not use it to force her tempo. To Violet, it was emblematic of his total and ruthless control over her.

The warlord groaned when he came. He pushed his cock to the back of the English whore's throat and let his spasm erupt there. Violet felt his hand take an even firmer grip on her hair. She was holding her breath desperately. She didn't want to choke and splutter, ruining her master's enjoyment, an eventuality which could only bode ill for her.

Finally, just as her chest started into a series of light convulsions in demand of sustenance, she felt the conscienceless instrument ease from her mouth.

Wang left her kneeling there, struggling to regain her breath, as he rang for his eunuch. Li Pao appeared as if by magic.

"*Take this one back*," Wang ordered him. "*Bring me Whore Number Two*," he added.

Grateful to be out of the fiendish man's presence, Violet let Li Pao escort her from the room. As soon as she was free of the warlord's bedroom, she began to sob. She found it hard to walk. They traversed the long, private corridor that led directly to the seraglio, Li holding on to her arm to keep her from falling. Her pussy throbbed and ached. She was still sobbing piteously when she was led into her small room.

Her maid, Lijuan, the smallest and most doll like of the three, was there to take care of her and watch over her for the night. When she saw the vicious marks the general had left on her she gasped and, after helping Violet lie down on the bed, fled from the room. She brought back with her one of the old chaperones who also took in her breath deeply when she saw the marks tiling up and down the English concubine's thighs. She ordered Lijuan to stay and hustled away. When she came back, it was with a large bowl of cool water, a cloth and a jar of salve.

Lijuan comforted Violet throughout the night. She rubbed the salve into her wounds and pressed the cool, wet cloth onto her sex. Every night that Violet slept in her room, her maids, or whichever one of them was there, always bound her ankles and wrists together in a secure, but comfortable tie. Concubines were not permitted to wander around the seraglio during the night on their own. And the confinement served both as a potent reminder of their status as mere property and the fact that drastically more harsh confinement awaited them if they sinned. This night, however, Violet was left unbound, and Lijuan spent the evening stroking and comforting her.

The next morning, Violet was dressed and fed her breakfast as usual. Li Pao, after examining her wounds closely, waived, for the day, his ritualistic shaving of her loins and the concomitant orgasm.

She spent most of the day lying listlessly around the common room. The other concubines smothered her with comforting caresses. Tatiana was in tears. She had suffered once thusly herself and she was well aware of the harrowing ordeal her slave sister had endured. Violet had discovered that Tatiana shared a mutual language, French, and Tatiana uttered soothing words of love and care for her in their only common tongue.

It was late in the afternoon and Violet was sitting cross legged watching the Chinese girls play one of their strange card games in the middle of the communal room. Tatiana was sitting next to her, her arm draped affectionately around her waist. All the concubines were dressed in silken finery, the maids, one for each of them and a couple extra to send on errands if need be, were dressed in the standard uniform, a light green cheongsam style blouse with tight, white, cotton pants. Violet's third maid, Ting, a tall, willowy girl with, like all of the maids, long black hair that descended in a ponytail down her back, was kneeling nearby as was one of Tatiana's maids.

Sitting near them was Qiao, the queen of the seraglio. She was the mistress of the older women, the chaperones, and the ultimate authority when neither Li nor the master was present. Usually, she wiled away her time gossiping with the other older women or playing mahjong and drinking green tea. She had dark grey hair pulled into a knot at the back of her head. Her face was lined with wrinkles. Her teeth were stained red, like all of the other older women's and she could usually be seen chewing betel nuts and spitting into a brass spittoon. She wore, as did the others, a coarse, grey and brown, cotton robe and withered sandals on her tiny feet. She also kept by her side a 3' long whippy stick, identical to the one that Li Pao carried, the symbol of her authority.

Until this day, her demonstrations of authority had usually been limited to certain administrative tasks, like deciding when all the women would go down to the colorful garden that sat between the fortress and its inner wall in the back. She also served as a kind of master of ceremonies, often giving instructions as to which two of the concubines, or maids, or combinations of the two, were going to provide the afternoon's entertainment by coupling, naked, in the center of the communal room while all the other women watched. Her duties included inspecting the concubines before they were brought down to one of Wang's many parties and doling out severe punishment to the maid who had not properly prepared her charge. She possessed the only key, other than in the possession of Li Pao or the master, to the door that led to the corridor outside and to the passageway to the master's bedroom. She was ever present, abandoning her post only when all the concubines had been put to bed.

On this day, Violet was watching the card game of the two Chinese slaves. She turned when the door to the seraglio opened. It was the general. All of the women stopped whatever they were doing, got to their knees and pressed their foreheads to the floor. Violet's stomach soured when she saw him. As she kowtowed, waiting for the disclosure of her lord's purpose in visiting, her innards quailed and her lips trembled. She heard the warlord's steps approach her. He paused and then she heard his harsh voice intone, *"Whore Number Four, lie down, spread legs!"*

She released a sob of misery and rolled to her back, spreading her legs widely, her knees slightly bent. As she had been taught by the others, she pulled the hem of her green and white colored, silk gown up to her waist, exposing her intimacy and her red, latticed, inner thighs. She closed her eyes tightly and awaited the general's pleasure, sure that he had come to visit more abuse on her.

While it was not unknown for the warlord to visit the seraglio, he rarely used any of his concubines in the communal room, instead, either telling her to follow him back to his chambers, or taking the whore to her little room and fucking her there. As she lay prostrate before her lord, her legs splayed open, her hairless vulva laid bare for his perusal, Violet prayed that he would not vary his routine today.

He stood there for a while, contemplating his handiwork. The lips of Violet's labia and inner self were still swollen. Long, red lines were laddered up and down her thighs.

Crouching down between Violet's knees, the general ran his hand over her damaged flesh. His hand was cool and while Violet abhorred his touch, the coolness was soothing.

He knelt between her thighs and made a close examination of her hairless sex. He stroked it where the red marks were and delicately spread her outer labia apart to examine the damage he had wrought. He held the lips open while he inspected the gate to her canal. It was an angry red. He then drew a thick finger gently along the line of the divide. Violet jumped as his finger came into contact with her damaged flesh. Tears had come to her eyes. She didn't know if she could stand any more abuse. She had thought about throwing herself out of the seraglio window all day.

Wang had no intention of visiting further pain on his English whore. For some reason, he had lain awake half the night, thinking about what he had done to her. It was his duty to discipline her, he knew that, and he did not regret beating her. Aside from the fact that it excited him to see a female totally owned by him writhing in pain that he had administered, how else was she to know the importance of obedience and of total, unreserved dedication to his pleasure?

There was something about this whore, though, that encouraged his sympathy for her. He wouldn't usually check up on a whore after whipping her, but he couldn't get her out of his mind today.

Now that he saw her spread thighs and her proffered quim, his sympathy had turned to lust. He was wearing a silk robe with blue, black and red, rococo style dragons on a field of green. He cast it off and let it drop to the floor.

He had noted her flinch as his finger came into contact with her damaged flesh and knew that he would have to be gentle with her. He leaned over and planted a soft kiss on her pudendum. He gently rested his hands on her tortured thighs and let the tip of his tongue drag softly between the swollen, reddened labial lips. Softly and gently, he lapped at her sex. He tickled the small digit at the top and delved his tongue further and further, by tiny increments, inside her each time it traveled along the delightful crevasse which beckoned him.

Violet, at first, cringed as she felt the cruel man's tongue press between her love lips. Slowly, but surely, though, her passions began to rise. She had not been held exempt from the lust provoking potion today and she had not had any release from its effects. All day, she had squirmed and burned. Now, to her dismay, the last person in the world she wanted to ignite her passions was delving his hot tongue inside her, reaping the reward of her prior self control.

The English concubine raised her arm and laid it across her eyes, trying to block out what was being done to her. She was conscious of the presence of all the other women in the room, all of them observant of what the warlord was doing to her. What more proof would they need of her sluttish nature than to see and hear her succumb to the ministrations of the man who had whipped her so cruelly not even twenty four hours ago? While she had often moaned in lust while engaged in a Sapphic embrace before the small audience of females, submitting to the lord's cock before them was different. It was a clear and unequivocal demonstration of her submission to him.

When the warlord had spread her labial lips and inspected her, she felt as if he were a little boy coming to see whether he had done any permanent damage to a toy that he had abused the day before. Not her, but her conch. That was the part of her that was of most interest to him. As his tongue pierced her inner self, she cursed her miserable fate even while she felt her blood begin to rise.

When she moaned, Wang's cock twinged. He was hard and his prick was needy. He continued to lick her sweet slit until her labia were fully dilated and the flower of her puss was wet and hot. He rose from his task and crept up until his torso was leaning over hers. Her brilliantly colored dress was mashed around her hips. Her breasts were soft, shimmering mounds under the silken fabric. Her head was back, exposing her long, luscious neck. A graceful arm was covering her impassioned face. Leaning on his left hand, he took hold of his rigid tool and positioned it at her gate, the tip just protruding inside.

Violet moaned as she felt the cock demand entrance to her inner place. She began to cry as she anticipated the pain that this brutal man was going to cause her. She lifted her knees anxiously and dug her heels into the soft, thick carpet.

Wang was aware of his slave's apprehension. He pressed forward slowly, incrementally, parting her inner lips bit by bit. He was not heedless of her pain, but was overwhelmed with the need to penetrate her, to be inside her.

She moaned as he slid himself deeper and deeper. Her left hand, the one that wasn't covering her face, instinctively pressed against the large man's hip, weakly trying to slow his penetration. Her pussy was suffused with pain, but, at the same time, welcomed the bulk and heat of his instrument. It was flush with her juices. Her heart was beating wildly in her chest. Her breasts had become tense and her nipples tingled. Her left hand abandoned its almost pathetic attempt at resistance and she spread her palm across her tormentor's lower back, feeling the heat and strength of his flesh.

Once the warlord had buried his cock to the hilt inside her, he began a slow, almost imperceptible motion of his hips. Violet moaned as her body was filled with an agonizing mixture of exquisite pleasure and pain. She took her right arm off of her face and circled it around the man's broad back, letting it lay listlessly on top. Slowly, but surely, his hip's motions increased in velocity. Soon, he was plunging in and out of her at a regular, but gentle pace. She could feel her orgasm rising from deep inside her. She cursed herself for her wantonness even as her body craved release. "Ohhhhhhhh! Ohhhhhhhhhh!" she moaned loudly. Her voice echoed off of the walls. She could not remove from her mind the fact of her display of lust before the other women in a circumstance where she should be rebelling against his callous use of her. It seemed that her need for her lord's cock trumped her body's need to be free from abuse and pain. Even as she felt her passions break from their containment, her bruised pussy burned.

"Ahhhhhhh! Ahhhhhhh! Ahhhhhhhhhh!! Ahhhhhhhhhh!" she called out into the room, her voice growing louder with each throbbing contraction of her womb. Her hips bucked and her legs thrashed. Her arms gripped her evil lover tightly. When his lips found hers, she welcomed them and intermingled her tongue with his. His motions continued and when she came the second time, she squealed and groaned animalistically. He roared as his cock sprang to life, jetting his hot cum inside her.

As it did each time he emptied himself there, a wave of self loathing passed through Violet, knowing that her inner self was just that much more despoiled, polluted by his seed. Her feelings of remorse and regret did nothing however, to dampen the unrestrained enjoyment of the pleasure that he brought her.

The general allowed himself to linger in his slut's hot pussy while his aftershocks wound down. He could feel her post coital tremors clench at his prick again and again, a little softer each time until they faded away.

He knew that he was treading on dangerous ground. Lust was one thing, but the sensation of completeness that he felt as he remained joined to the panting, still moaning slut was something else. He feared that he would grow to want her too much. His philosophies taught that all things were ephemeral, unreal, wisps of smoke. To need and want something or someone too much was foolish and weak. He was not foolish and weak. He was the master of literally all the land that he could survey from the upper floors of his hilltop fortress and more. He commanded an army, a horde of servants, slaves, minions, three whorehouses within walking distance, and, yes, a quarto of concubines, each one with a pussy as soft and inviting as hers, not to mention two beautiful wives. To feel any emotion for her was to undermine everything that he was. She was just a whore, a slut, and an English one at that.

Wang shook off the spell that his slave had cast over him. He slipped his softened prick from her womb and rose to his knees and then to his feet. He looked down at the flesh that he had conquered. He would need to be careful around this witch, he thought. Perhaps the old woman had a spell that could protect him.

Donning his robe once more, he uttered a command. *"Whore Number Three, come with me!"* The Russian whore would serve as the expiator of his obsession with the English one's flesh. He strode from the room, the terrified, blond haired concubine trailing meekly close behind him.

Violet laid there quietly crying for a long time. In many ways, this rape had been worse than all the others that had come before. She closed her eyes tightly, not wanting to look into the faces of the women she had disgraced herself in front of. Her pussy burned. She reached her hand down to comfort it.

"Whack!" Intense, sharp pain arose from her wrist. She looked up, alarmed. She pulled her hand back from her loins. It was the old woman, Qiao, the harsh, coarse headmistress of this strange gnyceum. She had struck Violet's hand viciously. She was staring down at her and was barking some command that Violet had never heard before.

Violet tried to edge away from her. Unconsciously, her hand began to descend once more to her damaged purse. The old woman became red in the face. She swiftly brought the whippy stick down on her wrist once more, shouting the same expletive again and again. She whipped her shoulder, her arm, and when Violet turned away from her, her back and her rear.

Violet was sobbing madly, striving desperately to discern what sin she had committed. The old lady barked a command to the maids who seemingly all swooped down on Violet as one. They took hold of her arms and legs and spread her out on the floor. Qiao towered over her. She barked an order to Ting, Violet's maid, who was holding her right wrist. Ting forced Violet's hand over her quim. Qiao struck it viciously. "*No touching!*" she yelled in Chinese. She gave Ting another order and the trembling, young girl brought Violet's hand to her breast. Qiao smacked her hand harshly once more. "*No touching!*" she screamed again.

Violet's hand was paralyzed with pain. She cried out. The demonstration had been sufficient, more than sufficient for her to understand what the old lady meant. "*No touching!*" Her sex and her breasts were off limits to her. Parts of her body had been taken away. She sobbed and cried from the pain and the aching feeling she felt inside her to learn that she had lost one more basic freedom.

The old harpy was not done. She took the whippy stick and poked it harshly at Violet's sex. *"Lord Wang's pussy!"* she cried and struck the already wounded flesh harshly. Violet howled. The old lady pointed the stick at her breasts. Violet cringed as she anticipated what was coming. *"Lord Wang's breasts!"* she shouted and laid the stick across Violet's tender mounds. Only the fact that they were still covered with her thin, silk dress assuaged the impact. Violet moaned with distress.

The young woman panicked when she felt the stick tap across her lips. She saw the fury in the old woman's eyes. *"Lord Wang's mouth!"* she shouted. She raised her stick back and hesitated as if having second thoughts about striking her there. Instead, she barked another command to the maids who deftly rolled Violet to her belly. The stick tapped against her naked rear cheeks. *"Lord Wang's ass!"* she yelled and brought the stick down brutally.

Violet moaned form the pain. She was sobbing piteously. She heard the old woman issue another command and the maids brought Violet again to her back. The woman stared at her sternly, almost maniacally. *"No touch pussy! No touch breasts! No touch mouth! No touch ass! Understand?"*

Violet nodded her head dolefully. Twice in the same day, the relative safety and tranquility of the seraglio had been disturbed. To see the old hag erupt like that was like discovering a monster in their midst. In her misery, Violet tried to parse the logic of why she was allowed, even encouraged to stroke and caress the very same body parts on her sister concubines and not her own. Then it became clear. By stroking and kissing the other concubines to pleasure, she was serving her lord by making them more passionate and lustful. By stroking herself, she was serving only her own needs which were, of course, inconsequential. Her body had been stolen in a very real sense. It existed, literally, only to serve her lord.

To emphasize the imperative nature of her ruling, Qiao ordered the maids to bind Violet's hands behind her back. She spent the rest of the day that way, even through dinner and until bed time. When Qiao calmed down, Pu and Me came to her and kissed and caressed her, holding her tight. Ting, her maid, produced a jar of salve and applied it to her still burning gash.

The next morning, Li gave her a double dose of the lust producing concoction. Violet, overwhelmed with a passionate need, made love with her sisters and her maids all throughout the day.

军阀 外家

CHAPTER THREE

Violet gave a start as the door to the guest room finally opened. She heard it close and then the sound of heavy footsteps as they slowly crossed the thick, oriental rug. She felt eyes peering down at her. Her legs were bound at the ankles and knees so she could not spread them for the enjoyment of her suitor, but she leaned back, as she had been taught to do, and exposed her pale, soft mounds for his pleasure.

On this night, which she considered her one year anniversary of enslavement, she had been trying to recall how many times her sex had been plundered and by how many different men. At the time she had been kidnapped, it had been only one. Within a short year it had become dozens. If she used an average of four per month, one a week, and discounted that figure by a third for repeat customers, that would be thirty two. Thirty two different men, not including her owner, had entered her soft, receptive channel and spilled themselves inside her. All of the men had fucked her pussy at least once and some had kept her over two or three days. If you added back all the men who had used her more than once, and then doubled it, for her pussy was rarely bathed with sperm only once a night, you would have about a hundred times that strange men, men she had no power to say no to, or to deny them access to any part of her that they deigned to possess, had injected her pussy with their fluids. Add that to maybe 250 times with Wang, a low estimate, and you had, at a minimum, over 350 loads of viscous, white sperm that had flooded her womb since she had been enslaved, almost one a day on average.

And that didn't count the men's use of her other holes, nor the many oral servicings she had given to the general and his guests at the dining table, or in his library or billiards room, or in his salon while the men talked business in clipped, hushed tones.

Yes, she was a whore now, through and through. She tried not to think about it and lived day by day.

Life in the seraglio was able to ameliorate, to some degree, her shame and self hatred for what she had become. She had made great friends with the two, somewhat dizzy headed, young, Chinese women. You didn't really need language for that, at least not too much of it. The fact that they served the same master and underwent the same humiliations and use that she did, although perhaps not to the same degree, gave them a natural empathy for each other's plight. But the one who had become her special companion was Tatiana, the Russian whore, Whore Number Three.

Tatiana had been one of Wang's sex slaves for two years when Violet arrived. She had moped dismally around the seraglio all of that time. She knew no Chinese other than the two or three word phrases she needed to know to perform her principal function. She had porcelain-like skin, large, fluffy breasts and a face that made her look as innocent as new snow. She was only 22 years old when Violet had been introduced to her the first morning that she had awoken in the seraglio.

It was a formal introduction. Her maids, after awakening her and letting her pee in the chamber pot in her room, brought her out to the communal area where her three sister concubines, the mistress of the seraglio and her cronies, and a bevy of maids awaited her. It was a little after the break of dawn and a soft light was pouring in through the windows of the expansive room. The maids had not dressed her. Violet was chagrinned to be naked, but for her demeaning, ringed collar, in front of so many other women.

Qiao, the seraglio overlord, called her over. The maids guided her to her knees in front of the daunting looking, old woman. Her stern look and the deferential way everyone was seated around her made it clear that she was the boss. Violet cringed as she felt the woman's eyes roaming her flesh. The old lady motioned for her to turn around. Violet hesitated. The woman picked up her 3' long whippy stick, tapped her harshly on her bare knee and repeated the order. Shamefully, Violet complied. She circled around on her hands and knees, her bare breasts dangling under her, swaying back and forth. She was conscious of her nudity, but also the remaining evidence of her harsh beating the night before; her skin still exhibited a faint shade of pink from her neck to her knees.

When Violet returned to her original position, the old woman motioned for her to come closer. Filled with shame and anxiety, fearful of the instrument of punishment that the old woman had laid down next to her, she crept forward until her body was only a foot or so away. Qiao motioned for her to lean forward and, when she did, took hold of her plump breasts and held them in her hands, palms up as if weighing them. She made a comment to the cronies kneeling to her right and left and they all laughed. She brought Violet's mounds to her lips and she suckled her teats, one after the other, as if she were sampling her. Violet moaned softly as the hot lips and the firm, outward pressure on them brought a tug to her womb. When the old lady was satisfied, she took hold of Violet's nipples and pulled her closer so that she could run her bony hands over her torso and thighs. She made her turn around again and caressed her rear and her flanks.

Violet could see that all the other women, the other concubines and the six or seven pretty maids in the room, were watching her. When she felt the old lady's hands spreading her thighs apart from behind, she blushed with shame.

"*Head down!*" the old lady commanded, an order that Li Pao had given her many times and one which Violet recognized. She placed her forehead on the soft rug. This caused her rear to jut upwards, exposing her delicate, love lips to the old lady's examination. Violet whined with unhappiness when she felt the bony hand slide over it and begin gently rubbing back and forth across its smooth, hairless surface. She closed her eyes to try and block out the shame at her submissive surrender to the old lady's dictates, and the humiliation of having her purse caressed in front of all these women.

The old lady's finger traced a line between her delicate love lips insistently, until Violet's divide obediently watered. Violet moaned when she felt the finger gain access to her inner self. The old lady made another witty comment to the others who knelt near her and there was more laughter. Violet felt the woman spread her moisture to her bud of pleasure and swirl her knowledgeable finger around it until the small protuberance became hard. She continued until Violet, after struggling with all her strength not to, gave out a low, guttural moan of pleasure. This brought another round of laughter from the old lady's companions.

Having satisfied herself as to the new slut's responsiveness, the old lady rose to her feet, the whippy stick in her hand, and ordered Violet to crawl in front of the youngest looking of the two Chinese concubines. "*Whore Number One!*" the old lady announced, pointing her whipping stick at the woman Violet came to know as Me Ling. Me Ling bowed slightly. She, like the other concubines, was dressed in a thin, shiny, colorful, silken robe. They all wore, as did Violet, General Wang's distinctive, black leather collar with the large, golden ring attached to its front. Violet bowed her own head in return.

She was brought in front of the older of the two Chinese girls and was told that this was, "*Whore Number Two.*" It was Pu Wei. She and Violet exchanged polite bows.

Then Violet was brought in front of the lovely, angelic, blond girl that she had seen at her induction ceremony. Her eyes were a starry blue, her face was pale and sad. Her hair was like spun gold. Violet noticed her heavy breasts behind her silken robe and two wet spots around the nipples. "*Whore Number Three,*" the old lady intoned. Violet, trying to keep her eyes on the beautiful apparition bowed her head in greeting.

Qiao then gave the young, blond woman a curt order and she rose immediately from her sitting position and went to the middle of the room. Violet watched as she shrugged her robe off of her shoulders and let it drop to the floor. She then knelt there, looking at Violet expectantly.

The old lady tapped Violet on the shoulder with her stick and pointed to the beautiful girl that Violet came to know as Tatiana. It was clear what the old lady wanted her to do. Violet looked up at her beseechingly. "Not in front of all these women!" she wanted to say. The old lady tapped her with the stick again a little harder and gave her an instruction in Chinese, one that Violet was to hear many times after this day.

Violet gave a sob and crawled over to where Tatiana awaited her. The voluptuous Russian's flesh was pale and inviting. When Violet came up to her and their knees were touching, the younger woman gave her a gentle, understanding smile and took hold of her hands. "I know what you're going through," she seemed to be saying. "I've been where you are."

For a moment, the two women stared into each other's eyes. Violet could see the vast sea of sorrow that lay beneath the young, blond woman's surface. Her eyes were soft, her skin almost translucent.

Tatiana took the initiative. She leaned forward and placed her small, soft hand on Violet's face. It was warm and comforting. She shifted herself on her knees until she was kneeling up and slowly brought her face forward. She closed her starry eyes and presented her thin, pale lips to Violet's. She let them make gentle contact, her hand still softly pressed against the side of Violet's face. Violet sighed as she tasted the hot air of Tatiana's mouth. The Russian girl's mouth delicately pressed Violet's open. Her tongue probed the inner portion of Violet's plump, red lips. Violet felt a wave of desire go through her. Tatiana withdrew her lips for a moment, uttered something soft and soothing in Russian and then, placing her hand behind Violet's head, brought their lips together again, sliding her tongue deeply into Violet's mouth.

It was as if the whole rest of the world had gone away. Violet leaned forward, accepting Tatiana's tongue willingly. She placed her hand on the younger woman's torso, enjoying the tender warmth of her skin. Their bodies pressed together. The wet tips of Tatiana's breasts pressed against Violet's. They held their passionate kiss for a long time, and then Violet felt herself being urged to her side. Their bodies slowly fell to the floor.

The two women made gentle but passionate love to each other. Tatiana suckled Violet's nipples until she groaned with pleasure. Her hand found Violet's quim and began to stroke it softly. She placed Violet on her back and dragged her tongue down her body, over her belly and down the length of her dilated purse. She took hold of the rigid nub at the apex and teased it with her tongue until Violet issued a violent moan.

Violet's consciousness of the appreciative, female audience had disappeared. She felt like she and the beauteous, blond woman were in a world of their own. She shouted out her pleasure when Tatiana's tongue and lips made her come. She clasped her body tightly against the blond girl's, hugging and kissing her in thanks and then began to return her affectionate favors. Her breasts were taut and filed with milk, to Violet's surprise. She suckled them, tasting for the first time since an infant the semi sweet flavor of mother's milk. She laid her blond lover on her back and supped at her pleasure gate until the woman moaned and called out her ecstasy. They ended their bout, head to foot as they exchanged feverish oral caresses of each other's sex until they were both moaning, their bodies writhing with fiery passion.

When their climaxes had dwindled to a warm, comforting reminiscence of pleasure, the women kissed each other lovingly. Me and Pu rushed over and hugged and kissed their new sister. Violet cried, knowing that she had successfully passed her initiation into the seraglio. There was a comfort knowing that her life would not be all harsh orders and humiliating submission. The gentleness and warmth of the other prisoner whores gave her hope that she would survive.

As she lay in the bed of the guest room one year later, Violet recalled with warmth her loving relationship with the blond Russian girl. Tatiana had been ordered to provide entertainment at the master's party tonight and Violet had said a sad goodnight to her before she had been brought down to the second level of the fortress. She knew that it might be Tatiana's fate to suffer her lord's vicious streak this evening, and she would, if she was permitted to return to the seraglio later, comfort the delicate girl in the morning.

It was coming up to Tatiana's turn to be in milk again, Violet's having started three months ago, her second tour of duty. Every time the master took his quarterly trip to Shanghai, the eunuch brought the other one into milk, giving the present one a three month's rest. The master always drank from the breasts of one of his whores in the morning.

When Violet had been made his slave, Tatiana had been in milk for almost a year. Spurts and dribbles released from her breasts every time that Violet suckled them while they made love. Tatiana needed to be milked at least four times every 24 hours anyway and, seeing how Violet enjoyed mouthing the large breasted blonde's nipples, Li Pao gave her the task of emptying them at least once a day.

Embarrassed, at first, to be taking sustenance from another woman's body, Violet came quickly to happily anticipate her feedings. It somehow felt right to be drinking from her lover's breasts. It was a warm, comforting feeling and lust inspiring as well. They varied the positions from which Violet was fed and whose turn it was to have the other stroke her puss until she came, a delirious, wrenching orgasm. Sometimes, Tatiana would lean over Violet while she was laying flat on the floor, proffering first one breast to her and then the other while massaging and teasing her cunt with her hand. Violet would suck and slurp at the stiff nipples, massaging the breasts so that she urged out every drop. Other times, Tatiana sat in Violet's lap while the other woman suckled her and manipulated her to a series of intense orgasms. Sometimes they lay down on their sides, facing each other, sometimes they knelt, Violet bending over and taking each breast in turn in her hands, suckling at it fervently.

The next time that Wang took his quarterly trip, Li Pao spent the time caressing, suckling and massaging Violet's breasts until, to her amazement, they began to produce. Li had begun giving her a dose of another of the old lady's potions every morning and at night. Violet's maids applied a sweet smelling lotion to her breasts three times a day, being especially mindful of her nipples. She felt her breasts begin to become heavier as the days went on. Then, one morning, they felt full and tight. Her milk did not release that morning, only a small dribble of lactatin. Li Pao squeezed and massaged her breasts until they were emptied out. This happened three days running. On the fourth morning, while Li Pao was suckling her plump, filled breasts, it happened. She felt the release in her breast and her milk begin to flow. Her eyes flitted back as a surge of warmth filled her body. Her uterus contracted and she felt almost dizzy as the eunuch emptied her with his lips.

After that, Tatiana usually had a daily turn at her breasts. At other times, her breasts were usually emptied by one of her maids, Li Pao, one of the other concubines, or, to Violet's dismay, one of Wang's avaricious wives. None of it was ever wasted.

She was as nervous as a cat the first time she was brought down to the master's table to serve him his breakfast. It was the morning after he arrived back from Shanghai. He had fucked her and the other three concubines roundly the night before in celebration of his return. She knelt on a small rug in the private dining room. Wang's two wives were kneeling at the two foot high table. Violet's robe was pulled back at her chest and her taut, bulging breasts were exposed. She was, as usual, of two minds about her serving as a milk cow for her master. One thing that was good was that she could now reciprocate to Tatiana the loving fulfillment that the Russian had given her. Tatiana's breasts were to lay fallow for the next three months and it would be her enjoying sustenance from Violet instead of vice versa.

The bad thing was that her cruel master had taken control of another aspect of her. She had no right to deny him the most salacious use of her breasts. No one had asked her if she wanted to be part of the man's breakfast every day. And she would have been ashamed if anyone in the outside world ever heard of what she had been forced to do. She was worried too, about how Robert would taunt her and the fact that he would certainly force her to feed him when he came on his next visit. The thought of it turned her stomach.

The worst part of it though was that it meant daily contact of the most intimate nature with the vicious warlord. He had just begun to get past the novelty of owning her and she now spent a few days every week where she did not see him at all, or, if she did, it was only to join him in one of his sanctuaries and suck his cock or one of his friends', or both. The warlord would now look at her in a whole new way. That it humiliated her to be forced to serve him this way would be, she was sure, a source of glee to him and would undoubtedly renew his obsession with her use in other ways as well. She knew from what had happened to Tatiana that her breasts would be offered to his guests at parties, or when they took her for the night. Violet hated the idea of feeding the man or his cronies her life's essence, but she had no choice. Or rather, the choice she had was to be sent back to his dungeon to be whipped and raped and tortured until she either conceded her cooperation or died.

It also placed Violet more at the mercy of the eunuch and, even, her maids. She needed to be milked on a regular basis to keep up her production. If she were to fail at pleasing the general there would be hell to pay. And, not being milked caused her full breasts to ache. She would be totally reliant on someone to feed from her. When Li or her maids withheld her use for any considerable time, her breasts would get so full and tight it would feel like her nipples were going to pop off her mammaries like corks from champagne bottles.

Wang hardly took note of her when he sat down cross legged at his place. She watched him drink from his tea and eat a sweet roll. Then, he turned his head, as if first realizing that she was in the room, and called her over to him. He brought her to his lap and, leaning her back in his left arm, took possession of a nipple and began to softly suckle at it, stroking and massaging it with his free hand, until her milk was released.

Within a few moments, her aversion to contact with the large, muscular general was forgotten. She even forgot that she was being shamefully used in front of the warlord's cruel and jealous wives. A feeling of warmth and contentment flowed through her body. She let her hand delicately rest on the back of her master's neck, gently holding his mouth to her breast as he consumed her body's production. He had taken hold of the breast closest to him first. When it was devoid of milk, he shifted to the one furthest from him, pulling her body closer to his. His free hand slid down her thigh and crept under the hem of her robe, pulling it up over her knees. It gently guided her legs apart and found its way to her warming crevasse. She sighed as he found her slit, dragging his thick fingers along her soft slice. He entered her with his digits and began a determined rhythm back and forth until she moaned. She groaned when he found her hardened bud of pleasure.

For Violet, it was as if her body had been placed in a warm bath. It was a feeling of total comfort and contentment. The pleasure from her pussy wafted through her, complementing the relaxing, mesmerizing experience of having her breast suckled. After a short while, her excitement started to rise. She started to moan and unconsciously spread her legs wider to giver her master better access to his toy. She groaned as she came, wrapping her arms around the warlord's neck, holding his face buried in her breast.

When she was done, and her breasts empty, she remained laconically leaning on her master's shoulder. Absent mindedly, her hand stroked his head and neck. He was holding her tightly as if he too was treasuring the moment.

Wang was, in fact, treasuring the moment. He had been drinking mother's milk from his whores for years. He attributed much of his manly strength and health from it. The sluts were always stupefied afterwards, especially if he stroked them to completion while he suckled them. This was something different. He reveled in the feel of the whore's delicate fingers on his head, the heat of her breath on his neck, the pumping of her heart that he could feel in his own chest. He wanted to fuck her right then and there. He placed his hand on her cheek and turned her face towards his. He married their lips together and gave her an impassioned kiss. The girl responded, her tongue lazily mixing with his.

All of a sudden, he felt two pairs of eyes boring in on him. He broke the kiss and saw that his two wives were staring at him and the whore with undisguised anger. He realized that he had done the whore a great disfavor. He had brought the wrath of his two cruel wives down on her. Well, there was nothing that could be done now. She was, after all, only a whore.

Violet heard the general give her a harsh command and she snapped from the spell that had fallen over her. She disengaged from his lap, returned to the small mat that she had been kneeling on, and dropped to her knees. Her breasts were still exposed. She kept her eyes pointed downwards. If she had only looked up, she would have been aware just what she was in for.

Violet was returned to the seraglio. Her maids took her for her daily bath, where they, too, brought her to pleasure. Counting the thrilling orgasm the eunuch had given her with his mouth after he had shaved her loins earlier that morning, she had already had three climaxes and it was only a little after nine o'clock.

It was after lunch that Li Pao came to get her. As usual, one of her maids, this time it was Lijuan, the pixie-like one, had fed her, her hands tied loosely behind her back by a silken cord, tipping succulent pieces of meat or fish or vegetable into her mouth and following them up with hot, strong, green tea. Her breasts were full again and getting sore. She looked forward to having one of the other women, preferably Tatiana, drain her, after which she planned a nice nap in her room.

Li Pao ordered her to her feet. She rose immediately. The eunuch ordered Lijuan to release Violet's hands and to remove her robe. Lijuan did so with alacrity, and then, at Li's instructions, bound her hands back behind her.

The eunuch had brought with him the ankle bracelets and the chain that connected them. He silently, without explanation, affixed them to her legs. After clipping a gold colored chain to her collar, He led her from the room.

The seraglio occupied the south wing of the third floor of the fortress, the master's bedroom, and those of his wives, occupied the north. When they got to the ever locked door at the end of the corridor outside the communal room, Li knocked. The soldier on the other side slid open a small panel and seeing the eunuch, unlocked the bolt mechanism with a key attached to his belt by a chain.

Aside from this main entrance to the seraglio, there were two other ways to gain access or to leave. One was by, after crossing a locked door, taking a small, dark corridor and descending some stairs. This led to the bolted door that would admit the concubines to the main reception room so that they could attend ceremonies there without mingling with guests on the second floor of the palatial fortress. This door, like the main door, could only be opened from the outside by someone with a key.

The third means of access to the seraglio was the corridor that led directly to the master's bedchamber. There were two locked doors one had to traverse. The first was the door that exited the seraglio. The second one governed access to the general's bedroom. Each door had a separate key. And then, again, the general's bedroom was also locked so that any slut who was able to escape down the corridor and gain entry into the bedroom had to overcome this lock as well. Once out in the hall, the bedroom and living areas on the third floor belonging to the general and his wives were closed off by yet another locked door. A guard stood outside this door perpetually.

Guards stood at the top of each stairway to the second and third floors. Guards stood at the foot of the stairs in the great hall. Guards manned the gate between the inner and outer walls of the fortress and also, of course, protected the main gate as well. The inner wall was a little over 20' high and the outer wall closer to 30'. The windows and the veranda of the seraglio looked over a 50' drop to the hard stone below.

The only women who were admitted to the fortress on a regular basis were the maids. Women did attend Wang's parties and his wives had guests from time to time. Careful track was kept of these females. The cooks and other servants were all men. Everyone entering or leaving had to have a pass signed by the officer of the day. The maids lived inside the fortress in their own dormitory on the first floor. Every woman who came and went had their necks inspected to make sure they did not wear the telltale collar which adorned the necks of the general's concubines.

Even so, Tatiana had managed twice to reach the outer walls in vain attempts at escape. On one occasion, she had been servicing one of the master's drunken guests in one of the guest rooms on the second floor. He had 'invited' a maid to participate in their jaunt. He had passed out while fucking Tatiana. The naked maid had been bound and gagged by the man on the bed. While the frantic maid watched, the desperate concubine adorned herself with her clothes. She took the key to the room from the pocket of the unconscious guest and slipped out the door.

There had been a large party and most of the guests were leaving. Tatiana was able to mingle with the crowd and her neck escaped inspection at the bottom of the stairs in the great hall. She passed similarly through the inner gate. Once outside, she ran all the way around the inside of the outer wall of the fortress looking for a way to ascend it. It was unfortunate for her that three of Wang's soldiers were drunk and had cornered a maid and brought her outside to fuck her. When they saw fresh meat, the two who were waiting their turn chased after her and caught her. Once they realized who she was, they turned her in. She spent a week in the dungeon, in addition to suffering several other harsh, disciplinary measures, as a result of her crime.

The second time was pure madness. She was being escorted to the general's salon to entertain him and a few guests. Li was busy with Me Ling and Pu Wei. A young steward had been given the responsibility of delivering her. They had descended the stairs from the third floor to the second. The steward turned right at the bottom of the stairs. He had neglected to fasten Tatiana's hands behind her back or to apply a chain between her ankles. She looked down the stairs to the first floor and saw that the post at the bottom was temporarily abandoned. Yanking on the chain that led to her collar, she whipped it out of the steward's hand and dashed down the stairs. She was dressed in a long, slinky banner dress, and had to pull it up to her waist to run.

At the bottom of the stairs, the blond concubine sped past the returning guard, who had gone for a smoke. She was able to brush past two startled soldiers who were entering the great hall from outside. The inner gate was open, admitting a delivery wagon and she dashed past that.

That left only the outer gate. Another wagon, which had just dropped off a load of coal, was leaving. Tatiana saw her chance. She ran frantically to get past the gates before they closed. She almost made it. An alert guard, seeing the blur of blue, green and gold that was Tatiana's dress fleeing across the outer courtyard, darted after her. She was just about to pass through the gate when he took hold of the long, blond, braided tresses that trailed behind her and yanked her backwards. Tatiana gave a loud scream and fell to the ground. And that was that. Needless to say, she suffered even more grievously for her second attempt.

The steward and the AWOL guard were beheaded the next morning. The guard who had saved the day was promoted to corporal and permitted to use her in any way that he wished for a whole day down in the dungeon.

Li had not made the mistakes of the unhappy steward. Violet's legs were joined by 18" of chain connected to bracelets on her ankles. Her hands were bound behind her and she was naked, something even the stupidest guard would be sure to notice. The eunuch led her across the landing outside the seraglio to the door that led to the private quarters of the generals and his wives.

Violet bristled at being escorted across the landing naked, the eyes of the guards on either side leering lasciviously at her. Of course, who she was naked before was an issue that months ago had been taken out of her control.

She kept her face pointed downwards in shame as the soldier unlocked the door to the north wing. She was relieved when Li led her through it.

Although she had been Wang's slave for four months now, she had never visited the wives' suite. The two bedrooms fed off of a large lounge area. The lounge had a pair of luxurious sofas set perpendicular to each other to form a corner, several overstuffed easy chairs and a dining table, 2 feet off the floor, with pillows strewn around it. The most important accouterment, as it pertained to Violet today, was a six foot long bar that stuck out from the wall. It had a chain with leather bracelets on the end dangling from it. When Violet entered the room, the bracelets were empty.

Wang's wives, Li Hua and Yu Ji, were sitting on one of the couches drinking tea, watching two of their maids make a two backed beast on the soft rug in front of them. Life as Wang's official mates was largely a boring one, especially after so many years. Yu had been married off to the general when she was only 16, the same year that Wang wrested control of his kingdom from his predecessor. She was now 36. She had given Wang three sons and two daughters. The sons were attending the British school in Shanghai and the daughters, 14 and 16, were being educated in the Christian school in Yeuyang run by European nuns. Wang insisted that they be kept away from the dissolute activities of the fortress as much as possible.

Li Hua was 45. She had been married to Wang when he was still a lowly lieutenant in the prior warlord's army some 30 years ago. She too had given Wang sons, three of them. Two of them ran rackets for Wang in Shanghai and the other managed one of his estates. The two daughters of their union were married off long ago to prosperous merchants.

Wang's wives had very little to do. Mostly, they drank gin, smoked opium and fucked their maids. Occasionally, Wang still visited them, the younger Yu more than Li. They were permitted, from time to time, to visit the wives of some of the other prominent families in Wang's empire where they drank gin, smoked opium and fucked their maids. Those wives, in return, often visited the fortress where they were similarly entertained.

Li and Yu were permitted to amuse themselves with Wang's concubines as long as they did not go overboard or damage them. Tatiana had been their favorite to torment, although Me Ling and Pu Wei also had their turns at receiving the business ends of the wives' floggers, a seven strapped whip that irritated, but did not mar the skin. To date, they had left Violet alone.

Yu jumped to alertness when she saw the British whore being led into their suite by the eunuch. He was the one who regulated their use of Wang's concubines, making sure that it was not too regular a thing. He had been given strict orders from his master not to let the wives' use of his sex slaves get too out of hand. He would stay in the wives' suite until they had finished taking their pleasure from Violet.

Yu shoved the virtually comatose Li Hua awake and then rushed over to the eunuch to claim their victim. She took the leash that led to Violet's collar and dragged the unhappy concubine over to the whipping stand. After removing it, she unbound her hands from behind her and attached them to the dangling bracelets. She then pulled on the other end of the chain until Violet was standing on her tippy toes, her arms raised high above her.

Li Hua had joined her and she reached out and tweaked Violet's nipples with glee. The concubine's white product leaked out onto her fingers. Li withdrew her hands and licked them, making a witty comment to Yu, who laughed.

Violet was trembling with fear. She knew what whipping stands were for. A whole new vista of torment was opening right in front of her. She knew that the other concubines sometimes served Wang's wives, but she had been hoping that she would be spared. On a number of occasions, she had comforted one of her sisters after returning from the wives' domain, her body scoured red. When Wang was away in Shanghai, the wife who had been left behind often kept one or the other of the concubines her prisoner for days at a time, taking out her anger on the younger woman.

The wives were wearing colorful, silk robes, tied around their waists. Their black hair was done up in pompadours on the tops of their heads. Their fingernails were long and sharp and were painted to match their robes. They wore cloth slippers embroidered in gold and silver on their tiny feet.

Violet took a panicked look around the salon. She saw the maids coupling frantically on the rug, and three other maids, all young with long, black hair, kneeling submissively on the side of the room. They were naked. The salon was decorated lavishly, with beautiful, hand carved, dark stained tables, elegant vases, a thick, hand woven rug. A large, crystal chandelier dominated the room.

The wives' hands wandered Violet's body. They played with her full, aching breasts, pinched her rear viciously, slid their fingers along the divide between her delicate love lips. Li Hua reached down and freed Violet's ankles from the bracelets. She spoke with Yu for a moment, both women giggling evilly. An agreement was reached and Li called over one of the maids who had been kneeling on the side of the room.

The girl scurried over and received instructions. She knelt down between Violet's legs and, after guiding her thighs apart, applied her lips to Violet's hairless gash. Violet moaned as she felt the tongue wind its way up her slit to the apex. It toyed momentarily with her clit and then descended again. The maid's hands rested lightly on the insides of her thighs and caressed and stroked them softly. Li and Yu were standing close by, watching for signs of lust in the English whore.

It too only a few minutes for Violet to be sighing and moaning with pleasure. The young girl supping at her gate was well experienced. She brought her tongue inside Violet's turgid tunnel and dragged it across the top, making her squirm and dance. She took Violet's now stiff love nubbin and sucked on it softly then harshly, softly then harshly, alternating the strength of her attentions to it and making Violet writhe in her bonds.

When red had broken out across Violet's upper chest and her hips began to rotate and push back against the tongue and lips that were playing with her conch, Li and Yu knew that the concubine was ready. Bending over slightly, they each took one of her nipples and began to suck on it while their hands surrounded the bloated mammaries, massaging and squeezing them.

Within a few moments, Violet's milk descended and she gave out a groan of pleasure. The active lips of her three assailants were stoking her passions. The flow of her maternal liquid through her nipples sent a tingling all over her body. A wave of contentedness flowed through her despite her fierce regret at being forced to feed the two callous and venal women. Her spread legs were putting pressure on her distended toes and they had begun to hurt. For now, though, her developing climax pushed her discomfort aside.

The maid was flicking her dexterous tongue across Violet's bud of pleasure rapidly. Her hands were working the sides of her labia and she plunged a thumb inside Violet's needy gash. It set Violet off. Her body shook and her legs trembled as her orgasm coursed through her. "Ohhhhhhh!" she moaned. She came hard, her pussy sending fierce, pleasurable contractions to her. She abhorred her reactions. The lips of the corrupt wives felt like leaches on her breasts, sucking and sucking and sucking. The tongue of the maid kept up its dance, drawing out and then renewing Violet's climax.

"Ahhhhhh! Ahhhhhhhh!" Violet moaned. Her knees had grown weak and she was dangling from her chained wrists.

Li and Yu were determined to supp in full at Violet's tits. They continued through her second climax. When the semi-sweet liquid finally petered out, Li's was finished first, they finally abandoned Violet's teats and signaled the maid to cease her adoration of the English whore's pussy.

The two wives giggled and laughed at their successful demeaning of the despised concubine. They had another conference while they pinched and played with Violet's body. They then came to a decision.

Yu issued the maid who had serviced Violet's pussy a command and she ran off for a moment, returning with the wives' floggers. They were seven tassled whips designed to bring about pain but not scar the body, much like the whip the general had used on her the first night as his sex slave. Violet tremored and whined when she saw them.

Li Hua and Yu taunted Violet with the whips by running their long, flat tassels all over her body while making deprecating sounds to her in Chinese. Violet realized that her special treatment by them had been triggered by their witnessing of her use by their husband that morning. It was so unfair, she thought miserably. She had had no choice as to whether to permit the warlord to nurse at her breasts. She would have gladly given up that duty. She wanted to beg the women not to whip her, to explain that it was not by her design that she should affront them so. She trembled at the thought that she would have to suffer every day that the master supped at her breasts. How would she ever stand it?

Li was the first to strike a blow. She dashed the whip fiercely over Violet's breasts, causing the concubine to dance and wail. It was followed quickly by a hard stroke by Yu across her belly. Li brought her whip down on Violet's back and then Yu struck her the front of her thighs. Violet was sobbing and wailing as the long, leather straps tormented her body in harsh counterpoint, one after the other. She danced and writhed in her chains, her hands clasped tightly above her. The harsh strokes went on and on in rapid succession from the two cruel women. They cried out imprecations of disdain toward the presumptuous whore as they repeated their assaults to her body again and again. It was literally a rain of blows.

Blossoms of red appeared on Violet's pale, tender skin everywhere that the two women struck. Her body began to burn. Each blow of the whips brought her a fiery message of pain.

The only consolation was that her torment was over quickly. She was sobbing heavily by the time that they stopped. Her body felt like it was afire. She saw the look of supreme satisfaction in the women's faces. She hoped that they would release her now and let her return to the seraglio and its relative safety, but it was not to be, not yet.

Li and Yu ordered the maid to release Violet from her bonds. When the maid lowered the chain over her head, she collapsed to her knees. The women had gone back to their elegant couches. The maid retied Violet's hands behind her back, took hold of the ring in her collar and brought her over to them. She guided the naked concubine to her knees before Li, who, as first wife, had the right of first use.

The venal woman lifted her pretty, silk robe around her waist and spread her legs, issuing a curt order to the concubine. Violet's belly revolted at the thought of pleasuring the woman who had just beaten her, but, her body still burning, fearful of more abuse, she obeyed the salacious order. Creeping up between the women's thin thighs, she placed her lips upon the hairless gash that was presented to her and began to service it.

Li's pussy soon watered and she began to moan and sigh as Violet used her tongue to pleasure her. Violet kissed and licked the woman's sex with alacrity, knowing that to act otherwise was to court another session with her whip, and in an effort to end the humiliating service as quickly as possible. Li, in this respect was accommodating. It was not long before the woman began to writhe and moan, her hands pressed firmly on Violet's head. When she came, she uttered a cry of pleasure at each hard throb of her pussy, her hands holding tightly onto Violet's hair.

Her service of the second wife, Yu, was not so easy. When Violet began to issue rapid lashes of her tongue over the woman's clit, Yu slapped her face and reprimanded her sternly. Violet, her face burning from the blow, tears rolling down her cheeks, her hands bound behind her, leaned forward once again and started over. She lapped her tongue along the woman's divide, tickled the nubbin at the top gently, placed her lips around it and gave it a soft suckle. Yu placed her legs on Violet's shoulders, and her thighs pressed against the side of her head. She sighed languidly after a time. Twice, she stopped Violet's efforts by pushing her head back from her loins until her passions cooled and then signaled her to resume. She ordered the maid, who had remained at Violet's side, to stroke the concubine's pussy from behind. When Violet felt the small girl's hand there, she obediently spread her legs.

The dainty fingers stoked her lust. Violet had, till then, resisted the exciting odor of the women's pussies. Over the last four months she had become quite enamored of the musky scent of female arousal between her reciprocal serving of her randy maids and in pleasuring her lover, Tatiana, or the Chinese concubines, Pu and Me. The hand on her quim broke down all resistance. Her nipples became tight, her breath labored. Her moans of pleasure, cast into the gaping maw that was Yu's cunt, echoed the venal wife's. The maid had her thumb deep in Violet's puss, sliding it in and out, while her fingers worried the little man standing at attention at the top.

Yu was a gusher, something that Violet had not encountered to date. When she came, a flood of her pussy's product washed over Violet's face, dripping down her chin. At first, Violet thought that the woman had pissed in her mouth, but as the taste revealed itself to be the musky product of the woman's loins, she felt relieved.

Yu's thighs pressed firmly against Violet's head, tightening at each throb of her pussy, accentuated by her cries of glee. Violet kept licking the sopping quim until the woman's thighs finally relaxed and she pushed her head away. The hand of the maid was still torturing Violet's purse exquisitely and she had not yet come. Li Hua had been watching as if fascinated by the concubine's efforts and she laughed when she saw her face emerge from Yu's thighs coated with her ejaculatory discharge. She also noted that, while she was panting and moaning from the maid's efforts, Violet had not yet crested her lusts. She issued a curt, harsh order to the maid.

The young girl abandoned her efforts and ran off to retrieve something. She returned with a leather harness. Attached to it was the wooden replica of the master's cock, something that Violet was well familiar with. It had been used on her in her forced seduction during her training period and since then many times by her maids and by her sister concubines at the order of the eunuch. It was an exact replica of the warlord's cock and there were several copies floating around. This was the one that Li Pao had given to the wives for their enjoyment. If they couldn't have their husband as often as they might like, at least they had his cock. And it was fun to use on the maids as well.

Li Hua leapt from the couch and threw off her red and blue, silken robe. She fastened the harness around her waist and knelt down behind the still impassioned concubine. She pushed Violet's torso down so that her forehead touched the rug and then insinuated herself into position to impale her.

Violet felt the cool object beg entry to her slash. She moaned with unhappiness, wondering miserably when her ordeal with the cruel women would end. She knew that she would soon be giving the women a salacious display.

The faux prick slid in easily. At first, its coolness made Violet shiver, but it soon warmed up to the task as Li began to saw it back and forth inside her. Her small hands were on Violet's hips, guiding her back and forth in harmony with her thrusts. She was making little, high pitched grunting noises each time she shoved the false cock home. It rasped against Violet's bud of pleasure, driving her lusts higher and higher. Yu had decided to get into the action and she slipped in front of Violet. Taking her by the shoulders, she lifted her torso from the floor until her face was made available to her. She seized the enflamed woman's breasts and placed her mouth on hers. Violet's belly turned as the woman drove her tongue into her mouth and squeezed her mounds harshly. She could not fight off, though, the building need to climax.

When Violet came, she grunted and moaned into Yu's mouth. Her body shook and she thrust back hard at her invader. "Mmmmmmmmm! Mmmmmmmm! Mmmm-mmmm!" she moaned as her pussy contracted and throbbed, sending jolt after jolt of pleasure through her. When she calmed, Yu withdrew her lips from Violet's and issued a complaint to her co-wife. Li snarled back, but withdrew the hard, wooden prick from Violet's loins. In her befogged state, Violet sensed Li unfastening the harness from around her waist and handing it to Yu. Yu strapped it on and then shoved Violet to her back.

As soon as the hard replica was slid into her canal, Violet's passion started to rise again. Her hands were crushed behind her back uncomfortably, but that did not halt or even slow her climb to lust. Yu had her arms under Violet's thighs, pushing them back against her chest and her face was inches from hers. Violet had a close look at the woman's cruel, lustful eyes. They were deep brown, almost black. She had a wide grin on her face. She said something to Violet in Chinese, something that made her laugh. When she saw Violet close her eyes and her mouth open, exuding a lustful sigh, she pushed the concubine's thighs back further until she could place her lips on hers. When her tongue began its dance in her mouth, Violet's pussy exploded in celebration of the woman's efforts. Violet grunted into the older woman's mouth again and again as her climax went on and on. For a moment, she had a respite as her rolling orgasm petered out, but it soon renewed and she was calling out her pleasure again. The false prick just kept going and going. Violet's mind screamed in protest as it seemed that the woman's assault would never end.

Finally, Yu deigned to give Violet surcease. She slowed her thrusts until the concubine's shouts of passion became mere moans and then murmurs. She halted her movements and then gave the still sighing woman a playful and insulting slap on the face, uttering some harsh message in Chinese.

Yu's blood was up. Li had taken the maid who had been assisting them and forced her mouth onto her steaming puss and she was writhing on the rug next to the formerly fornicating couple. Yu slid the solid tool from Violet's quim and issued a nasty sounding order to one of the maids who had been kneeling meekly at the side of the room. The young girl came over and Yu handed her the harness that had formerly been around her waist, ordering the frail, nervous girl to put it on. When that was done, Yu pushed the girl to her back and, throwing a leg over her thighs, lined her pussy up to the rigid prominence rising from the maid's loins and mounted it. She gave out a moan of lust as it sank within her. She pumped at it madly. She leaned over and took possession of the maid's lips and began to kiss her passionately. The ever obedient maid thrust her hips back at her mistress's and threw her arms around her.

Violet, limp and tired from her ordeals, listened to the groans and wails of the fornicating women. She had rolled to her side to relieve the pressure of her bound hands on her back. "What kind of a world am I in?" she asked herself miserably. She had been trying desperately to accommodate herself to her fate, making the best of a terrible situation. But new, harsh travails kept cropping up. Would she be subject to these women's salacious and cruel whims from here on out? Would they bring her back tomorrow, and the next day and the next? Was she really condemned to spend the rest of her life as a whore, her body used and useful to seemingly everyone's delight?

When the women had satisfied their lusts fully, they lay limp and spent on the floor. One of them signaled to the eunuch that they were done with Violet for the day and, after helping her to her feet, he escorted her back to the seraglio. There, she spent comforting hours in Tatiana's loving arms before being called to service her master for the night.

There had been no repeat of the orgiastic abuse of her by General Wang's wives. Their humiliation of her seemed to have satisfied them. On occasion, especially when Wang was away, she was called to one or the other of their beds and, from time to time, she was brought to their bedrooms to feed one or the other of them. The older one, Li, Wife Number One, actually began to establish a somewhat amicable relationship with her after a while. It was she who called her to their chambers the most. She used her gently and passionately, not in the salon, on view to all the maids and Wife Number Two, but in her sumptuous bedroom amidst her silken sheets.

军阀 外家

CHAPTER FOUR

The man who entered the guest room where Violet lay waiting took a moment to peruse her charms. It was what they usually did. Her maids maintained a strict diet for her and made sure that she toned her muscles every day to keep them taut and firm. She knew that her body was pleasing to the eye, not quite voluptuous, but finely curved and pleasantly soft. She had long, graceful legs and heavy, round breasts. All the men enjoyed taking in the sight of her prone and bound body, one clearly open to any and all of their lustful demands. Some of them used her roughly, some more gently. Some played her body like a violin, urging out all of her reciprocal lusts, making her scream and moan in pleasure. Others had no concern whether she enjoyed herself or not, were not stimulated by the experience of bringing a subservient female to ecstatic enjoyment, but, rather, merely wanted their cocks sucked and to finish themselves cursorily in one of her other holes.

But they all stopped and looked first as if burning into their brains for later retrieval the delectable sight of the warlord's English whore.

Some of the men cast off their clothes before approaching her, not wanting to delay their experience of bliss a moment more. Others took the time to examine her more closely first, cupping her delectably sized breasts, rubbing their hand over her taut belly, releasing her legs so that they could stroke her hairless puss into wetness.

This man, whoever he was, was of the latter variety. She felt the mattress depress as he sat on it. His hand reached out and his thumb and finger took gentle hold of the nipple on her left breast and pinched it lightly. He ran his hand down her arm and over her hip. She felt him loosening the ties around her thighs and then her ankles. Once they were free, Violet dutifully spread her legs so that he could have access to her font of pleasure. The hot hand brushed over her denuded mons several times and then insinuated a finger just inside her labial lips dragging it upwards to the little bud up top. He leaned over and took one of her teats in his mouth, suckling it softly. Violet had not been milked this afternoon and he was greeted with a small spurt of her fluid. He moaned in appreciation and, after placing his hand around her breasts, took a long, hard suck at the teat while squeezing the soft, heavy promontory until the milk began to flow freely.

Having satisfied himself that a wealth of pleasure awaited him, he stepped off of the mattress and began to disrobe. The pause in the man's attentions and the tingling in her breast brought her back again to her first days as General Wang's milk cow.

After that first time, Wang decided that he would take his breakfast alone. He didn't want his enjoyment of his English slut to be distracted again by the presence of the jealous women. He was tempted to have them both placed in milk and to let the guards service them three times a day. He had heard about the wives' use of his English whore later that afternoon from the eunuch and, while he would not, on principle, interfere with either his eunuch's regulation of her use or his wives' prerogatives, he was not happy about it. That night, he made sure that he fucked the English slut long and hard in compensation for her travail, bringing her to pleasure four times all told while discharging in her heavenly cunt twice.

Every day, for three months, the English whore was waiting by his breakfast table, on her knees, her breasts exposed, ready to serve his pleasure. He loved to hear her sigh as he fed from her, loved to feel her gentle hands on his head, her breath on his neck afterwards, as she reveled in her contentedness. He didn't always make her come, but when he did, her moans of pleasure stood his cock on end. When they were finished, he almost always had her suck his cock to completion while on her knees in front of him. And he was always somewhat wistful when he left her there to start his work day, wanting to take her back to his bedroom for a proper fuck.

He realized that his growing enthrallment by her boded ill for him. It was a weakness that he couldn't afford. It was for this reason that he started to select her to service his guests more often, much more often than his other whores, and proffered her oral services to them while they relaxed in his library or whiled away time in his salon. He needed to keep a distance from her, he knew that, or he would lose his soul. The more he saw her as just another whore, being used as one again and again, the easier it was to put his attachment to her out of his mind. He made it clear to the eunuch that no matter how enamored he was of her, the Russian whore should be returned to milk at the end of three months as scheduled.

Violet always cursed herself for letting herself be carried away when the warlord fed from her. There was something about his strength, the hardness of his flesh, the total control that he exerted over her that made the act of feeding him more than just pleasurable. At the same time, ironically, for a time, while he was drinking from her breast, he was no longer the cruel, rapacious warlord who had so callously enslaved her, who handed her out to his friends and guests like candy. He was, instead, a small, needy boy, suckling from his mother, gaining strength from her to face the day. When he made her come, and it seemed to her that he almost always did, her body and mind became enwrapped in rapture, a perfect blend of giving, her release of sustenance to him, and getting, the pleasure that his expert hand brought to her. She often lay listless in his arms afterwards and had to be stirred into wakefulness by his loud, rough voice.

When he demanded that she suck his cock following her feeding of him, she was actually glad to be reminded that she was just a whore to him, someone to use as his whims struck him. It made it just that more easy to maintain her implacable hatred of him and everything that he had done to her.

His long arm controlled everything that she did. If not through his stern and immovable eunuch, or the wrinkled old hag who ruled the seraglio, then through the three, often giddy, ever present maids.

At first, Violet had just thought of her maids as a gift, a consolation for her cruel slavery. They brightened up her day with their loving smiles and their gentle handling of her. That they also bent her to the seraglio's rules and kept her always beautiful and ready for her master's use had been beside the point.

She had come to know better, though. For disguised amidst the fawning attention that they gave her, the pleasure they brought her with their hands and mouths, the pleasure that they allowed her to find in their soft bodies and sweet quims, they were, when it came right down to it, just another aspect of her master's control over her. They were the velvet glove to his mailed fist. Through their amicable, doting attentions, they molded her day after day into the creature that was best designed to serve her master and theirs.

That their attentions were not always benign became clear to her one day, early on, just after Li Pao had administered her daily dose of lust producing elixir. While the feeling of resultant sexual need that permeated her day was exquisite and easily satisfied, Violet knew that it was a form of control over her. She rebelled against anything that prevented her from having a clear, rational understanding of what went on around her. She was always thinking of how she might escape, thinking of ways to make her servitude less onerous, trying to remember who she was and what she had been before she was transformed into a whore.

The lust driving potion interfered with all that. Her mind would drift into a fugue of need. She would eye her sister concubines with amorous intent. She would lose herself in a passion induced haze. And after she coupled, be it with Me Ling, Pu Wei or Tatiana, or with one of her maids, she would spend a long time luxuriating in the afterglow of her multiple orgasms.

She also hated how it made her into a lust driven demon when her lord and master used her or when he made her service one of his guests. It was like losing control of your own body. She would resist, at least initially, the hands that stroked her quim, the lips that teased her teats, the musky odor of the men's loins while she suckled them, but always to no avail. She quickly began to hate the potion and all it did to her.

For a couple of mornings, she got away with it. She would take the two ounces of thick, pleasantly tasting concoction into her mouth and pretend to swallow it. Then she would, as nonchalantly as she could, go to the chamber pot behind the silk screen and, before her maid could come and assist her, spit it out into the porcelain bowl.

It was heaven to her to be able to spend her days with a clear mind. She responded dutifully when appointed by the seraglio mistress to comport lustfully with her sisters, and received her maids' caresses and kisses readily. But her mind was clear and that was what was important. She could remember what it was like when she was free. The yearning for freedom was like an itch that she loved to scratch, an ache that she loved to feel, since, by feeling it, she could know that a spark of her old self sill lived.

It was on the fourth day that she was caught.

It was Lijuan, the pixie like maid, the sweetest of all three, who found her out. It was possible that someone had suspected what she was doing and had tipped Lijuan to look for it. After Violet spit the hateful concoction into the chamber pot and tried to quickly crouch over it and fill it with her urine, Lijuan stopped her and looked inside. When she saw the greenish substance at the bottom, she looked up at Violet with dismay. It was as if Violet had committed some grievous sin against her. Her lips trembled and tears came to her eyes. Before Violet could stop her, she jumped to her feet and ran over to Qiao, the wrinkled mistress of the seraglio. When Violet emerged from behind the screen, she saw the girl tearfully telling the old hag something and pointing to her.

The old woman looked at Violet sternly. This was a serious matter, one that she could not resolve herself. She ordered the maids to take hold of Violet and bind her arms and legs together. There were five of them in the communal room and they all sprang at Violet at once. She tried to resist them, but they were unusually strong for such sleight creatures and there were too many of them. In a few moments, she was lying belly down on the rug, her ankles and feet up in the air. The old hag brought over a gag and blindfold and had Lijuan apply them to her.

It was about a half hour later that Li Pao reappeared. Violet had been laying there ruing her fate when she heard him come in. Only he and the master, beside Qiao, had the key to the door from the hallway and Violet could tell from his distinctive footsteps that it was him and not the warlord.

She heard Qiao giving the eunuch an explanation of what had been discovered. Li ordered Violet to be brought to her knees and her gag and blindfold removed. At his instruction, she was dragged over to where the jug of elixir was stored.

Violet fully expected to be beaten, but the punishment that he had in store for her was much different.

Li poured a dose of the substance into a cup and presented it to Violet's lips. She was determined to resist him. She wanted no part of it and kept her lips sealed tight. Li looked at her sternly and gave an order to Lijuan who was kneeling next to her. Lijuan hopped up and retrieved from a cabinet a large ring wrapped in thin, stiff lengths of dried rattan. The ring had straps attached to two sides. Li ordered the other maids to assist her. They converged on Violet at once and with Lijuan taking the lead, forced her mouth to open. Violet moaned and struggled while the young women jammed the ring into her mouth. She groaned when she felt it lodged behind her teeth and then the straps tied off behind her head.

Violet was crying and struggling at her bonds. She knew that they were going to force her to drink the liquid and she raged within her at the unfairness of it. She didn't want to be a languid whore, sucking and fucking all day until her mind dwindled to nothing. She wanted to be bright and alert and free to determine her own actions.

Li handed the cup to Lijuan. The dainty maid, sadness on her face, nodded to the other maids, who held Violet's head still and tilted back. She poured the contents of the cup into Violet's mouth and then clamped her hand over it. She put the cup down and placed her fingers at the top of Violet's throat, pinching it slightly. She then dragged her fingers along Violet's throat. Before Violet knew it, she had swallowed.

She gave out a dispirited moan. She knew what the result would be. Although she might have the power to resist the potion's compulsion to copulate, she would spend the day in intense need until satisfied and then again soon afterwards as the lust built up in her once more. Her mind would be fogged, her thoughts dulsatory.

Violet whined when she saw Li Pao pour another cup. She struggled futilely as Lijuan poured it into her mouth. She used the same trick of her hand to make her swallow, like she had done this before with some other recalcitrant whore. Violet was crying when she felt the liquid flow into her stomach. She gave out a groan and tried to plead with the eunuch when she saw him pour out a third cupful.

When the third cupful was on its way to be digested and spread throughout her body, the eunuch ordered Violet to be released. The ring gag was removed and her limbs freed. Disheartened, she retreated to the opposite side of the room and leaned against the wall, her arms around her knees. Lijuan followed her dutifully, but Violet warned her off with a look of hatred. She sat there for a long time. Lijuan knelt there dolefully, sniffling, watching her.

The potion was quick acting. Within fifteen minutes, Violet felt her lust start to build. After a half hour it became stronger, more compelling. She was determined to fight it, determined to defeat it with her will. After an hour, the drive to passion became so strong she could taste it. A little while after that, it became a crisis.

Violet's pussy burned with need. Her breasts were taut, her body hot. She squirmed and pressed her knees firmly into her chest to try and resist it. She closed her eyes and bit her tongue. She clamped her hands into fists. She hung her head and moaned.

Tatiana and the other concubines had apparently been instructed to leave her alone. Only Lijuan knelt by her side, commiserating with her, though she made no move to relieve or comfort her.

Finally, Violet could stand it no more. She was crying from frustration and sorrow at the condition she had been reduced to. She looked at the forlorn Lijuan. She had stripped herself in anticipation of her mistress's needs. Her pretty, dainty breasts beckoned, her hairless sex sat invitingly between her outstretched thighs. Her lips looked fat and luscious. Defeated and in anguish, Violet reached out her hand to her. The child-like maid took hold of her hand gently. She brought it to her lips and kissed it and then worked her lips up Violet's bare arm slowly until she reached her shoulder. She placed her hand on Violet's face, stroking it softly. She uttered a phrase in Chinese, soft, amorous words. Then she placed her lips on Violet's and kissed her.

It was as if a switch had been pulled. Violet grabbed the dainty maid and pulled her to her body. She crushed her lips with hers and delved her tongue frantically into her mouth. They fell to the floor and Lijuan struggled to remove Violet's soft silken robe. When she was nude, their bodies melded together and they were off.

They made love furiously, right there in the communal room. Violet moaned loudly when she felt the girl's soft lips on her teats. She spread her legs widely when she felt her hand reach for her puss. She screamed with delight when the girl's lips found her quim and began licking it passionately. Violet writhed on the floor, welcoming the build up of her passions. Her chest rose and fell in laborious breaths as she moaned and groaned her ecstasy. Her thighs began to quiver. Her hands were buried deep in the coal black hair of her lover. When she came, she screamed and her whole body contorted.

After the third orgasm, Violet had calmed. She castigated herself for her weakness. She rolled away from the maid and cried. Soon, she felt the need come upon her once again. Defeated thoroughly, she rolled back to the maid and crawled atop her. She pressed her pussy upon on the willing, Chinese girl's and dragged across it again and again until the young maid moaned with pleasure.

The whole day was spent in delirious copulation. Tatiana, finally freed from inaction by Qiao, held her and kissed her for the longest time, manually bringing her to pleasure, kissing her breasts and licking at her slit. When Tatiana was called away by the eunuch to serve their master's will, Me Ling and Pu Wei joined forces and gently gave her comfort and release.

After dinner, Jinjing, the taller, more voluptuous of her three maids came on duty relieving the sorrowful Lijuan. She kissed and fondled her mistress sympathetically and brought her to her room so that they could fuck in private.

That night, it was Me Ling's turn to satisfy the master's libido, but Li Pao mercifully allowed Violet to serve him instead. When the warlord pierced her quim, Violet melted with joy. After their first bout, she mounted him while he was on his back and fucked him fervently.

Following her sweat inducing, tumultuous session with her master, Violet was led, exhausted to her bed. Ting, the thin, willowy wisp of a maid was on duty. After she bound Violet for the night, she made her come twice with her hand and then lay next to her on the bed, holding her all night long.

In the morning, the effects of the multiple dose of the potion had mostly passed. Violet's pussy was sore. Her muscles were tired and strained from her ordeal. She was brought by Ting to the eunuch for her daily vaginal shave. He was gentle with her, but made her come with his mouth nonetheless. When it was time for her dose of the old lady's aphrodisiacal potion, he made her bend over first and gave her, to her dismay, three solid whacks with his whippy stick, just to remind her of the gravity of her sin. When Ting had finished pouring the concoction into her mouth, he made her spread her lips to make sure that it was all gone.

After that, the role of her maids became clearer to her. Jinjing, who seemed to act as the leader of her squad of caretakers, took a firmer hand with her, insisting that Violet interrupt her card playing or lolling around with her blond lover and come to her bedroom to be fucked. The other maids followed her lead. Afterwards, they would leave her bound, blindfolded and gagged on her bed for an hour or so to contemplate her subservience and to enjoy the after effects of her orgasms. One of them always sat on a cushion near the door watching over her.

Violet always looked for the eye of the old hag that ruled them when Jinjing or one of the other maids ordered her gently to "*Stand up*," so that she could be given some sexual exercise in her room. The old woman had begun to watch her closely and her eyes burned into her whenever there was even a slight sign of resistance.

But if the maids were the velvet that covered the warlord's mailed fist, Violet eventually forgave them, especially the forlorn Lijuan. They had their roles and she had hers. It wouldn't due to take it out on them. They were all subject to the warlord's whip if they failed in their duty.

* * * * * * * * * * * * * *

The man's return to the bed interrupted Violet's reminiscences. He lay down next to her and pulled her to her side. His lips circled her teat and began the pleasurable process of emptying her breast. He was a large man, definitely Chinese from his smell. The Europeans smelt of butter and meat, while the Chinese men had a smell redolent of marjoram and cinnamon. His belly was rotund, but not so much as to make him obese. Violet sensed that he was older, not a young man, a fact supported by his relaxed, unhurried use of her. He was strong and his breath smelled like rice wine. His hands were soft, unused to physical labor. From what she could tell, he had never fucked her before, although she could have been wrong. He could have been one of the thirty five or so different men she had had coitus with over the last year. She couldn't be sure.

Violet moaned softly as she felt the liquid passing through her sensitized nipple. The man had captured her needy crevasse with his free hand and was stroking it gently and knowingly. She had her left knee up in the air to ease his access to her.

When her left breast was emptied, he shifted to her right. It was so strange to be feeding an unknown man, so strange to be receiving pleasure from him. It had happened a few times before, that one of Wang's guests wanted to use her blindfolded. Each time that it happened, it felt like she was being fucked by a ghost. Nonetheless, Violet felt glad that she did not have to look into the face of her abuser to see her shame reflected there. What difference did it make to her who used her anyway?

The man's agile fingers soon had Violet moaning with pleasure. When she came, it was like a wave rolling over her. The milking of her breasts, as it always did, made her lightheaded and dizzy. Her climax merged with those sensations and brought contentment to her entire body.

When the man finished supping at her breasts, he lay back for a time, apparently relishing the feeling of her rich, creamy output in his belly. After a while, he rolled back to his side and released Violet's hands from behind her. She took this as her signal to play a more active role in her ravishment. She slid her hands down his chest and urged him to his back. Kneeling at his side, she placed her lips on him, suckling his nipples, teasing them with her tongue. Her hand drifted south and brushed across her tangle of pubic hair until she found his stiffened wand. It was thick and long. The man moaned when she took hold of it.

Violet caressed the steel-like pole gently as she worked her mouth towards it. She laid her lips flush against the man's skin and washed it with her tongue. His belly flinched when she flitted across it. Her head towards the man's feet, her left thigh pressed up against his side, using her hand as her guide, she rose and took the steely instrument into her mouth. He gave a pleasured groan when she subsumed it into her, keeping her lips taut against it while they descended to its base.

She pleasured him slowly, expertly. Me Ling and the other concubines had long ago shown her all of their tricks and she had come up with a few herself. If she were pressed, she would have to confess that she drew a mild enjoyment from sucking pricks. She liked to hear the men moan and groan helplessly under her ministrations. It gave her a feeling of power over them if only so briefly. When they fucked her, she became just as much a prisoner of her passion as they were of theirs. Sometimes, though, like now, her customer, that's how she thought of them, if she was a whore, well, that's what they were, would seek out her usually already dilated and needy purse and begin to stroke it, sending her into her own realm of passion. When she felt the man's hand exploring behind her, she spread her legs to give him access to her center of delight.

Violet cupped the unknown man's soft stones with one hand while her other delicately caressed his lower belly. She varied the strokes of her lips on his rod, going slowly then speeding up, then slowly again. When his belly started to quiver and his thighs spread wide and shook, she ceased her oral manipulation of his tool and waited until he calmed before resuming again. Three times, she brought him to the edge and back. Meanwhile she was getting ready to blow herself. The man's fingers plunged in and out of her fevered canal, rogering her and driving her lusts higher and higher. When she felt her passions close to overboiling, she flicked her tongue a few times at the tender tip of the sleek prick and then went to town, sucking and caressing it with her lips madly.

The paroxysms of her pussy shook her whole body when she came. She was, barely, able to continue her adoration of the man's cock. The man's back arched, his thighs spread wider and he groaned. A moment later, his thick jism poured from his cock in spurts. Violet drank it all down while her body tremored with her own delight. She kept suckling the spasming prick until its dance slowed and then faded. She took one, last suckle of its end, absorbing the remnants of his spendings and then released him.

The two lovers, if one could call them that, lay spent for several minutes. Violet's heart was beating wildly. She knew that their session was not over. For all she knew, he would keep her all night. It would take him a while to rise again to hardness and so she took the time to recover from her own crisis.

They were laying with their heads facing opposite ways. The man's hand caressed her naked rear cheeks languidly. After a while, perhaps a little more than fifteen minutes, she rose and, turning around, draped her body over his, letting her breasts drag across his belly and chest. She started slowly. She kissed the man's chest here and there. She gave his nipples a slurp or two. She had her legs insinuated between his and she was able to capture his soft yet still engorged cock between her thighs and squeeze it. Slowly, but surely, she worked her way down his torso once more. When she got to his cock, she caressed it several times with her lips and then, lifting it, took his sac into her mouth, warming it with her oral heat.

The man sighed and his hips rose. She had her hand on his tool, coaxing it, stroking it, squeezing it, until she felt its hardness begin to return. She released his balls from her mouth and exchanged them for his cock. She stroked her lips up and down it, suckling it gently until it was firm and straight once more. Then she crawled up his belly until her purse was opposite his hot wand. She took it in her hand, rubbing its tip along the moist, dilated gap between her love lips and then, aiming at the entrance, slowly let herself down atop of it.

The man reached out for her hips and moaned with pleasure. Violet started a rocking motion, slow but steady, drawing his cock up and down her hot tunnel. The man had, for the moment, surrendered control of their coitus to her. She reveled in the feel of the stiff meat as it dragged across her energized clit, enjoyed the sensation of his thick member splitting her turgid, lower lips. Another climax was coming on.

Holding it off as long as she could, Violet rode the man like a cowgirl riding a bronco. Her climax overwhelmed her. She was drinking in great gasps of air. Her hands were on the man's chest, using it to push herself up and down on his wonderful tower. She felt the man shift his hips and begin to turn to his side, his signal that he wanted to be on top. For Violet, and the other whores, the customer was always right, and she let herself be flipped onto her back without breaking coitus.

Having achieved his objective, the man commenced a driving rhythm in and out of her gash. Violet had her legs splayed wide and was thrusting back up at him. He leaned forward and took possession of her lips, driving his hot tongue into her mouth. She came again and her pussy gave the cock a series of intense squeezes. "Oh! Oh! Oh! Oh!" Violet moaned into the man's mouth. His forearms were on the bed to each side of her head, his lips were married to hers. He pumped away madly. Violet gave the cock a squeeze each time that it tried to withdraw from her, something that the eunuch had taught her to do at the end of a whip. The man groaned, his body stiffened, and then he came.

The man's orgasm set off another for Violet. She could feel his hot juice flooding her passageway, yet one more load of jism poisoning her soul. But she would think on that later. For now, she was doing her best to please her master's guest lest he give a bad report, something that would bring her a whole world of pain.

When the man's emissions ebbed, his body came to rest. He lingered there, his softening cock slowly retreating from her canal. He moved his hips and it slipped out. After a few moments, he gave her lips another kiss and he rose from her embrace. Without as much as a word, he flipped Violet to her belly and refastened her hands behind her with the silken cord that had confined her when he came into the room. He joined her ankles and tied them off to each other and then to her hands. He reinstalled the bond around her thighs, sealing her legs shut.

Violet heard him dressing. She knew that there was a huge party going on, it was General Wang's birthday again. He was fifty one today. Violet recalled suddenly that she had met him on his birthday exactly one year ago. She tried to block from her mind all thoughts of their meeting. The memory of her lost freedom was too hard to bear.

Obviously, the man wanted to get back to the festivities after knocking one off with the English whore, a whore whose whole face he never deemed necessary to see. She heard him unlock the door and then it closed behind him.

During the act of sex itself, and usually before it, Violet kept up a brave front, sealing off her feelings, making the best of things. When it was over, though, and she heard the door close, returning her user to the free world, leaving her behind in her imprisonment, she always felt like yet another little piece of her had died. It was no different tonight. She squirmed in her bonds and she felt her eyes well up with tears. She recalled the enthusiasm with which she had sucked the unknown man's prick, had used her canal to excite him, and she hated herself for it. She knew that she couldn't help it. The potion she had been dosed with before she was brought to the guest bedroom was largely at fault, she knew that. She also knew that she should be grateful for it. Without the benefit of a mind clearing passion, she would never be able to do what she did and she would pay dearly for her defect.

About a half hour after the man left, Li Pao came to get her. He was a busy man since all four of Wang's concubines were at work tonight.

He brought Violet upstairs to the bathing room where her maids were waiting for her. After they cleaned her, perfumed her again, and oiled her body, Li brought her back downstairs. There was another of General Wang's esteemed guests to service.

军阀 外家

CHAPTER FIVE

The long, hot summer of 1923 was over. Fall was in the air. Tomorrow was a red letter day at General Wang's fortress. Tonight, the general was getting a head start on the celebrations.

The first class bordello he had started a little over a year ago was a smashing success. The French slut who ran it had been a birthday present from his sons to commemorate his fiftieth. They had presented the unsuspecting whore to him at the dock in Shanghai just before his steamboat began the journey back to Hunan Province. He had whipped her first thing, of course, as you would any new slave. She had proven adept at her profession and he decided that she would serve as the madam of his yet to be built, new, house of delight. He controlled or licensed all of the whorehouses in his domain. But they were mostly pedestrian affairs, and some rather low level ones where a farmer or a farmer's son could get his pipes cleaned at relatively little cost. Prices were kept down because, since they were treated as virtual slaves, the whores were paid nothing. There was only the cost of feeding and cleaning them and, in the poorer houses, the latter was not much of a consideration at all.

This one was to be first class. While the French whore spent a week or two in his dungeon learning the principles of obedience, he looked for an appropriate setting. He found it very quickly. It was an old mansion on the edge of Yeuyang, his port city. An elderly man and his three daughters lived there. The man, Zhou Xaiojian, was a former Imperial Official from back when the Emperor's writ ran here. Since 1887, when Wang's predecessor took control of the region, he had continued to work as a bureaucrat, helping to collect taxes, recording the sale of properties, the filing of wills, and other civic duties. He had been a thorn in Wang's side for many years, complaining of over taxation, the loss of any semblance of civil rights, slavery, drumhead justice, the monopolies on sugar and salt, the death tax on peasants, etc., etc. Since he was the last vestige of Imperial rule, and he knew how to make the place run, Wang had tolerated him.

Zhou had married late in life and his three daughters ranged from 18 to 23. Their mother was an attractive 39. The eldest daughter, Jingfei, was following in her father's footsteps, learning from him the in and outs of municipal administration, studying Confucius, reading history, learning mathematics. She had refused several offers of marriage to stay with her father. The middle girl, Shu, was just twenty. She had let it be known that she found none of the eligible bachelors in the area, most of them merchants' sons or the sons of landowners, within the class of suitor that she would entertain. One of the local boys had gone off to Beijing to study at the Imperial School there, and she was waiting for him to return. The youngest and prettiest of the three, the 18 year old, Jia, was in love with a shop owner's son in Yeuyang. Her father had forbidden her to see him, ruling that she needed to marry someone who was more refined and educated. She still saw the boy secretly and had pledged to him that she would end her life if her father didn't relent. The boy agreed, but suggested that they both do it after a night of torrid lovemaking.

The girls were all beautiful and, as far as Wang's spies could tell him, pure, except for perhaps the youngest one.

As the supreme leader of a virtual duchy, Wang was always conscious of the risk to his rule from subversive elements. It was true that he could put down any uncoordinated, spontaneous peasant revolt, and had ruthlessly, twice, but if somehow they all got organized and someone gave them weapons and leadership, his 350 men, although armed with high powered Mauser rifles, machine guns and two French 75's, would be hard pressed to defend him. Also, it was all the central government would need to hear that he was in crisis and their constant threat to send a battalion or two of Nationalist soldiers up the river from Nanking might become real.

So everyone who might be a threat to his rule was watched very carefully. Long ago, Wang had insinuated a spy in the man's household. Reports had gotten back to him of late night meetings with men from Shanghai, a meeting of some of the village elders of the province, a printing press that had been shipped to Zhou surreptitiously but not yet assembled.

The spy in Zhou's household was none other than his private secretary, Qin Guoliang. Qin was the answer to Wang's prayers. He could not depose the old man unless he had somebody suitable to replace him. Wang was biding his time, letting his spy gain as much experience as he could in the old man's employ before he acted.

The appearance of the printing press and the men from Shanghai was what broke the camel's back. He knew that he needed to act. And he needed an appropriate setting for his whorehouse as well as inmates to staff it.

He had brought with him back from Shanghai three young virgins who, having reached the age of 18, were graduated from the Golden Bough Orphanage, which Wang sponsored in Shanghai. They and the administration of the orphanage were under the impression that Wang was going to obtain suitable employment for them in Yeuyang. He had assumed responsibility for a number of the graduating girls over the years. They got jobs all right, but mostly working on their backs or their knees. If he had not needed the fresh blood for his new bordello, the girls would have been auctioned off to the highest bidder or sent to work in one of his other houses. He had decided that they would help initiate the opening of the house by offering up their virginities on opening night to the highest bidders. But four whores, including the French one, of course, were not enough to staff a whole house.

As a result, three nights after his return from Shanghai, almost a year and a half ago, he had had the old man, Zhou, and his whole family arrested. It was a simple thing, not that he really needed it, to produce the evidence to justify his actions. The bonus had been the list of coconspirators and the three agitators from Shanghai that were found there. The coconspirators and their families were rounded up in short order. The executioner at his fortress was kept quite busy. The females who were marketable, after entertaining his troops for several weeks, were sold off to whorehouses in Shanghai and Nanking. The rest were set adrift with dire warnings to all that no one should give them food or shelter within his domain.

Three of the peasant girls who were among the families that were arrested fit the bill nicely. But even seven whores were not enough if the place was really going to prosper.

To ensure the cooperation of the wife and daughters of the old bureaucrat, Wang kept Zhou alive in his dungeon for many months after his arrest. The females of his family were told that he would be allowed to live as long as they performed adequately as whores in his new bordello. Zhou lasted only six months, but by then the women were sufficiently acclimated to their new life, and sufficiently afraid of the whip, that it didn't matter any more.

The house was perfect. There was a nice garden in the back with various fruit trees and a stream fed pond. The upstairs levels of the house had five large bedrooms and three rooms which had served as Zhou's office, library and the family shrine. There was a spacious dining room in which revelries could be held, and even a basement where the maids could be housed and recalcitrant whores punished.

As his reward, the secretary, Qin, assumed the man's post. It was amazing how much tax collections improved. He imposed a duty on all commercial transactions and a tax on marriages and births. He was also given a large bonus, a house in the town which had belonged to one of the conspirators and one of the rebels' daughters as a concubine, after, that is, she did some duty in the fortress.

The rumors about the eighteen year old had been true. Jia had dishonored her family by giving herself to the merchant's son. That still left Wang, however, with eight virgins. He would auction off one a week until they were all pierced and ready to serve regular customers. The girls from Shanghai would go first, saving the best, the Imperial clerk's two virginal daughters, Jingfei and Shu, for last. The French whore, assisted by his eunuch, Li Pao, needed some time to break them in. Who wanted a whore who didn't know how to suck a cock, even a virginal one?

Wang took it upon himself to show the 18 year old how to be a whore. Her pussy was tight and sweet, her moans of unhappiness exquisite. He fucked her roundly for almost two weeks running, a major feat considering that he was breaking in the English whore at the same time. The house needed some renovations before operations could start, such as locks on all the doors, large, accommodating bathrooms with luxurious tubs, renovating the eight upstairs rooms into sixteen bedrooms, the installation of some cells in the basement for punishment purposes, stocks of liquor and comestibles. He even built a small pavilion out in the garden so that the rich merchants could fuck there under candlelight in the summer months.

When Robert came and told him that his Chinese girlfriend, Qua Li, needed to disappear, it was a gift from the gods. Now he had four working whores: the Imperial clerk's wife and youngest daughter, the French whore, Estelle, and Qua Li. He also had eight virgins to peddle.

It had come off like a dream. Every week, the bidding for the virginal whores got higher and higher. As each one had her cherry busted, she joined the crew of regular working girls. When it came to the Imperial clerk's two maiden daughters, the bidding went through the roof. And since then, they and their mother and sister were most popular. There was something about them being whores in the same house where they lived and grew up that made fucking them more exciting.

Tonight, Wang was paying a special visit to the youngest sister, Jia, who was now nineteen. She had been somewhat ethereal in her demeanor when she was first put to work, but she had filled out nicely. Her breasts, which had been somewhat on the small size had developed, with the help of a diet prescribed by Wang's old, witch woman, into prizes. She had waist length, black hair. Her hips were narrow and her belly taut. She had a well proportioned face with a small nose and a dainty mouth. Her brown eyes were limpid and alluring.

Wang was in her room on the second floor. She had been waiting, kneeling naked on her bed when he entered the room. Hatred flashed across her eyes when she saw him. He laughed to himself. It was, ironically, what he relished about her.

A bright, steel chain led from the foot of the bed to between the girl's thighs. It was long enough so that she could move around the bed with ease, pressing her breasts and thighs against the headboard for a whipping if need be. None of the other whores were chained to their beds. Jia was something special.

Two months after the whorehouse opened, Jia managed to slip out one night in a bid for escape. The only clothes that she had when she left was a silken robe that she used to present herself to customers. Her boyfriend from the village was waiting and had peasant clothes ready for her. Together, they fled on foot easterly. The boy had hired a fishing boat from some smugglers to take them down to Nanking where they hoped to enlist the assistance of the nominal regional governor in saving Jia's family. Amazingly enough, they made it to the small village 10 miles outside of Yeuyang without meeting up with any of Wang's patrols. The boat was there. The boy paid the money, stolen from his father's store, and it pushed off.

They were out about an hour on this moonless night when the smugglers, there were four of them, began to eye the young girl salaciously. Although she was dressed in peasant's clothes, her beauty shone through, even in the dark, and she was still redolent of the expensive perfume she was forced to wear in the bordello. She had forgotten, in her haste, to remove the shiny, gold earrings that were part of her regular costume.

When the leader of the smugglers demanded she show him her breasts, the boy protested. One of the smugglers cut his throat and threw his body overboard. It had been in the plan all along. They were just waiting to get far enough away from the port so that the boy's body would float downstream. Jia screamed and tried to jump over the side to share her boyfriend's death, but the men were too quick for her. She was soon stripped and bent over a wooden crate, her hands and ankles tied off to the deck. She entertained them with her three holes all night. It wasn't until the morning that they spotted the tattoos on her lower back and belly. There were four, three inch high ideograms front and back, marking her as "General Wang's Whore."

Wang had gotten the idea originally from Li Pao, his eunuch. He had suggested that the general adorn his concubines with tattoos to demark his ownership of them and to make their reduction to slavery more permanent. Wang had balked at that. He loved their pure flesh too much and had settled for the virtually irremovable, black collars with embossed, gold ideograms announcing them as "General Wang's Concubines." He had used the idea, however for his new whorehouse. He had the inscription tattooed on each of the new whores' lower belly and back with the idea that whenever they were fucked, either in front or in the rear, his ownership of them would be suitably displayed for their customer before he sank his cock home.

None of the smugglers wanted to fuck with General Wang. Wherever they sold the girl, which had been the plan, if the girl showed up anywhere that the general could find her, the trail would lead right back to them. Two of the men wanted to wait until dark again and slit her throat. They could fuck her all day in the hold of the small ship first. One of the remaining men wanted to bind her ankles and wrists, weight her down with some rocks and throw her overboard immediately. He didn't want to take the risk of one of the general's patrols searching the boat and finding her.

Luckily for them all, it was the leader that made the decisions. At his direction, they turned the little boat around and made their way back to Yeuyang. Once there, they sent word to the whorehouse that she was on board. A delegation came to collect her right away. The men were rewarded, after a bath, of course, with a night in heaven with the finest whores in Hunan Province and $100 in cash, American money to boot, four times what the naïve and unfortunate, young boy had paid them.

As a result, Jia spent a couple of weeks in Wang's dungeon in a cell right next to her father's. She was whipped and raped daily by the gremlin like guards. They were careful not to exceed their brief by scarring her. When she was released, a hole was punched into her lower right, outer labial lip and a gold ring was soldered in place. The ring had a ten foot long, steel chain attached to it. Since then, she was only permitted out of her room once a day in the afternoon when she would be tethered to a ring pounded into the earth in the garden and allowed to get some fresh air and exercise by walking around naked in small circles. That, and to be washed and cleaned. Her status and price in the whorehouse went up, since fucking a girl whose pussy was chained to a bed was a great attraction.

Wang stripped himself of his general's uniform. He took hold of the chain and slowly drew the pretty, little whore towards him. She shuffled over on her knees, pursuing her advancing cunt. He was standing at the foot of the bed, and when the girl came within arm's reach, he took hold of the hair on the back of her head and rudely forced it down level with his cock.

"*Suck cock!*" he ordered her brusquely.

He had a tight grip on her shiny, black hair making the girl whine with pain. She opened her dainty lips and took hold of the as yet, limp instrument. Wang held her face tight against his loins while she manipulated his crank with her tongue, encouraging it into hardness. As it expanded, it started to push against the back of her throat and she began to whine and squeal. The harsh general let her squawk for a minute or so, and then withdrew her face from his loins and allowed her to open her air passage.

The girl held her lips tightly against Wang's now steel hard cock as he used her mouth to jerk off. He pushed and pulled her captured head back and forth, reveling in the unhappy girl's use of her tongue. She knew better than to disappoint the general. He had had her down in the basement of the bordello a number of times for poor performance. She didn't want to go there again.

Wang alternated between giving himself long, languorous strokes of her mouth and drawing it up and down over his prick rapidly. His body was enjoying her blowjob, but his mind was on Me Ling. Tomorrow, Me Ling would cease to be his concubine. He was marrying her off to Major Won as a reward for many years of fine service. She was to be Won's second wife, Wang having gifted him his first one from his seraglio about five years ago. Won's loyalty was crucial to the maintenance of order in his realm. They were from the same village and were cousins. Wang had made him a wealthy man. He owned a large estate and had two concubines of his own, also gifts from Wang. One of the women was a dark eyed Russian swept up off the streets of Shanghai. Wang enjoyed whipping her whenever he came to visit.

While Major Won was his second in command, there were two captains under him. Both were also Wang's cousins. Won knew that if he ever took it into his head to try and overthrow the warlord, one or both of the captains would probably contest succession with him. The landlords who owed personal fealty to Wang would revolt and seek the aid of the National Government. He would be without the vast flow of cash that Wang maintained in Shanghai that helped keep the army together and paid for the weapons of war. Most importantly, he would need coconspirators and he could never be sure whether any of the younger officers, there were twelve lieutenants, could be trusted not to betray him to their master. A painful death would be the result and a sure promotion for the lieutenant. Why risk it when he was living in the lap of luxury already?

Tonight, when he returned to the fortress, Wang would give his number one concubine one last, good fucking. He had had the witch prepare one of her special potions made up of rhinoceros horn and selected, secret herbs. Last time he had used it, he had come five times. That was certainly enough to plow all of the young woman's holes. He would make especially certain to have her use her mouth to bring him to completion at least twice since he knew that she hated it so. He had told Li Pao to give Me Ling a double dose of the old lady's lust inducing potion.

"Mmmmmmmmmmm," he moaned languidly as his cock worked towards completion. He turned his attention back to the whore on his cock. She was making amusing little choking sounds each time that he rammed his cock deep into her throat. Her tiny hands were on his thighs, trying, futilely, to regulate his use of her. He could see his upside down tattoo on her naked, lower back. He would fuck her ass when he was done. It was only eight o'clock and he had plenty of time to recuperate before he went back to the fortress.

This afternoon, he had held a huge party for all of his officers. They had all gotten immensely drunk. The fortress' maids were called into service to attend to the sexual desires of the lieutenants and, while the bride to be languished upstairs, his three other concubines were brought down to service his senior officers.

While a merry orchestra played, the naked men ate, drank and fucked for three hours. He had let Major Won have the use of Whore Number Four, at his request. It had amused Wang to watch him plow the English whore's front and rear orifices on the floor of the dining hall and then trade her for a round with the Russian.

And yet, there was something about the innate fragility of the English whore that clung to his heart. It was her turn to be in milk again, and each morning, after he drank from her, he felt this strange, bedeviling attraction. She was beautiful, yes, but so were all of his whores. She was very skilled, but that did not really differentiate her from the others. Me Ling had been her superior with her mouth, and Pu Wei's cunt was like another hand the way she could manipulate her muscles. No, it was something else.

The second time that Robert had come up, about a year ago, he had brought with him the letters she wrote during their long distance courtship. It had amused Wang at first to read them. The gap between her anticipation and her reality could not have been more extreme. Later, though, he was sorry. It was difficult enough for him to maintain his emotional distance from her. Now that he knew all her hope ands fears, had read her elegant, almost poetical prose, he had gotten a window into her heart. Her personhood had started to take form in his mind. This would not do. He thought of burning the letters, but he could not do it. Some nights, before he retired to his bedroom, he would sit in his library and reread them. If it was her turn to service him, he would fuck her like a lion. If not, the unfortunate whore whose turn it was would get a taste of his whip.

As the deceased Imperial clerk's daughter's mouth rode his cock, his mind returned to this morning's oral servicing by the English whore. He had rested his hand lightly on her head as she knelt on the floor between his thighs. He had leaned back and let his eyes roll back in his head. She was patient, letting his lusts build slowly. She had a little thing that she did, fluttering her fingers faintly on his rigid pole while teasing the sensitive opening of his instrument lightly with her tongue. It was a secret that she had apparently kept from her sister whores, since none of them did it. It made him sigh with pleasure every time.

Wang shook himself from his reverie. Why should he moon after her like a school boy when he had this perfectly adequate and, in some ways superior, whore on his cock now? His feelings for her were like a disease. Maybe he should sell her off, or, better yet, bring her here to his whorehouse and have her service twenty five or so men a week. She would be a good moneymaker.

His cock was approaching sartoris. He was stroking it with the young whore's mouth harder and harder. Her squeals were getting louder and louder. He thought of Jia's delectable pussy, tethered like a wild animal. He would fuck her there, he decided, not in the ass. From behind. The picture of her bent over, the remorseless chain dangling from her quim, set him off.

"Arrrrrgh! Arrrrrrrgh!" he moaned mightily. He would chain the English whore's cunt to a bed like this one and have her whipped every day! He would come and fuck her mouth like he was fucking this one! "Arrrgh! Arrrrrrgh!" he went on, his lust magnified by the vision of the English whore in chains. He would drive all feelings for her out of him. "Arrrrrgh! Arrrrrrgh!"

When his passions subsided, he noticed that the little clerk's daughter was choking on his wand. She was whining piteously. He pulled her head from his cock by her hair and slapped her twice harshly across the breasts. She needed to be whipped!

* * * * * * * * * * * * * *

Tears were the order of the day the next morning in the seraglio. All the other concubines knelt and watched while Me Ling received her last ceremonial shaving of her pussy by the eunuch, Li Pao. Afterwards, he took his time in pleasuring her, using his mouth to bring her to the brink of completion several times before letting her lusts cascade over. The young girl's body shuddered and she gave out sweet, little yelps of pleasure.

A special, ceremonial breakfast was served with a variety of delicacies including sweet rice cakes, dried apricots smothered in a tangy sauce, candied plumbs, apple slices covered with cinnamon, a thick porridge flavored with honey and raisins and, for each of Wang's sexual slaves, a glass of rice wine. The four women knelt naked in front of the short, lacquered table in the seraglio's dining room, their hands bound behind them with soft strands of silk, their maids feeding them bits of this and that with their chopsticks or porcelain spoons. A hearty, black tea had been brewed.

The maids had all caught celebratory fever and were giggling and stroking their charges. Me Ling's maids, however, had their joy tinged with melancholy since it would be the last meal that they would be serving their mistress and, after that, they would be reduced in rank to that of regular house maids.

After the meal, one by one, they were escorted off to their daily baths. Me Ling would go last so that the perfumes and oils with which she was anointed this day would be the freshest. Her maids took the opportunity to drag her back to her room for one last session of delight.

While she waited to be escorted to the bathing room, Violet stood by the window of the communal room and looked out over the splendid view, her heart heavy. Today, Me Ling would be liberated from slavery. True, even married Chinese women had few rights. One of them, however, was not to be handed around by their husbands to every Tom, Dick and Harry who happened to come by. She would be able to go to market, visit with her neighboring wives, go see her family, decide what to wear, what to eat. While Major Won, she understood, already had one wife, Me Ling was pretty enough and sexually accomplished enough to hold her own.

Violet knew that no such fate awaited her. General Wang had told her as much when he had pronounced his sentence of enslavement over her. She would be his whore until he tired of her and then she would be somebody else's, and then somebody else's, etc. It would be a great affront to a man's ancestors to marry a woman who was not Chinese. Besides, every Chinese man knew that Western women were born to be whores, showing themselves off in public, drinking and smoking like the men, wearing lascivious dresses that showed off parts of their breasts.

Me Ling's departure brought home to her in a dramatic way both the power that the warlord had over his concubines and the slender thread on which her own future hung. Robert had said that Wang would discharge himself in her mouth a thousand times before he got rid of her. Wang had suggested two thousand. It had probably been a few hundred already. And their humored suggestions were just hyperbole anyway. Wang would get rid of her when he wanted, no matter how many times she had sucked his dick or how well.

And then there was Tatiana. She was standing by Violet's side, holding her hand, thinking the same thoughts. She had been Wang's whore for three years now. It was just a matter of time. Violet couldn't stand the thought of losing her. She looked over at her blond lover and squeezed her hand. When Tatiana looked back, she saw that she was crying. Violet took her free hand and stroked her cheek lovingly and then leaned over and gave her a soft kiss. Tatiana rewarded her with a slight smile.

When it was her turn to bathe, Violet listlessly allowed her maids to clean her and adorn her body. Her baths always ended on a soft mat, soothing oil being rubbed into her body and a comforting orgasm to follow. She held little Lijuan closely to her body as Ting mouthed her to completion. When she came, tears flowed down her face.

She had serviced the warlord this morning. His attitude seemed cold and distant. He had not stroked her to climax as he usually did and when he was done emptying her, he shoved her rudely to the floor and told her harshly to, "*Suck cock!*" To Violet, it was a sure sign that her days were numbered.

While she did not rue the opportunity to be parted from the man who had so cruelly enslaved her, there was no telling what her next duty station might be like. Like most people, she preferred the devil she knew to the one she didn't. And would there be a Tatiana there wherever she went? She doubted it.

After her bath was done, Violet was led through the hallway back to the seraglio's common room. As when she was escorted outside the seraglio, the maids always bound her hands and affixed the chain to her ankles when moving outside the seraglio proper. Inside, she could stroll to her room, the dining room or the communal room without restriction. She had spent most of the last year and a half in those three rooms.

They dressed her in a beautiful, dark blue gown with golden floral designs flowing all over it. It came with a light blue, gauze like shawl that draped over her shoulders. The gown covered her feet so that the chain she would wear would not be seen. She waited kneeling in the communal room while the other whores got ready.

When Me Ling emerged from her room, she was wearing a long, bright red dress. It had large, loose sleeves that covered her hands. Behind it was a train several feet long that her maids would carry for her. Her black hair was wound up on top of her head and held in place with long, thin golden needles. She carried a red parasol. Her face had been powdered and she looked almost ghost like as she entered the communal room. All of the women stood up to greet her. One by one, Me Ling said a tearful goodbye to them all. Her maids had tissues in their hands with which they were assiduously wiping away her tears so that they wouldn't ruin her beautifully made up eyes.

Violet had to suppress a sob when it came to be her turn. Tearfully, she tried to tell the soon to be bride how much she had meant to her. Me Ling had helped her a great deal with her Chinese lessons and had taught her several Chinese games to help while away the time. They had spent a year and a half together in an hermetic environment. She had loved her many times. It was like their flesh had melded together when they coupled. They would never do so again.

"*Violet love Me Ling,*" she said to her friend and lover in Chinese. "*No forget Violet. Violet no forget Me Ling. Be happy long time me wish you.*" She was holding the slender, graceful woman's tiny hands in hers. Her heart was breaking.

Me Ling too, suppressed a sob. She gripped Violet's hands tightly.

"*I'll never forget you Violet, Whore Number Four,*" she said tenderly. "*I will pray for you to find happiness every day. You have a great soul and the gods will not abandon you.*"

Like most people learning a new language, Violet understood more than she could speak. She saw the earnestness in the young woman's face, a face she was looking into for the last time. Suddenly, she was overwhelmed with sadness. She collapsed to her knees, sobbing plaintively, sobbing for herself, for Tatiana, for everything she had lost, for all she had had to endure and most of all, for what the dark future had in store for her.

Me Ling crouched down before her and placed her delicate arms around her neck, pressing her face into her youthful bosom. Her maids, ever her ruler until the last, bent down and guided her up lest she stain her pretty wedding dress with tears, a bad omen indeed. Violet's maids helped her to her feet. She felt her maid Jinjing's strong arm holding hers.

"*Be brave, Whore Number Four,*" Jinjing said kindly. The maids never used her real name. "*Do not cry or the master will surely beat you. Everybody today is happy for Whore Number One. You should be happy too if you love her."*

Violet nodded her head, fighting back her tears. She gave Me Ling a smile. "*Goodbye, Me Ling,*" she said.

After all the goodbyes were said and all the tears dried, Qiao, the mistress of the seraglio, tapped her whippy stick on the floor several times to get everyone's attention. She uttered a command and leather bracelets were placed around Violet's and Tatiana's ankles, connecting them with their 18" long chains. Lijuan brought Violet's wrists in front of her and she tied them tightly together with a silk cord. She then wrapped a matching silk belt around her waist and, after tying it once in front, wrapped it around her joined wrists several times and then pulled it behind her where she tied it in place. Violet's hands were now bound firmly in front of her at waist level.

Even Pu Wei was bound today. The wedding would take place in the meeting hall on the second floor. There would be more than 200 guests. A clever concubine might just find a way to slip into the crowd and disappear. Li Pao, who dictated the arrangements for the concubines, was not going to let that happen.

Me Ling's marriage to the major did not bode well for Pu Wei. She was a year older than Me Ling and had been in the seraglio longer. It might just mean that the warlord had not yet tired of her sexual skills or pretty face. It also meant, however, that her stock in trade was not as high. Major Won was the second most important man in the warlord's domain. He was a prize for any wife. Pu's mate would therefore be of lesser status. And the older she was when Wang released her from her bondage, the further down the scale she would go.

They were all waiting for the arrival of Li Pao. While Qiao had the key to the door that led to the other service rooms in the seraglio, she did not have the key to the doors that led to the master's bedroom or to the meeting hall. Only Li and the master had those.

Qiao inspected them all closely, especially Me Ling. She found no fault, luckily for the maids. Li Pao came in soon afterwards. He found no fault either, a lucky thing for Qiao. He had one last security measure to apply to the whores. From a small basked he was carrying on his arm, he produced what appeared to Violet to be a small ball of leather. He ordered her to open her mouth and he plopped it in. It was just big enough to fill her mouth, but not so big that it bulged out her cheeks or that she would have any trouble closing it. If Violet decided to shout out for help at any time that she was exposed to the public, her voice would produce only a garbled noise.

The second feature of the ball was that it loosely wrapped a smaller ball of opium. It had been ground and mixed into a slurry like solution. Violet's saliva would mix with the drug and she would swallow it. There was enough so that she would be in a dull haze for a couple of hours.

Li administered a ball to Pu and Tatiana as well. He waited until he saw that their eyes had glazed over. Violet felt dizzy and her mind was confused. She realized that the mixture she was given every day must contain a small amount of opium because she was feeling somewhat like she did after she drank it. She had not been given her potion this morning, Li didn't want the concubines to be squirming and wriggling their asses all through the wedding ceremony.

The procession to the meeting room on the second floor was led by Li Pao. Qiao held up the rear with Me Ling's maids and then Me Ling in front of her. The concubines followed Li Pao in order of rank, each one followed by her personal maids. The maids had all been dressed in pretty banner dresses matching the colors of their charges. Violet's wore blue, Pu Wei's wore yellow and Tatiana's wore green.

Silently, they walked down the hallway and down the stairs to the second floor. When they reached the door which led to the meeting room, Li Pao knocked on the small wooden panel window and it opened. A guard was on the other side. They exchanged some words and the panel was slid shut.

The procession waited in the cramped hallway for about fifteen minutes. It was hot and stuffy with so many people in it. The rush of the drug that she had been administered had worn off to some degree, but Violet found that she could duplicate it at any time by squeezing the leather ball in her mouth. She was going to try and avoid it, but the rush was so delicious that she didn't think that she could go long without doing it a few times.

Finally, there was the sound of the Chinese orchestra beginning to play. Its muted sound floated through the door. Violet had become enamored of the strange harmonies and chord progressions that the music contained. In the last year and a half, she had heard them play many times at parties. She came to understand that what sounded at first to be cacophonous and random was actually quite well ordered. While the instruments at times seemed to be playing different songs, after careful listening she had come to appreciate how the differing lines of melody complemented each other. It seemed singularly appropriate to the dream like state that the opium had put her in.

Violet felt her body give a little shiver. This was the room she had been enslaved in and she had not been back to it since. On that day, she had come in through this very same door by herself behind Li Pao and she had been the center of attention. She had been forced to strip for all of the audience to see and so that the general could appreciate all of her charms before he formally made her his concubine. As a gesture of submission, Violet was ordered to crawl on her hands and knees to the warlord and suck his cock. At first she refused, but was beaten down by the news of how she had been betrayed by Robert. Alone in the world, forlorn, she had surrendered her pride and honor and performed the deed.

The music stopped and the door to the hallway opened. As Li Pao stepped through it, the orchestra began again. The women followed, walking in small, timid steps. There was a crowd of people filling the large room, many more than had been present at Violet's formal enslavement. They were standing silently as the women marched in, all eyes turned towards them.

The procession went down an aisle between the two groups of people. At the end of the aisle was a two level, raised dais. It was covered in green felt and had a red runner up the middle. At the top sat the general, bedecked in his dress uniform, his chest full of medals, his gilt laden, military cap tightly on his head. To either side of him sat his wives, Li Hua and Yu Jie. They were bedecked splendidly, wearing long, elegant gowns of blue, silver and gold, fine slippers brocaded in silk, large, golden ear rings and rich, bejeweled necklaces. Their hair, like Me Ling's was piled atop their heads and held in place by golden needles.

As the processional music continued, the women were guided to positions to the left of the platform. Pu, Tatiana and Violet took up kneeling positions on large, fluffy cushions on the first level. Their maids knelt behind them. When Violet was fully kneeling, she felt one of the maids slip her hand under the back of her dress near her ankles and clip the bracelets together. If Violet felt a sudden urge to run across the room, she would fall flat on her face.

Me Ling stood alone in the center of the aisle. Her face was radiant. Major Won, in his dress uniform stood to the right side of the first level of the platform. A priest stood next to him dressed in a flowing, light green robe. He wore a square, black, leather hat on his head and his grey beard descended to his waist. Behind him stood an acolyte. He was much younger and was dressed in a similar but plainer robe. He was carrying a large scroll with a red ribbon on it.

Slowly, Me Ling approached the dais. The music had stopped. She stepped up on the first level and bowed lowly to General Wang. The general nodded his head back slightly and then rose from his chair. He stepped down to the first level and approached his concubine. She knelt on the dais in front of him and bent her neck forward. One of her maids, who had been standing behind her, lifted her hair from her neck revealing the black, leather collar that she wore. Earlier, in the seraglio, with great effort, Li Pao had torn though most of the threads that held it together with a pair of sheers. It had taken more than an hour to first scrape away the enamel covering and then to cut the thin, copper wires. It now hung by a single strand. One of Wang's servants brought him a silver platter with a small, shiny pair of sheers on it. Wang picked it up and snipped the last thread. The maid who had moved Me's hair took hold of it and slipped it off of her neck.

When Me raised her head, she was smiling broadly. General Wang regally offered her his hand and, grabbing it, she rose to her feet. Leading her by the hand, he led her to where Major Won was standing. He proffered to him her dainty hand and he, also smiling, took it in his. General Wang resumed his seat. Won led Me Ling to the center of the platform and they both bowed lowly to the general. He gave then a nod in return.

The orchestra started up again and, as if jolted into action, the priest began to move around the stage. There were four urns, one at each corner, and he lit them one by one, sending clouds of incensed smoke into the air. He picked up a set of bells and shook them while walking around the couple, reciting some prayers. When he was in front of them again, he motioned for the acolyte to bring the scroll to him. Holding his hands over the happy pair, he recited long passages from it. He asked Major Won several questions to which Violet heard the man answer, "*Yes.*" The priest turned to Me Ling and asked her some questions. She answered them affirmatively. Violet, with her limited knowledge of Chinese, and amidst her foggy haze, heard the word obey.

With that, the priest rolled up the scroll and handed it back to the acolyte. Won and Me bowed their heads in front of him and he placed his hands on them. He uttered some words and then stepped back. Won and Me turned to each other, smiling. They gave each other a perfunctory kiss and then turned to the crowd and bowed.

The crowd erupted in applause. Some of the people had brought noisemakers: bells, small drums and other percussion instruments. They rattled and shook and banged them now exuberantly. A maid came from the side and strewed flowers over the red part of the carpet and then towards the main door to the room. Me Ling and Won followed her. People in the crowd threw more flowers at them as they passed.

Li Pao snapped his whippy stick on the green marble floor and Violet and her sisters were urged to their feet by their maids. Their ankles were unclipped and they began the procession out of the meeting room led by Li Pao. He took them to the door to the seraglio. The soldier unlocked it and they entered the passageway behind it. Their part in the day's festivities was over.

* * * * * * * * * * * * * * *

Gloom settled over the seraglio when the women returned. Qiao ordered the women out of their fine dresses and into their slinky robes of silk. They were told to leave the balls of opium laced leather in their mouths.

They had nothing to do. Violet spent much of her time on the balcony off the communal room. From there you could see into the garden below where the wedding couple and the celebrants were feasting. Me Ling, or a tiny version of her, was sitting at a table with her new husband and his Wife Number One. The former concubine stood out easily from the color of her dress.

Violet's heart was heavy. For about twenty minutes, her world and the free world had intersected. The people who had attended, and Violet had not been able to get a good look at them, she thought that she had seen some Europeans, were able to walk from that room and return to their free lives. They had the entire world to roam. She had but these three rooms. The events of the world held meaning for those other people, they meant nothing to her.

It was early in the afternoon, and the fall sun glinted on the meandering Yangtze River. There was the normal river traffic, junks and sampans flowing down or struggling upstream, an occasional fishing boat. They looked like little toys from her perspective, but she knew that there were people in them, people who led relatively free lives. She could see the docks of the town of Yeuyang, tiny laborers busily loading and unloading the boats, wagons and carts, and even an occasional truck pulling up or leaving.

Beyond the docks, there were stores and streets and beyond them houses. There was one house that she often watched. A large family lived there. It sat on a spacious plot and had several outbuildings. On sunny days, she could see the laundry hanging from a line in the back. There were children who played in the yard. From what Violet could tell, there were two girls and two boys. Sometimes, they held picnics out there and had parties. At night, the house was all lit up until around nine o'clock when one by one the lights in the rooms would extinguish. The last were always two rooms on the second floor. Violet supposed one of them to be an office where she imagined the man, who she saw sometimes coming and going from the house, worked late at doing his accounts. Always at about eleven, by her calculation, she only knew that it was about an hour before the midnight bell sounded in the seraglio, a signal for all the concubines who were not busy elsewhere to go to bed, the light in the office would go out. Within five minutes, the light in the other room would blink out as well. This, she imagined, was the master bedroom. She pictured the man sliding into bed next to his loving wife, them kissing, sometimes making love, but always snuggling up next to each other before they went to sleep.

Sometimes, watching the ritualistic extinguishment of the lights, she would cry. The simple act of being joined at night with a man she loved, giving and receiving gestures of affection before sleep, would always be denied her. She would never be surrounded by a loving family, never picnic with friends and family, never watch her own children play games and laugh. She was an owned whore and would never be anything else.

Why did she go on? She didn't know. Perhaps it was her faith that God somehow would redeem her. Me Ling had said that the gods would not abandon her, that she had a great soul, whatever that meant. She didn't feel that she had a great soul. She spent her days mostly lonely and afraid. Her love affair with Tatiana helped her survive, but it was clear to both her and the Russian girl that their liaison was only temporary and essentially tragic. It could be sundered at any time.

The October breeze wafted up to the balcony the muted tones of the orchestra. Colorful ribbons and banners decorated the garden. She could see the Chinese ideograms painted on them. She could not read Chinese at all. The only writing she was familiar with was the ideograms on her collar declaring her as the property of General Wang.

The party went on late into the night. Colorful lanterns dangled on strings drawn across the garden while the people ate and drank. Apparently, there was to be no fucking of guests for the concubines tonight. There were probably too many of them to be accommodated by just three whores. Too many noses would be out of joint as a result of not being so honored.

Normally, Violet would have been ordered to couple with one of her sisters in the middle of the communal room at least once and taken to her room by her maids for lovemaking. The only things that had happened all afternoon and into the night were that Tatiana had come and drunk from her breasts shortly after the ceremony and Jinjing, her maid, had supped from her after dinner. It was as if Qiao and the maids knew that it was better to leave the concubines alone to process their unhappiness.

Violet missed her piano terribly. One of the crones who acted as a chaperone in the seraglio played a mandolin shaped Chinese instrument called the liuqin. It had a pear shaped body and four strings. She was teaching Violet how to play it. Over the last 10 months or so that Violet had taken lessons, she had learned a number of simple songs, five or six verse things which put some ancient and revered Chinese poetry to music. It had been a struggle to learn the words and to understand the feelings that were being conveyed, but the old woman was a good teacher and Violet was a quick learner. There was a song she was trying to get right. It had sad notes. As far as she could understand the language and the chaperone's explanations, it was about a lost love. The chaperone who was teaching her, Yanyu, had pantomimed as much of it as she could. The notes told her the rest. The song was as sad and lonely as she felt now.

> *"At last year's Lantern Festival*
> *The flower market was bright as day.*
> *The moon had climbed the willow tops.*
> *At twilight end he came my way.*
> *At this year's Lantern Festival*
> *Moonlight and lamplight shine no less.*
> *I have not seen my last year's love.*
> *Tears wet the sleeves of my Spring dress."*

Yanyu had told her that it was a very old poem and that the man who wrote it was a very great, ancient, Chinese poet. Violet didn't know about that, but it made her think of home, her lost life, what might have been.

The only other break was when Li Pao arrived with a maid following him. She was carrying a tray from the party. On it were a dozen pieces of Me Ling's wedding cake. The women ate it in silence.

Li Pao had renewed the opium spiked balls of leather several times during the day. Whenever Violet had felt particularly sad about the day's events and what it meant to her, she gave the ball a little squeeze and within a few minutes, her head would begin to swim and she would calm. She had received permission form Qiao to remove hers while she practiced the mandolin like instrument. All of the women sat and listened and a few cried. When her practice was over, she handed the mandolin back to Yanyu, replaced the ball in her mouth and bit down on it. She laid down on the floor, letting the soothing sensations flow through her.

At twelve midnight, when the seraglio bell was sounded by Qiao, the party had diminished. Occasional peels of laughter wafted their way up to the third floor. Violet could still see the colorful lanterns stretching across the garden. She let her maids lead her to her bed. Jinjing and Ting laid on either side of her, stroking her face, kissing her, caressing her breasts while Lijuan made oral love to her. Violet was thankful for the calming effect of her orgasms, which came soft and pleasant, undoubtedly because of the drug she had been imbibing all day. Afterwards, the maids tied her ankles and wrists together and drew a soft, silk sheet over her naked body. It was Lijuan's night to watch her. Jinjing and Ting left. Within a short while, Violet fell off to sleep.

军阀 外家

CHAPTER SIX

It had been a stupendous party. Wang really knew how to throw one. Even the guards had gotten into the spirit of the thing, rice wine being spirited out to them regularly. At midnight, when the shift changed, the guards who had been drinking all day came on duty. Most of them fell asleep within the hour, some finding some quiet, unobtrusive place to lie down, some right on their feet.

As a result, no one noticed a slight figure dressed in black when he slipped over the inner wall at about 2 A.M. He carried a long rope with knots along its length every few feet and a large, iron, grappling hook on the end. He had wrapped it in leather to deaden the noise it would make when he used it. It made a dull thumping sound when he tossed it up and caught it on the edge of the balcony to the general's salon on the second floor. The man waited cautiously to see if anyone would respond. No one did. He quickly scampered up the rope.

The balcony to the seraglio was about twenty feet away from where the salon balcony jutted out. The black clad man got the hook to catch on the third floor balcony on his first try, as if he had been practicing it. The next part was tricky. He had to jump from the salon balcony and let his body swing wide under the balcony above it and twenty feet away. It required a tight grip on the rope and immense strength not to fall off. He had come this far, though, and he was not about to turn around now.

He stood on top of the railing and jumped. His body swung out in a huge arc. It took a good three minutes before his body finally came to rest. His shoulders ached and his hands burned from the friction on the rope. Ignoring the pain to his hands, he pulled himself up, helped by the thin, leather slippers that he wore and the knots that he had presciently tied there. When he reached the railing, he took a quick look through the glass door to the seraglio before jumping over it. There was a woman asleep on the floor. His grappling hook had not awakened her. It had been a simple thing for the man to tell the guard outside the seraglio door that the general had sent up a bottle of wine for the chaperones to drink after the concubines had been put to bed. The wine had been heavily laced with opium.

Flipping himself over the railing, the man landed quietly on his slippered feet. After pulling the rope up so that it would not be spotted by anyone roaming the grounds below, he tiptoed over to the door. It was unlocked as he expected. Who would bother to lock a door on a third floor balcony? He slid the door open and stepped inside.

Lieutenant Cheng had been burning for a year and a half. He could not get the English concubine out of his mind. He had taken care of her every bodily need for ten days on her trip up the Yangtze. He had washed her naked body, seen her cry her heart out with abandon. On the day that he saw her suck the general's cock in the meeting room when she had been inducted as his concubine, he had vowed that someday she would be his.

After a while, his lust for the beautiful European woman had faded. She was the general's property and to covet her invited death. Then one day, about nine months after she had disappeared behind the seraglio's doors, he saw her again.

He had been officer of the day in the fortress in charge of all the guards. He was on the third floor making sure that the guards were alert at their posts and that they were properly dressed and outfitted. He had just been chastising one of them for unburnished buttons on his uniform when there came a knock on the door from inside the seraglio. He ordered the guard to see who it was. It was the eunuch. The guard opened the door and the eunuch led her out.

She was naked, her hands were bound behind her and she wore bracelets on her ankles connected by a chain. Her head was pointed downwards and their eyes did not meet. He actually gasped when he saw her. She was as beautiful as he remembered her. Her hair was longer and her pubis was shaved. She wore makeup on her eyes and her nipples and sex lips were outlined in red as were her lips and fingernails. He watched, stupefied, as the eunuch led her across the landing by the golden chain that was affixed to her collar and gained admittance to the wing housing the bedroom suites of the general and his wives. As he watched her disappear inside, shuffling along on her bound feet, his heart ached.

That night, after he got off duty, he got good and drunk. And the next night too. And the next. Then, he pulled himself up. He would gain admittance to the seraglio and make love to the Englishwoman if it meant his life. He knew that he could not just break in; the other guards would be called within moments and he would be apprehended before he even had the opportunity to kiss her. No, he would have to break in somehow surreptitiously. Week after week went by, month after month. He planned to go three times. He had it all worked out. Each time he was frustrated by an over attentive sentry or a diminution of his nerve. It was Major Won's wedding that finally gave him his opportunity.

He had seen the whore, for that's what she was by now, servicing the major with her mouth, her rear and the fulcrum of her thighs at General Wang's party the day before the wedding. He watched angrily as he saw him pass her off to the Captain and the Captain fuck her in her rear portal. She had screamed and cried with lust. His heart turned black. He had been practicing his plan for months. He knew he could do it. But now his plan was altered slightly. He knew he could never get her out of the seraglio. She would not be able to climb down his rope and he would never be able to carry her, even if she was willing. Seeing what a slut she had become, he doubted that she would be. He could never provide her with the luxuries of the seraglio. And once he had taken her, she would have to abandon her wanton ways. From the ecstasy on her face when she orgasmed the day before the wedding, he knew that she was committed to her life of sexual abandon. No, the only solution was that she must die. He would rape her, plow her every hole, and then slit her throat. After that, he would take his own life.

Once inside the door, Cheng reached down and lifted the head of the crone who was sleeping the sleep of the dead by the door. He slit her throat from ear to ear. She barely gave out a murmur.

Cheng had bribed one of the maids into giving him the floor plan of the seraglio. She was a silly girl and he had told her that it was just so that he could feed his imagination, dream of the beautiful concubines asleep. They met in one of the warfside taverns in Yeuyang. The girl had been slightly drunk and gave up the information easily in exchange for a paltry sum. She was enamored of him. He had fucked her afterwards in one of the upstairs rooms.

He crept silently through the communal room and tip toed down the hall. He saw the door that led to the whore's bedroom. All the interior walls of the inner seraglio were merely opaque rice paper stretched over wooden frames. The door was no different. He slid it open quietly. From the maid he had bribed, he knew that the Englishwoman's personal maid would be kneeling by the door watching over her. She was, as he suspected she would be, fast asleep. He slipped into the room and, after clamping his hand over her mouth, prepared to slit her throat.

Violet had awoken during the night and she had not been able to get back to sleep. She was just too disconsolate about the day's events and the thought that tomorrow morning she would have to let the warlord feed from her breasts again. He would order her to her knees once more and have her suck him off. There was at least 45 days until his next voyage east to Shanghai, when it would be Tatiana's turn again. She didn't know how she was going to be able to stand it.

Her arms were bound behind her and connected to her ankles in a loose tie, so she was unable to leap from the bed when she saw the intruder enter. There was always a lantern burning in her room through the night so that the maid could watch over her and she saw the light glint off the blade of the man's knife. "No!" she called out frantically.

Cheng heard the Englishwoman's voice. It was the first time that he had actually heard her speak other than some muffled syllables through her gag on the voyage up river. He had not expected her to be awake. He realized that if he slit the maid's throat, the whore would scream for help. His plan to fuck her for hours at his leisure, until someone discovered the dead body of the chaperone in the communal room, would be set awry. He didn't know what to do.

The maid was whining desperately. The knife was poised against her throat, the edge drawing a little trickle of blood. The English whore spoke to him again.

"*No hurt, please! No hurt!*" she whispered in Chinese.

Violet was frantic that the man, whoever he was, was going to murder sweet Lijuan. She tried to think of how to forestall it. Why had the man come, she asked herself. He must be suicidal! What did he expect to accomplish? Was he there to murder her? Kidnap her? Rape her? She saw the hesitancy in his eyes. He looked familiar in the dim, yellowish light. She didn't care what the man did to her; she couldn't bear the thought of the kindly, little maid dying because of her. She decided to bargain with the only thing that she had, her body.

Her body was covered by the silk sheet. Straining her shoulders, she quickly used her legs to kick it down to the end of the bed. When it was off of her, she turned onto her back and presented her naked breasts.

"Whore Number Four fuck you! Me suck you cock good! No hurt girl, please!" she whispered just loud enough so that he could hear her. If she spoke too loudly, she would awaken one of the other maids or one of the chaperones and they would come running. The man was certain to slit Lijuan's throat the moment someone poked their head through the door.

The man heard the pigeon Chinese spoken by the woman. That was why he'd come, wasn't it? If he used the girl as a bargaining chip, he could secure the whore's cooperation and silence. And there was no particular reason the maid had to die. It was the whore he was after.

Violet saw that she had hit the right button. The man had come to fuck her. There was some hope. Then she recognized him. It was the man from the junk that had taken her to the general's fortress. All of the memories of that harrowing journey flooded her mind. He had been stern and cruel, forcing her to lie on her belly, her wrists and ankles tied to a ring in a beam above her, kept virtually motionless for days and days and days. He had slapped her and beaten her when she broke his rules. On the other hand, when he had washed her and fed her, lying on her belly like a beached whale, she had sensed some kindness in him. She hadn't seen him since the last day on the boat. Now she realized that he must be one of General Wang's soldiers. He had harbored a lust for her all this time and had finally gotten the courage to act on it.

If it was fucking that he wanted, she would give it to him, anything to save Lijuan's life. She turned her back so that he could see her bonds. "*Cut me, me help you,*" she said. She cursed herself for not having more Chinese words.

Cheng considered what she had asked. He understood that she wanted him to free her from her bonds. The maid was issuing little whines of panic. There was nothing to bind or silence her with. He decided that he had nothing to lose.

He dragged the unhappy maid closer to the bed. Tightening his grip on her face, he leaned over and slipped the point of the knife beneath the silken cord that was holding the English whore's wrists bound. It sliced through it easily. He watched as she shook her hands free. Her breasts moved invitingly. Her eyes were excited. His cock was hard.

Violet moved quickly. Her gag was kept in a cabinet by the bed. She freed her ankles and slid over the bed to it. Once she had it out, she showed it to her assailant. He nodded his head.

Bringing the gag to where his hand covered Lijuan's pretty mouth, Violet proffered it to her. The maid's eyes were as wide as saucers. Violet's eyes softened in entreaty. The frightened maid had to understand that it was the only way that her life would be spared. Tears were flowing from the young girl's eyes and, to the extent that she was able, she nodded her head.

The impassioned lieutenant was watching the two women carefully. If either of them tried to pull a trick, he would kill them both on the spot. At least part of his self imposed mission would be fulfilled. He carefully released his hand from the maid's mouth. She opened it and Violet slowly, gently, slid the nefarious instrument in. Her shoulder brushed against the soldier as she buckled the gag behind Lijuan's head. She looked at him. She could feel his excitement, his lust for her. But there was something else there too. A look of hatred? Where did that come from? What had she ever done to him?

Once the gag had been installed, Violet crept back to the bed and retrieved the silken ropes. She motioned for the man to drop the maid to the floor. He complied, warily, not taking his eyes off of his ultimate target. Violet drew the maid's hands behind her back. Lijuan moaned softly in her distress. Once her wrists had been joined together tightly, Violet leaned forward and whispered in her ear. "*Whore Number Four love Lijuan. Man no hurt Lijuan. Me fuck man good.*"

There was ample cord left to take care of Lijuan's ankles and tie then off to her wrists. When Violet was done, she knelt there and paused. She looked at the man. Was he going to kill her? A vast empty space opened in her belly. "I might as well die right now," she thought to herself. Her heart was pounding and she could feel the sweat emanating from her body. She realized that if she did anything to frustrate the man's purposes, reneged on her promise, he might kill the little maid out of spite. "No," she thought, "I have to go through with it."

She had fucked so many other men, what difference did one more make? And if by fucking this man she could save Lijuan's life, she would do it. The prospect of her own death did not bother her. She looked at the broad, red tinged knife and wondered how much pain there would be. She then realized, as she took in the traces of red in the grooves of the sharp, steel blade, that someone had already died. This man had nothing to lose now.

Violet saw that the man was hesitating about what to do next. She reached down for the hem of his jet black shirt and urged it up. "*Strip,*" she said as quietly as a coconspirator, a command that had been given to her often but one that she never thought she would be using herself.

Cheng wanted to strip, but he realized that he would be vulnerable while the pullover shirt went over his head. He placed the edge of the blade at Violet's throat. "Maybe I should kill her now," he thought. But, in a second, Violet, literally, disarmed him.

A placidity came over the enslaved concubine. She reached out her hands and placed them on the hand that held the knife. She pushed it away gently, her eyes locked on those of her captor. Almost tenderly, she pried it from his hand. Cheng was paralyzed. The contact between their skin sent a rush of excitement through him. She was kneeling in front of him, so naked, so beautiful. It took his breath away.

When she tossed the knife on the floor, he stared at it stupidly. This woman had put a spell on him! How did she do it? He looked back at her. They were kneeling inches apart on the soft rug. If he leaned forward, his chest would rub up against her heavy breasts. The woman took one of his hands in hers and lifted it to her chest. She placed it on her breast, smiling invitingly. The heat of the rounded orb traveled from his hand, up his arms and throughout his body.

"*Strip,*" she said again.

Cheng wasted no time. With the woman's help, he lifted his shirt over his head. She spread her hands over his chest and then leaned forwards and placed her lips on his skin. He closed his eyes and sighed as he felt her mouth's heat. She took one of his nipples in her mouth and suckled on it until it was stiff and then did the other one. Her hands roamed over his arms, down his belly, over his hips and thighs. She raised her head and kissed the fulcrum between his neck and shoulder, pressing her naked torso against his. She smelt of sweet perfume. Her body was hot. Her skin was soft and her breasts mashed enticingly against him.

He felt like he was in a daze. He had dreamed of having her in his arms so many times, for so long, that it hardly seemed real that she was kneeling naked before him. She was like a river sprite who had enchanted him.

Violet placed her hands under the lieutenant's arms and slowly brought him to his feet. When he was standing, she turned his back to the bed and pushed him until he sat down on it. Her hands descended his sides and then found the buckle to his pants and undid it. One by one, she freed the buttons of his fly. When she was done, she pushed him gently until his back was on the bed. She drew his pants over his hips and down his legs. She crouched down and slipped his leather slippers from his feet and pulled the pants over his ankles and off of his feet.

Violet looked at the body of the naked man. He was strong and fit. He was no boy, probably over 35. He had short, black hair. His chest was bare and black hair surrounded his rampant cock. It was long and thick. The dim light of the lantern gave the room a dream like quality. His body seemed to be aglow. She leaned over, ran her hands down his thighs and lowered herself between his knees. Her mouth found his rigid organ and she slowly drew it in, keeping her lips pursed against it and letting her tongue swirl around the shaft.

Cheng moaned with pleasure. His right hand found her head and stroked it lightly while his left took hold of the sheet below him and absorbed it in his grasp. It was a dream come true, better than he had ever imagined it. As her lips and tongue worked his needy piece, wave after wave of exquisite sensation flowed through him. Her mouth left his shaft, supplanted by her soft, adventurous hand. Pressing his cock back, she lowered her lips until she had captured his twin, soft stones. She suckled on them softly, stroking his cock gently with her hand.

"Ohhhhhhhhhh!" he moaned.

Violet heard him moan and her head perked up. Had anyone heard him? She waited for a moment, keeping a languorous pace on his cock with her hand. When she was satisfied that no one was coming, she whispered to him, "*No talking,"* the best thing she could think of to approximate "Keep quiet!"

The man's legs were hanging over the edge of the bed. Violet lifted them up and placed them on the mattress, turning his body so that his head was at the head of the bed. She climbed on after him and brought herself between his thighs. Leaning over, she brushed her lips on his cock and then raised herself past it. She let the manly projection slide along the cavern between her breasts. She kissed his belly, then his chest, then his neck. She raised her hips and took hold of his prick with her hand. She rubbed its tip along her pussy's divide, spreading the moisture that it found there. With a sigh, she lowered herself slowly, relishing the feeling of his pole brushing aside her labial lips.

Violet tried to figure out why she was so excited. Her breasts ached and her heart was beating heavily. Her pussy was wet and she trembled as the man's heat filled it.

And then she knew. This man had fallen in love with her. She had become an obsession with him so intense that he was ready to throw his life away for one night of passion with her. She thought of General Wang, who was passionate, but whose passion was cruel and domineering. She thought of the men who had used her so casually. This man, whatever his name was, had seen her at her most degraded, in her most helpless state. Yet, he adored her. He seemed to melt when she put her hands on him, brushed the tips of her breasts against his chest. And now he lay here, overwhelmed by the experience of the meeting of their flesh, tamed from his anger and vindictive passions. Who wouldn't be excited?

If this was to be his last night on earth, if he had given all to spend this time with her, to partake of her flesh, she would use all of the skill and wiles she had been taught or had discovered, to make his experience seem just short of paradise.

The man's hands grabbed her hips tightly as she began to raise and lower herself over his cock. She leaned over so that her breasts were crushed against his chest. She placed her hands against the sides of his head and melded her lips with his. He opened his mouth and accepted her tongue, issuing a muffled groan of passion. Rocking her hips, she stroked his cock with her cunt. Not General Wang's cunt. Her cunt. By pleasuring this virtually condemned man, she felt as if she had reclaimed her sexual organ, liberated it. She was using it for her own purposes. Even though the man clearly had her involuntary ravishment on his mind when he entered the seraglio, she had accepted and adopted his purposes as her own.

The man's hands tightened on her hips, his hips began to buck. He groaned into her mouth, "Arrrrrrgh! Arrrrrrrrgh!" His climax triggered hers and she cried out her pleasure back to him, stroking his cock wildly with her conch. She pressed her lips down on his madly as wave after wave of mind numbing pleasure flowed through her.

For a few moments, they laid there, stunned by their lust. Violet recovered first. She rolled off of him and he rose to follow her. She laid back, laying herself open to him. His hand moved towards her breast, cupped it, stroked her nipple. He looked up at her with wonderment. Was she real? Was this really happening? he asked himself. She ran her hand over his face. Her eyes were inviting him to explore her flesh. He leaned over, placed his mouth on her nipple and kissed it.

For the next half hour, Cheng kissed and stroked and suckled virtually every part of her body within reach. It was if he were trying to consume her. He pleasured her breasts until she moaned. He ran his lips and tongue over her belly, her thighs. When he dragged his tongue along her crevasse, Violet spread her legs widely, giving out a soft moan of pleasure.

Cheng was, in fact, close to heaven. He drank in the smell of her musk joyfully as he licked and kissed and suckled her bud of pleasure. He wrapped his arms around her thighs, locking his mouth in place and drank at her essence. Violet's hips bucked and shook as her orgasm overwhelmed her. She had clamped her lips tightly to suppress the sound of her joy. A long, high pitched whine escaped. Her hands were grasping tightly at the head between her thighs.

After her third climax, Cheng rose from her loins. His lusts had been renewed. He crawled forwards, greeted by Violet's welcoming arms. He poised his rock hard cock before her gate, his hand circling it. He pressed the head between her enflamed outer lips and then slid himself in.

Cheng was no neophyte when it came to fucking. Down at the Bamboo Teahouse in Yeuyang, he was well known for fucking its denizens for hours on end. His first burst of lust had come upon him quickly. He would not make the same mistake now.

Slowly, lovingly, he stroked his cock back and forth within Violet's canal. Violet succumbed to the mesmerizing pace of his rocking hips. She wrapped her arms around him. She had lost count of the number of men who had possessed her since her enslavement. There were maybe sixty or more. This was the first one that she could truly say was making love to her. She was overcome with happiness. She had despaired of ever having a night of real love again. To feel the member of a man sunk within her who was willing to lose everything for a single night of bliss made her mind spin. She knew not what consequences she would face tomorrow. She knew that she would have to face punishment for not resisting the man, for not fighting and screaming to protect the general's property. She had actually assisted him in subduing her maid. The warlord, her master, would not care that she had surrendered herself in order to save Lijuan's life. To him, she was sure, the life of the maid was meaningless. Even Violet's life was meaningless when it came to protecting his rights of ownership. She would face whatever punishment he laid out for her gladly in exchange for this man's love.

Timing her motions with his, Violet thrust her hips back at him. His head was buried in her shoulder, her thighs were wrapped around his. His hips had accelerated their pace. He was breathing heavily. Violet strained herself to withhold her lusts. She wanted to match his, to have her pussy explode in rapture at the same moment as his cock began to throb and pulse inside her.

The man was pumping his hips quicker and quicker. His cock rasped across her bud of pleasure, sending fierce, electrical charges to her sex. Her fingernails dug into the man's back. She felt her whole body contract in preparation for the explosion of her passions. She fought it, fought it, fought it, and then the man grunted. He gave out a series of short, emphatic groans. She felt the warmth of his discharge begin to spread inside her. She let go and her pussy came to life. Intense, hard contractions sent jolts of pleasure through her. She held onto the man for dear life. She buried her face into his chest and smothered her shouts of ecstasy. His cock kept going and going, driving her near to delirium.

The lovers clutched fiercely to each other's bodies as their orgasms faded. Violet could feel the man's heart beating hard through the wall of his chest. Their bodies were slick with the sweat of passion.

For the next hour or so, they lay in each other's arms wordlessly. Cheng stroked her breasts from time to time, ran his hand down her taut belly and drifted his fingers across her hairless puss. It was not an act of demand, or even of lust. It was an act of exploration, an attempt at gaining full knowledge of the flesh that he had pined for for so long.

All thoughts of murder had been wiped from Cheng's mind. He could not bring himself to destroy such a wondrous creature. He rolled her to her belly and explored her broad expanse of skin. He caressed her rear cheeks, massaged her muscles, tasted her flesh. He caressed her the length of her long legs.

When he rolled her back over, Violet took possession of his manhood and pushed him to his back. It was her turn to explore him. She kissed his chest, his belly, his thighs, all the while giving his member gentle, loving strokes. When he was good and hard, she brought herself between his knees and wrapped her hungry lips around his shaft.

Before becoming Wang's whore, Violet had never performed such an act for any man. Since then, who knows, maybe a hundred. But she had never taken within her mouth the cock of a man for whom she felt affection and love. Her mind reeled with bliss as she felt the thick cylinder fill her. She could taste the remnants of their previous bout on him and she reveled in it. She wanted to drive the man wild with ecstasy. She licked, she sucked, she kissed his tool. He writhed and sighed madly. She stroked his thighs, his belly, his chest, drawing all of his body parts within reach in to his cock. It was when he could no longer hold in his violent groans of passion that she brought him to completion. His cock jetted shot after shot of his viscous fluid into her mouth. She swallowed it hungrily. She exulted in the throbbing of his meat against her tongue and her lips. His hands had taken hold of hers and he squeezed them tightly as his body gave up his lust. When his paroxysms slowed and then halted, Violet gave his cock one last, gentle suckle and then rose to lie next to him.

His body drained, Cheng soon fell asleep. Violet nestled him in her arms, watching his peaceful face. It was a face that would be soon wrenched with pain. Wang would torture him before he killed him, she knew that. She felt a stab of fear for him and for herself. It would be dawn soon. Already there was a trickle of light through her window. She shook him gently, reviving him. His eyes sprang open and looked at the window. He looked back at her with sadness.

Violet's breasts were full with her milk. She wrapped her arm behind the man's head and proffered her teat to him. A drop of milk dangled from her nipple. He looked at her strangely at first and then, smiling, took her teat in his mouth and began to suckle her.

She realized, as did he, that this was probably his last meal on earth. She was happy that it could come from her. She knew that she was giving away General Wang's due, but she didn't care.

The feel of the milk flowing through her breast brought Violet a wave of contentment. He was lying beneath her and his hand was gently massaging her breast, encouraging her flow. When her right breast was empty, Violet shifted herself and let him drink from her left. While his one hand stroked and massaged her mammary, his other drifted down her thigh, trolling softly along her skin. Violet sighed and spread her legs, ready to receive his caress of her puss.

Violet was in the throes of lust when the man finished supping at her breast. He pushed her to her back and slid between her thighs. When he entered her, they both moaned. He fucked her long and slow. It was their last time, they both knew it. But their lovemaking was not desperate. It was the copulation of two old lovers, familiar with each other's flesh. They gazed into each other's soft, unfocused eyes. When Violet came, her body shuddered and she grasped him tightly. It passed through her like a meandering river. It passed and another slow, languid climb to completion began. Cheng was giving her the whole length of his cock, drawing himself out until the tip laid barely inside and then descending slowly, ever slowly so that they could both feel joy from every square millimeter of contact between their sexes. Violet's arms encircled him, holding him lightly against her. His passions were building quickly, she could sense it. She squeezed his member with her pussy's muscles, maximizing his pleasure. Finally, he caressed her face with the tips of his fingers, leaned down and took her mouth as his cock poured his soul into her deep, welcoming chasm. Violet closed her eyes as her responsive climax was triggered, and held her lover tight.

* * * * * * * * * * * *

They had been lying there holding each other peacefully for about twenty minutes when they heard the scream. The body of the chaperone had been found. Violet felt sorrow for the dead woman, whoever she was. She prayed that it was not Yanyu, the chaperone who had been teaching her the Chinese mandolin.

A tumult broke out. Footsteps could be heard dashing to and fro in the hallway. Cheng sprung to alertness. He jumped from the bed and retrieved his knife from where Violet had tossed it. He looked at her. She looked back at him.

He did not want to kill her, but he knew that he probably should. She was unaware of the full extent of General Wang's cruelty when his anger was aroused. They had committed a great crime against him. She had not shouted for assistance, given her life in protection of her virtue, such as it was. She would face harsh punishment, maybe even death. It was the possibility that she would somehow survive that halted his hand. If she lived, their night together would live on too. He had no doubt of the genuineness of the English whore's affections. Her lovemaking had been too pure for mendacity.

He thought of taking his own life. He was going to die anyway. But if he died by his own hand, General Wang would have no victim on whom to vent his anger. Undoubtedly, he would then visit it upon her. No, he would take whatever tortures that Wang could devise. He owed it to her for all that she had given him.

Little Lijuan had remained silent through out the night. Violet had forgotten all about her. When the maid saw the man pick up his knife from the floor. She gave out a desperate whine. She prayed that he wasn't going to kill her. She had heard them making love all night, their moans of lust, their groans of joy. She realized that her mistress had saved her life, but she knew that what had gone on between the concubine and the invader had been very wrong. She would be asked about it. She could lie, but knew very well that her body would be tormented until the master was sure that she was telling the truth. If she were dead, there would be no witness to their night of lust.

But Cheng had no intention of killing her. Her mistress had earned her her life. A head poked itself through the door to the bedroom. It was one of the chaperones. When she saw Cheng, she screamed and ran off. Cheng looked down at Violet and gave her a fatalistic smile. He grabbed his clothes and quickly put them on. He didn't want to be naked when the soldiers came for him.

It did not take long. The rice paper door slid open and Cheng saw Lieutenant Wong standing there, his pistol drawn. Two guards stood behind him, rifles at the ready. Cheng threw the knife on the bed and stepped forward to surrender. He knew Wong very well. They had gone out drinking and whoring together many times. They had been like brothers. Wong stepped forward to meet his old friend. The pistol was in his right hand. He drew it back across his left shoulder and then swung it at Cheng's head. He went down like a shot, unconscious.

军阀 外家

CHAPTER SEVEN

General Wang was in his second floor salon. It was where he often went when he wanted to be alone and think. Over the last two weeks he had done a lot of thinking. It was all the English whore's fault.

He was still asleep when he received news of the invasion of his seraglio and the death of the chaperone. He had ordered the offending lieutenant, the maid and the English slut to his dungeon pending further investigation. Actually, he wanted to have them beheaded right on the spot, all three of them, after personally scouring out their intestines with a dull blade. He had learned, however, from bitter experience not to act hastily in any situation if it could be avoided.

Some might say that ordering his concubine and her maid to the dungeon was putting the cart before the horse, that it was imposing the punishment before the trial. To a large extent, that was true. On the other hand, they had been caught en flagrente delicto. The English whore, may the devil take her eyes, and the stupid maid had let the man ravish his property without his consent and without him achieving a single benefit from it. It was true that he handed the whore out plenty of times. That was his prerogative as her owner. He did it, though, when it brought him some kind of personal gain, be it financial, strategic, tactical or psychic.

Sometimes the use of one of his concubines was the sweetener to a deal he was making. That was a financial reason for whoring them out. He liked to keep certain of the larger estate owners friendly to him. That was strategic or tactical depending on the situation. The psychic benefits ranged between his feelings of aggrandizement in having the power to do it, to the excitement, as in the English whore's case particularly, of forcing them to submit to the coarse and unrestrained demands of unknown men.

Since he had not approved it advance, the use of his whore by the lieutenant failed to provide him any enjoyment. It served no strategic or tactical purpose and it did not profit him in any way. Therefore, it was wrong on all counts. Moreover, there was the matter of alerting every swinging dick in his duchy that violation of his concubines without permission would result in a travail of pain and outrage and then death.

As to the concubine, regardless of her complicity in the matter, she was now despoiled. She had let a man not of his choosing possess the cunt that belonged to him and not to her. The only way that her violation could be considered nonculpable on her part would be if the man had killed her first. It was her duty to defend her lord's honor unto the death. That had clearly not happened since she was still alive. So, the likelihood of her being found innocent was virtually nil.

In the case of the maid, it was clear that she had been asleep. If she had been awake, she would have had the opportunity to cry out. Once she had done so, it was her obligation to place her life in the way of any transgressors to the seraglio. Since she was still alive, she was guilty as well.

It should be a simple matter then to set the execution date of all three offenders. No trial would be necessary.

Lieutenant Wong was condemned as well. He had done nothing directly wrong, but he had been the officer in charge on the night in question. It was his duty to protect his lord's property. He had failed egregiously.

In his mind they were all tired and sentenced. And yet, he had let them all linger on in his dungeon for two weeks. Suffering outrageous torments, it was true, but alive nonetheless. And all because of the English whore.

He had wanted to kill her with his bare hands. The eunuch, with his better knowledge of his master's mind had gently led him to the decision to wait. The whole story needed to come out, he said. There may be more conspirators. Let the ghouls in the dungeon work on her a while. And the others too.

Li Pao had been right about that. That Cheng was one tough bastard. It took the men in the cellar of his fortress eight days to get it out of him. He finally gave up the maid who had revealed the layout of the seraglio to him. Li Pao had her arrested later that day. So then there were five awaiting execution.

Whore Number Four must die, Wang knew that. But he couldn't bring himself to give the order. If he didn't do it soon, it would be academic. Sooner or later, one of the dungeon guards would go too far with her or she would just die of hopelessness. He had seen it happen. Why couldn't he do it?

Li Pao came into his salon. He had the maid Lijuan in tow. She was sniffling and sobbing. She looked a mess. Her naked body was striped like a zebra, except that her stripes were bright red. There were black and blue marks where she had been punched or beaten with something more substantial than a whip. Her eyes were red and her face gaunt. She had her arms tied behind her. Wang had sent for her because he wanted to hear for himself what had happened that night.

At first, after her arrest, the maid had tried to cover up for her mistress, as any good maid would. That had lasted for a day and a half, much longer than he would have expected considering the abuse his jailors were capable of. He had read the reports of her interrogation by his eunuch, how the English whore had saved her life. How she had bargained for her with her body. How long and passionate was her subsequent lovemaking with the lieutenant.

He had to turn his head away. It was one thing to exchange ribald tales with the men who had used her, them telling him how they filled her mouth with their cocks or how she squealed with unhappiness when they beat her. The thought of her passionate embrace with that lowly monkey, Lieutenant Cheng, drove him mad. He had reached a part of her that he, her lord and master, her owner, would never see. How could that be? Had they been lovers before? On the boat from Shanghai? He had had Li Pao cross examine the rest of the crew. There had been nothing to suggest that he hadn't followed orders.

The maid fell to her knees in front of him. She must have been a tasty morsel before her vacation down below, he thought as he looked at her. He was familiar with most of the maids in his fortress. He helped pick them out and had fucked most of them too. Somehow, this one had escaped him.

"*Your name is Lijuan?*" he asked her, his voice rough and deep.

The girl looked up at him piteously.

"*Y,yes, Lord,*" she eked out.

"*You are under a sentence of death. Did you know that?*"

A loud sob filled the room. Apparently no one had told her. He let the information sink in. Her lips were trembling and her neck was bent. Her long, straight, black hair made a curtain around her face.

"*I want you to tell me what happened that night,*" he instructed her. "*If you hold anything back or if I think that you are lying, I will set the torturers upon you again. You will beg them to kill you. Do you understand that?*"

She looked up forlornly, her face was a curtain of tears. "*Y, yes, Lord,*" she whined. "*Please don't let them hurt me any more, please! I'll tell you everything!*"

She told them abut the day up in the seraglio, how everyone was sad about the departure of Me Ling, especially her mistress. They had put her to bed, all tied up according to the rules. Someone had brought a bottle of wine for the chaperones. They shared a little bit with the maids. She had had only two mouthfuls. Later, when she was guarding her mistress, she fell asleep. "*I didn't mean to, my Lord! I didn't mean to! There was something in the wine! I would never leave my mistress unprotected! Never!*"

This was getting tiresome. "*Go on!*" Wang ordered using his voice of command.

"*I woke up with the man's hand around my mouth. He had a knife to my neck. He was going to kill me, but the mistress was awake. She told him, 'No!'.*" Lijuan's voice was panicky, strained. She looked back at the quiet, patient eunuch to see if he were about to strike her. When she saw that he wasn't, she continued her narrative.

"*She offered him her body so that I might live,*" she sad, her voice tremulous. She broke out into tears. "*Oh, Lord, please don't kill my mistress, please! It's all my fault! Kill me! Kill me!*"

"*Silence!*" Wang roared. "*If you don't tell me what happened, I'll have you boiled in oil! Do you know what that's like? It will take you three days to die! Your skin will boil off and your flesh will slowly cook! Do you want that?*"

"*Nooooooo!*" the girl cried. "*Pleeeeease don't, please! I'll tell you! I'll tell!*"

She was a miserable figure. Her naked breasts quivered. Her chest was heaving. Her face was a paragon of fear.

"*She asked him to untie her and he cut her ropes,*" she continued. "*She got the gag out and put it in my mouth. Then, when he put me on the floor she tied my hands. When she was done, she whispered in my ear, 'Whore Number Four love Lijuan. Man no hurt Lijuan. Me fuck man good.' She never knew he was coming! I swear it! She offered herself up to save me!*"

Wang was stunned. "*She spoke in Chinese?*" he asked, incredulous.

"*Yes, Lord,*" she answered. "*She's been learning it ever since she joined us. She plays the liquin as well. She sings beautifully. Please don't kill her Lord! She'll sing for you! She'll serve you! Please!*"

Wang looked at Li Pao. "*Why wasn't I told?*" he asked him.

"*You never asked, Lord,*" Li replied. Since when did the warlord care what went on between his sex slaves when he wasn't using them? To even ask the question was to answer it.

The warlord looked back at the frail, sorrowful girl. "*What did they talk about?*" he asked her.

"*Nothing, Lord,*" she answered forlornly.

"*They didn't say a word?*"

"*Only my mistress talked. She said, at the beginning, 'Strip.' And later, when he was groaning as she sucked his cock, she told him, 'No talking.' That's all, Lord. I swear!*"

"*So, she conspired with him to cover up their treachery?*" he shouted at the condemned maid.

"*Noooooooo!*" the maid responded desperately. "*It wasn't like that at all! He was going to kill me if she didn't! If she yelled for help, or if he was discovered before he had his way with her, he would have killed us both!*"

"*What did he do with the knife while he fucked her?*" Wang asked insistently.

"*She took it from him, Lord. I saw it. He had the knife at her throat and she put out her hand and just took it and threw it down on the floor.*"

"*He just gave her his knife?*" This tale was sounding stranger and stranger as the maid told it. Everything that she was saying, though, was consistent with what she had finally told his eunuch while under the whip.

"*Why didn't she call for help then?*" Wang asked her. "*She could have, couldn't she?*"

It was the one question that Lijuan had been hoping the warlord wouldn't ask her. Even from the floor of the bedroom, her mouth gagged, her hands and legs bound, she had sensed the passion pass through them. It had been remarkable. It was like watching a play where the characters fell in love at first sight.

"*Yes, Lord,*" Lijuan admitted sorrowfully. "*But you don't understand, Lord. It was like they fell in love at just that moment. Something came over them both. At first, it was like listening to two teenage lovers and then, as the night wore on, they seemed to join as if they had discovered all that they needed to know about each other. They fucked then like lovers floating on a sea, unaware of the world around them. It was beauti....*" The foolish girl stopped. She had said too much. Way too much. She could see it in the warlord's face.

"*Take her away!*" he yelled. Li took a handful of her hair and dragged her from the room. She kept shouting as they left, "*Please don't kill her, Master! Please! Please! Please!*"

A deep blackness seized his soul. He cursed the day that Robert had ever convinced him to claim her, cursed the moment that he had set eyes on her. Her victory over him in roulette had been an omen. She was his slave, but she was the victor. She had found love, despite being locked away, despite all the abuse she had suffered. The lieutenant's obsession with her had triggered it, he was sure. Everything he had done with her had blown up in his face! She had to die! Tomorrow, and all the others too! He would assemble all of the troops, all of the staff. The other concubines would be made to watch from the windows of the seraglio! They would watch and see what happens to someone who betrays him! He would whip her until she bled in torrents and then he would turn her over to the executioner after watching her lover die first!

* * * * * * * * * * * * * *

Down in the dungeon, Violet had no idea how much time had expired since she had been dragged from her room that morning. She had been bound and gagged, blindfolded and taken directly to the cell she now occupied. It was the same one that she had been in when she was first brought to the warlord's fortress. And she was bound in it in the same way. He knees were on the floor and her ankles bound to two iron rods set into the cement. Her bound hands were tied to another iron bar set in the floor behind her. And her neck was dragged down, a rope leading from her collar through the iron bar beneath her chin to one about three feet in front of her.

For the most part, she was left this way in the pitch darkness of her cell. When the door was closed, it was like she had been transported to some strange new world where there wasn't sound or light. She had to moan and sob every once in a while to remind herself that she was still on earth.

The men had whipped her savagely. They had used her three defenseless holes repeatedly. She was fed only a watery gruel and she had to eat it where she knelt, her face buried in the bowl. When she was done, they left the evidence of it on her face.

It was the same two evil gremlins who had cared for her during her first stay. She had named them Scylla and Charybdis, after the mythic Greek monsters. They were the ones who fed her, took care of her wastes, fucked her and, except for once, whipped her. They loosened her bonds only so that she could shit in a pail. Sometimes, after a whipping, they would, for a while, let her lay on the thin, greasy, cotton pallet that lay in the corner of her cell, her hands bound to her ankles, gagged and blindfolded.

Mostly, they had beat her out in the common area of the dungeon, where they had their option of a dozen different weapons of terror and pain. She would be strung up on a gibbet, her hands above her, her feet tied off to the floor so that she wouldn't try and dodge the blows. She would scream and beg, plead for mercy, promise them all the pleasure she could bring them. Nothing availed her. They would beat her until they were satisfied with her suffering and return her to her cell.

Sometimes, they didn't bother to take her from her cell. There was a hook in the beam in the middle of the 10' by 10' room. Usually, they hung their kerosene lantern there so that they could see her. But, when they tied off her hands to the hook so that they could whip her right where she was, they left their lanterns on the floor. They always came together and they always brought two lanterns. The light from them, shining up, cast demonic shadows on the walls as she twisted and turned to try and avoid the blows.

Once, she had been whipped by the eunuch. It had been the worst of all of them. It was the one time that she was gagged. The two gremlins had mounted her on the gibbet and left her there. She hung there for an hour or more while they made their rounds and fed and tormented the other denizens of their hell. The lanterns on the walls made the room bright and Violet could see all of the instruments of torture and pain displayed and ready for use, some of which she had yet to make the acquaintance of. She was naked, standing on her toes, desperately afraid, hungry, lonely, tired and without hope. When she saw the eunuch emerge from the long hallway that led to the punishment room, her body began to shake and her stomach flipped over.

She had wondered when she would see him.

When she was here last, an eight day stay, he had seen her every day, usually several times, to feed her and stroke her, to bring her upstairs to his bedroom to train her as a receptive whore. Now, there had been no trips upstairs to be pampered by her three maids, no lust driving sessions on his bed where she learned to ass fuck, suck a cock and make love to women, skills that had served her well. The last time she had seen him was when she had been dragged from her bedroom in the seraglio to the communal room. One of the soldiers was tying her hands behind her. The other was readying her gag for use. Li Pao entered the room from the hallway. He had stared at her demonically. These days she had spent in her cell, she had awaited his arrival with dread in her heart.

The eunuch approached her calmly. He was dressed in his standard uniform, a shiny, silk sheath of blue and gold. He had a matching, round cap on his head. He was tall for an Asian, about 5'9" and although wiry of physique, strong. He was 50 or so years old, had spent years in the Imperial Seraglio before being cast out in a general cost cutting measure. After that, he had done some time at a Shanghai whorehouse, running the girls for a local gang. Wang had won the right to his contract in a poker game. Li had been with him for most of his twenty years as ruler of this 400 square mile kingdom. They were the best years of his life.

Li was fanatically loyal to his master. Anyone who threatened him was his enemy. He was more than a whoremaster for him. He was also a kind of intelligence officer, with tendrils that reached all the way to Shanghai and Nanking. Nothing of note happened in Yeuyang without his knowledge. Nothing passed up or down the river without his okay and a percentage for his master. No one did business with the master without dealing with him first.

But ruling the warlord's seraglio was his first love and primary duty. He trained them, disciplined them, shaved their pussies every day. If General Wang was like a god to the enslaved women, he was like the avenging archangel.

He looked at the battered and bruised body of the English whore. It was too bad. She was an excellent concubine. He had encouraged the chaperone, Yanyu, to teach her to play the mandolin, and Pu Wei and Me Ling to teach her Chinese.

He remembered well the concubines in the Emperor's court, although that was all gone now. They were not just whores; they were elegant courtesans, most of them. They were poetesses and singers and storytellers of great repute. Some painted or were accomplished at calligraphy. This one had the potential to be one of those. She had the spirit and the eagerness to know. He too had read her letters to that foreign devil, Robert. What a fool he was to let her get away and all because of that slut Qua Li. The woman was well educated, had a heart, was clear of thought and expression. And she was beautiful. A perfect courtesan! Once he had her developed to her peak, there was no way that the lord would ever let her go. She would calm that madness that seemed to be in his soul. And now, because of that stupid lieutenant, she had to die. What a waste!

Aside from what he thought of her, though, he had his duty to his master to perform. The slut had sinned and she had to pay. Although it had occurred to him that he should go easy on her under the circumstances, she was not totally at fault, he had rejected that. A sin had been committed and justice must be meted out. His first loyalty was to his lord and his lord's honor. If he didn't whip her brutally, the guards would let it be known around the taverns and bawdy houses of the district. That would be bad for the general. If people thought that he was soft, the warlord would become vulnerable. No, he had to give her a proper whipping.

He had selected a long, thin whip. It was made of steel, but wrapped in leather. It was narrower than the one he used before on her and this one, unlike the other, would leave fiery lacerations on her skin. She would bleed. The cuts would take a long time to heal. But it didn't really matter. She would be dead long before that.

Violet saw the evil instrument that the eunuch had selected. She groaned in fear. Her belly did flip flops as he strolled around her, looking for an appropriate place to begin. Her body was sweating heavily and her mouth and throat were dry. With every ounce of strength that she had left, she wanted to cry out and beg the cruel man not to do it, not to whip her. Her voice was silenced by the thick cylinder of leather in her mouth. There would be moans and whines of pain, but no begging, at least nothing that would be intelligible.

The whip made a, "tszzzzzz!" sound as it cut through the air. The eunuch's first target was the small of her back. Violet stiffened her back and screamed into her gag. It felt like the whip had sliced a gap into her skin. There was a count of four beats and the whip was let fly again. "Tszzzzzzz! Snap!" This one struck her across the front of her thighs. To Violet, it felt like some feral beast had drawn its razor sharp claw across her skin. She moaned and cried out again frantically; her body was jolted rigid by the blow.

Li Pao counted out four to himself and the struck her once more, on the underside of her ripe breasts. "Ooooooooooouuuuuuuuu!" she cried out. Four more beats and, "Tsssssssszzz! Snap!" Then "Tsssszzzzzzz! Snap! Tsssssssszzzz! Snap! Tssssssszzzzzz! Snap!" Each ravishing blow was separated by four seconds from the last. Violet kept screeching at her voice's highest range. Her body writhed and twisted to the limits permitted by her bonds. Little rivulets of blood were flowing from her wounds.

"Tssssszzzzzzzz! Snap! Tszzzzzzz! Snap!, Tsssssszzzzz! Snap!" the rain of blows continued.

"Please! Please! Stop! Please! For god's sake! Please!" Violet screamed into her gag. Her throat was growing hoarse from her shouting. Her words emerged from her gag as garbled noise. It provided little distraction for her assailant. He covered her rear cheeks, her thighs, her breasts, her back. Each blow was perfectly timed to keep the slut at a high pitch of continuous agony. Li Pao was keeping count carefully. Twenty five was the limit. He would reach it soon.

"Tsssssszzzzt! Snap! Tsssszzzzzzzz! Snap! Tsssssszzzzzz! Snap!"

Violet felt like she had been dumped into a thresher and was being attacked by its unforgiving blades. All her mind could do was pray that her ordeal would soon end. All other thoughts and sensations had been swept away. "Ooooooooouuuuuuuu! Ooooooouuuuuuuuuu! Ooooooooou-uuuuuuuuuu!" she screamed.

Finally, it was over. Her body burned everywhere it had been struck. She couldn't stop sobbing and wailing. It was as if the switch in her brain that governed it had become stuck at on. She clamped her teeth down fiercely on the gag in her mouth. She shut her eyes tightly. Her heart was beating a hundred miles and hour and her lungs were searching for air through her nose, making loud wheezing sounds. And yet, when the pain subsided enough to allow her thought processes to begin again, they turned once more to her forbidden lover locked into a cell no more than ten or twenty yards away.

She didn't know which cell was his. She knew that he was still there though because just that morning she had heard him scream and cry with pain as the two ghouls tortured him. Her heart broke every time she heard it. There was another man there too, she knew that. She could tell the difference between them. Her lover, and she still didn't know his name, had been brought to the cells first and the men hard started working on him right away. She could tell the difference in the voice as he cried out. The torturers left the door to her cell open much of the day while they took their pleasure with all the inmates. One of them, she was sure, was Lijuan. Poor, little Lijuan. Maybe she should have let her lover slice her throat. If she had known, Violet thought, what she would be subjected to, maybe she would have. There was another young woman too. Violet didn't recognize her anguished pleas for mercy. They were pitiful nonetheless.

Li Pao signaled the guards, the men Violet had labeled Scylla and Charybdis, to release her from her bonds and return her to her cell. Charybdis, the stockier of the two, caught her as Scylla released her wrists from above her. He then released her ankles and they dragged her the fifty feet to her cell. She had hoped that they would set her down on her pallet for a while, but the men had other instructions. They took the end of the brown, leather strap attached to her wrists and tied it off to the hook in the beam above her. They left her standing on her tippy toes when they left. They had left a lantern behind them and, a moment later, she saw the eunuch coming in. He was carrying a bucket by its handle in his left hand. He put the bucket down next to her. Violet looked down and saw a brownish mixture inside the pail. She didn't know what it was, but she knew that it would not be pleasant for her.

Li Pao dipped his hand into the pail and came up with a handful of the thick, slurry like substance. It was a mixture of salt and vinegar. He began to rub it over the English whore's wounds. Violet screeched in pain as the fire that had finally subsided all over her body broke out again. He covered each and every wound with it. Violet felt like she was surrounded by fire. "Oh, god," she called out, her voice emerging muffled, "please don't leave me like this! Please!"

When Li Pao was done, he picked up the pail and the lantern and stepped through the door. He put them down, swung the big, heavy wooden door shut and locked it.

The intense fire that had been lit all over Violet's body lasted for a good hour. She whined and cried and begged someone to help her. In the darkness, it seemed like her body had been overwhelmed with an evil spell that kept her in constant pain. Her body shuddered and shook in agony. What a cruel world she had been plunged into! She prayed that they would kill her soon.

She had watched the occasional beheading in the inner courtyard below the windows of the seraglio. Her heart had always gone out to the poor people. It was gruesome to watch. Soon, it would be her turn. She understood now why the people let themselves be calmly led to their doom. After a sojourn in the hell that was General Wang's dungeon, death was a welcome friend.

The pain from her exacerbated wounds eventually reduced in intensity, but they continued to burn. The salt was drying in the wounds making them itch terribly. Violet's knees had gone weak and she hung from her wrists for the longest time. She cursed the darkness, cursed General Wang, cursed Robert. The only person of consequence that she did not curse was her lover. He had given her something that was worth suffering for. She felt as if her torment was merely the bill that was being delivered for her hours of joy and delight. Death would be a fair exchange.

Now, a week later, Violet wondered when her time would come. She knelt motionless as she had for hours and hours in the absolute darkness. Her abuse had seemed to taper off as if she had reached her point of saturation. The interminable wait for her fate to be revealed tore at her insides. She would rather have the whipping than this dreadful, lonely suffering.

She heard the key jingle in the lock and she steeled herself for renewed abuse. It couldn't be the gremlins, they had come in and fucked her about an hour ago, one in her mouth while the other plowed her rear entrance. They had stopped milking her the moment she had been brought to the dungeon so it couldn't be that. She couldn't say how long it was since she had eaten, time had little meaning in her dark hole, but she felt no hunger pangs. Then again, she rarely did.

Violet had refused to eat when she was brought down to the dungeon. She knew that she was damned and she wanted to get it over with. Scylla and Charybdis beat her unmercifully, but she still refused. She was on her knees, her ankles and arms tied off. Scylla, the more slender one, had pressed her face into the bowl of mush until she almost suffocated, but she would not eat a single mouthful.

Then, he had gone away. Charybdis stayed in the cell, laughing. He knew something that she didn't.

When Scylla returned, he had a long, bamboo tube, about two inches in circumference. It was fitted at one end with a broad scoop. The other end was tapered and the edges had been rounded off by sanding and then enameled, making them smooth. Scylla placed the tube on the floor. He and Charybdis sprung suddenly into action.

The man behind her grabbed her hair in his large, tight fist, pulling her head back while circling his other hand under her chin. Violet was so surprised that she didn't realize that her mouth stood agape. In a flash, Scylla had inserted a ring much like the one used to force feed her the potion that time in the seraglio. He plopped it in past her teeth. Charybdis released her chin and hair and buckled it behind her head.

Violet whined and moaned as she realized what the men had done. Her mouth was distended in a round 'O'. She looked at the bamboo tube with more understanding. The two gremlins laughed and mocked her, pushing their dirty fingers into her mouth and pulling at her tongue. Soon, though, they tired of this. Scylla picked up the tube. The other man poured some water in her bowl of mush, diluting it, and mixed it with his fingers so that it had a loose, fluid consistency.

The big man pulled her head back again by her hair. He held her chin in a vice-like grip, keeping her head still. Violet was looking up at the ceiling. Scylla moved in front of her and introduced the smooth, tapered end of the tube into the 'O' of her mouth. Violet squirmed and whined, tried desperately to free her head, but Charybdis held her tight. She felt the tube hit the back of her mouth and then ease slowly into her throat. She coughed and gagged as it went down. It went lower and lower. Her whole body was shaking with the terror of having the invader within her. Scylla held her in place while Charybdis reached down for the bowl of liquefied mush. He placed the bowl near the scoop at the top and began slowly pouring it in.

Violet moaned as she felt the liquid entering her belly. As the flow descended, she tried desperately several times to shake off her captors. They held her too tight. Charybdis kept pouring the mush at a steady, slow pace, like he had had a lot of practice doing this before. When the bowl was empty, he slowly pulled the tube from her esophagus and then released her.

Violet bent her head to the floor and cried. Refusing to eat had been the last vestige of rebellion left to her. Her whole body ached from despair. She felt a pull on her hair and her head was lifted up again. Scylla had his stiffened cock out. He pressed it into the forced opening that was her mouth and slid it to the back until it touched her throat. He pumped it back and forth, back and forth, sliding it over her tongue, forcing the end into her throat. He groaned when he came and then it was the other cruel man's turn. Violet wept and whined as she suffered the callous use. She had to let his slime descend into her belly when he came. He eased his cock out when his spasms stopped and slapped her cheek playfully. "*Whore Number Four sucks cock good,*" he told her. "*In the morning we'll do this again.*" He chuckled.

Scylla knotted the rope around the ring of her collar and then passed it under the iron bar embedded in the floor below her chin. He pulled it tight, forcing her head down. It was then tied off to the ring three feet in front of her. The men picked up her empty bowl and their lanterns and left.

They had fed her four or five more times with the ring in her mouth, each time fucking her mouth after they were done. They didn't bother taking it out when they left. When they whipped her later that day, her voice made an "Ooouuuuu! Oooouuuu! Oooouuuu!" sound as she screamed in pain.

On the third day, Scylla came in with her food. He had the bamboo tube with him. Charybdis was right behind him.

"Do you want the tube, Whore Number Four, or will you eat right now?" he asked her after he let her head up, in his rough, peasant's voice, a hint of amusement in it.

Violet wanted to tell him that she would eat every drop if only they would take the ring out of her mouth, but her voice came out, "Oouuu oouuu oouuu oouuuu!"

Scylla and Charybdis laughed. *"I'll take that as a yes, Whore Number Four,"* Scylla said. *"But you must promise to give me and my mate a good blow job when you're done. Otherwise, the ring goes right back in. Yes?"*

Violet nodded her head desperately.

She licked up every drop in her bowl, her face mushed into it, her hands unavailable to assist her. When she was done, she serviced both men as well as she was able. After they finished with her, they installed her gag in her mouth and tied her off again face down. When they left, she was in darkness once more.

Two weeks into her imprisonment, Violet tried to look up as the door to her cell opened. She could see only feet and a little bit of silvery blue fabric. It was Li Pao. She hadn't seen him since her whipping. He loosened the tie that held her head down and she rose up to get a full view of him. Her stomach fluttered as she considered whether he had come back down to whip her again. Then she saw the maid behind him. She recognized her as one of Me Ling's former attendants. She had a bucket of water, a jar of soap, a towel and a brush.

It had been two weeks since she had been cleaned and she knew that she stank horribly. But what was this bucket bath preliminary to? Was it her time and they wanted to make her look a little more presentable before they chopped her head off? She tried to figure out what time of day it was. She knew that the executions always took place in the mornings. Was it morning or night?

Maybe they're taking me back to the seraglio, she thought hopefully. Then her hopes were dashed when she realized that if she were returning to the seraglio, they would just give her a bath there. No, something was up. What could it be?

Li released her ties and told her to stand up. Weakly, she brought herself to her feet. The maid had put the bucket down by Li's side. He leaned down and pulled a large, rough sponge out of it and squeezed out the excess water. He held it out while the maid poured some soap onto it and he proceeded to scrub her body.

He was rough and cold as he cleaned her. He soaped her breasts and belly, her legs and her loins. He did her buttocks and back, her arms and her face. When she was all soaped up, he ordered her to her knees and then, after wetting her hair, poured some soap into and massaged her scalp until all her hair was filled with soapy bubbles. He then picked up the bucket and slowly poured its contents all over her head and body until all the soap was washed away.

It was the maid's turn now. She dried Violet's hair with the towel until it was slightly damp and then poured a sweet smelling lotion into it. She worked it in gently with her hands and then she brushed her long, brown hair until all of the knots were out. Once she had tied her hair back in a ponytail, the eunuch ordered Violet back to her feet. He tied her hands behind her back, reinstalled her gag and blindfolded her.

Violet felt him fasten a chain to the collar around her neck. He tugged it and she followed him out of the cell.

Violet's heart beat heavily as she stumbled up the stairs. The coarse stone of the dungeon's stairs became the smooth slate floor of the grand hall and then the soft, rug surface of the stairs leading to the living areas of the fortress. When they reached the second floor, she was pulled to the right. They walked down the hall and she heard Li opening what sounded like a large door. The surface under her feet became smooth and cool again, and there were echoes as they walked.

"*Kneel down!*" Li ordered her.

After she complied, he released her bound hands and withdrew her gag. Then he drew off her blindfold.

She was in the huge, ceremonial meeting room. She could see from the windows that it was dark outside. The room was dimly lit by lanterns on the walls. Then, to her fear and surprise, she looked up and, sitting on the top of the dais as she had seen him twice before, was her lord and master, General Wang Ku.

General Wang looked down at his concubine. He was appalled at what he saw. Two weeks in his dungeon had practically ruined her. Her body was bruised and covered with red stripes. Her face was gaunt. Her body was shaking. She looked defeated.

It broke his heart to see her this way. Why had this happened? What tricks were the fates playing on him now? He was a firm believer in fate and just desserts. It was his turn to suffer, he knew that. Suffering came following joy in his world as sure as the night followed the day. This was the first time he had ever been confronted with it so directly.

He wanted to forgive her. He wanted things to be as they were. He knew that they could never be. This upstart lieutenant, who was to die tomorrow, had given her in one night what he would never be able to give her: love. And she had given to his minion what she would never give to him.

He had been startled to hear that she had learned to play the mandolin. He remembered the first time that he had fucked her, looking into her eyes afterwards and seeing the strength and the character within. She had fought him admirably, with great courage the day that he had reduced her to slavery, only surrendering when confronted by the worst kind of betrayal. He ruled over 400 square miles of territory, made men quail at the sound of his voice, but he could not defeat this powerless Englishwoman. In all the times that he had used her, he had hardly touched her soul.

She had touched his though. Despite all that he did, she had pierced his heart. For the first time since he was a youth, he had become enraptured by a woman. He wanted to hear her play the mandolin. He couldn't bear the thought of her going to her grave without ever having played for him. He nodded to Li Pao who came over to the trembling woman and proffered her the instrument. "*Play!*" the eunuch ordered her.

Violet was taken aback. It was the last thing that she had expected. When she saw the cruel warlord, she had thought he had brought her here to rape her one last time. She had resolved to deny him as long as she could. But when the eunuch held the mandolin out to her, she was completely disarmed. She broke into tears. She took the pear shaped wooden instrument from the eunuch, bent over it and began to sob.

For several minutes, the only sound in the room was her fierce wails. She held onto the instrument tightly. Slowly, she regained control of herself. She made a quick decision. She would play all right. But it wouldn't be for the cruel general. It would be for her condemned lover, whose name she did not even know.

Having found some composure, Violet carefully adjusted the four strings until they were tuned just right. Her throat was constricted and her mouth was dry. She couldn't sing like this. She turned to the eunuch, ignoring her master's presence. "*Lord,*" she said, "*may Whore Number Four water to drink have so she please Master?*" she said in Chinese.

Wang was overwhelmed. She had not spoken a word to him, under threat of severe punishment, since her enslavement. He had forgotten the sound of her voice other than her moans and imprecations of passion when she came or her forlorn begging when he had whipped her. To hear her speak Chinese, even imperfectly, was like being in a dream. He felt like the gods were playing tricks on him.

Li Pao left the room to get the concubine a glass of water. They were alone. She held her head down respectfully. It would take a simple two word phrase to order her to come and please him, but he was afraid that she would not do it. Then he would have to have her whipped and sent down to the dungeon without hearing her play. He remained silent.

It seemed like many minutes, but it was actually a little over thirty seconds that Li returned with a small pitcher and a crystal glass for the concubine. He poured the water out into the glass and handed it to her. She gave him a bow of thanks and drank it slowly and deliberately, not giving away any of her fear. Calmly, she handed the glass back to him when she was finished. "*Whore Number Four thank Master Li good,*" she said softly.

Wang watched as the naked, battered woman adjusted herself so that the mandolin was placed comfortably on her lap. She gave the instrument a strum, picked at a of couple notes and then delivered her opening chord.

Her voice rang sweet and clear. It filled the empty room, echoed off of the cold, stone walls, reverberated in General Wang's heart. She sang of love lost, friends forgotten, homes left far behind. The song was a medley of the writings of several ancient poets. Wang recognized them all. The concubine's pronunciation of the words was perfect, her timing exquisite. Each verse was followed by a series of chords and notes, reiterating the theme with which she opened.

She sang,

> *"I'm saddened by the peonies before the steps, so red.*
> *As evening came I found that only two remained.*
> *Once morning's winds have blown, they surely won't survive.*
> *At night I gaze by lamplight, to cherish the fading red."*

Her voice held the last note a long time and then she strummed and picked a series of chords and notes. Her technique was still very raw, but Wang, who had heard some of the best play the linquin, was moved by her earnestness and patience. She sang the next verse.

> *"You ask me what time I'll return, but I cannot give a time,*
> *The rain in the hills of Ba at night overflows the autumn pools.*
> *When can we trim the candle together by the western window,*
> *And talk together of the rain in the hills of Ba at night?"*

And then the next,

> *"From whose home secretly flies the sound of a jade flute?*

It's lost amid the spring wind which fills Luoyang
City.
In the middle of this nocturne I remember the
snapped willow,
What person would not start to think of home!"

It was more than the unhappy warlord could bear. He raised his hand in a signal to the eunuch to have her stop.

"*Enough!*" Li Pao ordered her. "*Stand up!*" His voice was stern and cold. Violet carefully placed the mandolin down in front of her and rose to her feet. Yanyu had taught her the meaning of the words. Her heart ached for her lover, for England, for Tatiana who she knew she would never see again. Her songs had been for all of them.

Li Pao covered her tear filled eyes with the blindfold. He then administered her gag and tied her hands behind her. Taking hold of the chain affixed to her collar, he led her back to her lonely, dark, prison cell.

In his deserted meeting hall, General Wang looked down sadly at the abandoned mandolin.

军阀 外家

CHAPTER EIGHT

When the door to her cell opened the next morning, and she saw the black boots of the soldiers, Violet knew the day of her death had come at last.

She had been tied off on the floor of her cell when the eunuch had brought her back and had spent another long and lonely night in rigid confinement. Her sleep had been, as usual, fitful, and she was half awake when the sound of the key in the lock made her jump. Due to the tie on her collar, she was only able to raise her head slightly. She had hoped, ironically, to see the coarse sandals of her warders. Her heart fell when she saw the polished, black boots of the two soldiers instead.

She was trembling mightily as they untied her connections to the floor. They took hold of her arms and raised her to her feet. Her knees went weak with fear and the men had to help her stand. After a moment or two, she noticed that a high pitched whine was escaping from her gagged mouth and she concentrated on trying to stop it. Above all, if she had to die, she wanted to die with dignity.

She looked at the soldiers forlornly. They were just boys, maybe 18 years old, dressed in the olive brown, coarse uniforms of men. Their faces were scarless and smooth; no razor had ever been drawn across them. Their business like demeanor was belied by the sidelong glances they gave to her naked body, her heavy breasts, her loins. She moaned sadly when they covered her head with a black, satin sack. "I won't even be able to see the sun one last time," she thought miserably.

She had resigned herself to her death. Last night had seemed to seal her doom. The warlord's moroseness bespoke no willingness to forgive. From her point of view, of course, there was nothing to forgive unless she conceded his right to own her body and soul. On the other hand, she understood that she had violated his asserted right to control every aspect of her existence. It was a blow to his pride, his image of all powerfulness and an affront to his reputation. She had been hoping the harsh punishments she had received would redeem her. She wanted to live. But after last night, she knew there was little chance of that.

The two soldiers took hold of her bound arms and led her from her cell. She was barely able to walk and their strong hands kept her from falling.

She stumbled several times coming up the rough, winding, stone stairs. Her gag suppressed her cries as she scraped her bare feet. When they reached the ground level, she was hustled out the door to the Great Hall and into the inner courtyard. She could hear the sounds of a large crowd. A chill was running through her body. She was dragged along about a hundred feet or so and then made to kneel on the cold, wet cobblestones. It had apparently rained during the dark, lonely night.

Violet took in what she could of her surroundings. She sensed the eyes of the large crowd upon her. She imagined what she must look like to them. Her nakedness brought home her powerlessness over her fate and the fact that the warlord was not inclined to make any provision for her pride in the last minutes of her life. He had taken all that away from her a long time ago. In her projections of what her execution would be like, she had made no provision for being turned into a spectacle. The fact that her body was being displayed so brazenly for the people's prurient interests made the fact of her upcoming demise so much worse. That the sight of her naked body and her brutal execution would be a subject for titillating conversation, perhaps for years, for so many eyewitnesses, made her feel sick. She recalled the warlord's threat at the time of her conversion to one of his whores to have her body burned and her ashes cast into the wind. It had seemed a terrible prospect at the time, a year and a half ago, before she knew what being General Wang's whore would really mean. Now it did not hold the same disquiet for her. She wanted no memorial to what she had become.

Her back was pressed up against a post and her neck was tied off to it. It was chilly and her nipples had stiffened. She could feel, though, the sun beginning to beat down and realized that in an hour or so the morning chill would be burned off and it would be a beautiful day. She would not live to see it.

General Wang sat on a five foot high dais overlooking the courtyard, his back to the fortress. On his right stood at stiff attention, in precise ranks, about 150 of his soldiers, called to observe the executions and serve as a symbol of his power. On his left stood approximately the same number of civilians, members of the household staff, civil officials from Yeuyang, merchants, and other citizens whom his soldiers had rounded up to be witnesses. Wang was sure that word of the invasion of his seraglio had spread far and wide and it was essential that his harsh retribution against those responsible be a matter of public record.

Kneeling to Wang's left in a row were the five condemned: two men and three women. Their heads were all covered with black satin hoods and their necks were all confined to posts behind them. Their hands were all bound. The men, Lts. Cheng and Wong, were in uniform, but their epaulettes and other insignia of rank had been cut off. The olive brown uniforms hid most of the evidence of their travails over the last two weeks.

The women, Shushun, the foolish maid who had sold Cheng the map of the seraglio, Lijuan and Violet, were all naked, their battered and bruised bodies exposed for all to see. Violet was the last to be brought out, and the civilian audience had craned their necks to get a good look at the still beautiful, naked body of the condemned concubine. Their buzz had fallen to silence as she was dragged to her post and tied off to it. The soldiers remained stiffly at attention, in neat, orderly rows.

About a hundred feet in front of Wang's perch sat a 5' high platform. In its middle was a heavy block of blood stained wood, about three feet high and two feet wide. Behind it was a 6' long bench polished by use. In front of it, was an expansive, two foot high, wicker basket. Next to the bench stood a mountainous man. He was over 6' tall with broad shoulders and had foreboding, rough features. His head was shaved. He was naked to the waist and although it was chilly, his chest was gleaming with sweat. His black, cotton pants were held up by a wide, black, leather belt with a large, silver buckle. Sandals adorned his feet. The gleaming head of his upside down axe rested on the platform at his side.

It was not every day that Wang's executioner performed for the public. Most executions were carried out beyond prying eyes with only a few soldiers as witnesses. That was not what had him sweating. It was rare indeed that he was called to execute three women at the same time, and especially attractive ones at that. His conscience gnawed at him. He was certain that somehow the gods would make him pay for this affront: the destruction of so much beauty. But he had his job to do and he would do it.

The master of ceremonies was Major Won. He had returned from his honeymoon three days ago and that was the first he had heard of the invasion of the seraglio. His new wife, Me Ling, had slapped him across the face and spat virulent invectives against him when she learned of his role in the upcoming death of her former lover and friend. She had retreated to her bedroom and he had been denied admittance ever since. General Wang had refused to relieve him of this duty.

It was the beginning of a beautiful day. The sky shone a deep blue and small puffs of clouds drifted across it. There was a slight, early morning, chilly breeze, a harbinger of the fierce winds that winter would bring. A flock of birds was circling above the courtyard, a tribe assembling for the journey south. The cobblestones were shiny and clean from the brief shower that had fallen just before sunrise.

Violet's heart was pounding hard, her breath was labored. Her bound hands writhed behind her. She was trying not to cry. What was she losing, really, she tried to think. Her life had been a trail of tears ever since her kidnapping so long ago. She wished that she had had the chance to say goodbye to Tatiana. She imagined her up in the seraglio looking out the window, crying at the sight of her lover, naked and on her knees, prepared for death. She sent a silent goodbye to her, hoping that she would receive it.

Major Won looked at his master, the general, and received a nod. It was time to begin.

Standing next to Won was a young boy in military uniform wearing a black brimmed cap. He was carrying a silver and red snare drum. Its broad white straps ran over his small shoulders. At the major's signal, he released a long, loud tattoo, "Bidididididididididididididididididididididididi-didididididididip!" When it stopped, the public crowd behind the condemned, which had become noisy with muffled conversations after the concubine had been tied off to her post, became silent again.

Won strode purposely down the line of prisoners, Violet first, removing their hoods. They all blinked and scrunched their eyes as they were admitted to the bright daylight. Then, their attention was swiftly captured by the platform some fifty feet away from them on which sat the instruments of their death.

All of the prisoners were gagged. There would be no last second pronouncements, no screaming and yelling of frantic pleas to be spared. Shushun broke out into loud wails that emerged despite her covered mouth. Violet looked to her left. Lijuan was kneeling next to her. Her eyes were filled with tears and her chest was heaving. Shushun was to Lijuan's left and then Wong and last Lieutenant Cheng.

Violet looked across the courtyard at the assembly of General Wang's army. Their uniformity and rigidity was an implacable sign of her hopelessness. She could not see the crowd behind her and was grateful for that. She imagined their Asian faces, their colorful dress, their morbid curiosity. When she was dead, they would go on their merry way to their houses, stores or offices. Later, they would have lunch and discuss what they had seen while stuffing their faces. She resented their hold on life. It was strange to think of the world without her in it.

Won snapped to attention and barked an order. Two soldiers marched forwards and approached the kneeling Cheng. He was to be first. Violet watched with unhappiness as they untied his neck and brought him to his feet. They took hold of his arms and advanced him to the platform. He held his body erect and proud and he walked with an efficient, military air. When he was standing behind the bench, looking at the fortress and his master, the general, his body stiffened to attention. While the two soldiers kept a firm grip on his arms, a third bent down and tied his ankles together. Violet caught his eye. His face was expressionless, the lower half covered by the leather shield of his gag. His eyes though, reached out to her. They softened and seemed to be conveying to her his invitation to meet with him in paradise.

When his ankles were tied, the men tilted his body and lowered it to the smoothly polished bench. They slid him forward until his chin rested just over the far edge of the execution block. There was a frame there and it was closed around his neck, just below his head, leaving a five inch band of flesh exposed. His body was strapped to the bench in three places: his knees, his waist and his chest.

One of the soldiers nodded to Major Won who gave a signal to the drummer boy. He beat out a brisk tattoo, "Bididididididididididididididididididididip!" When it stopped, the executioner lifted his axe in a wide arc and delivered a swift, hard blow. Violet heard a 'thump!' as the axe struck wood. Cheng's head gave a little jump and then rolled off of the block and into the waiting basket. Blood poured from his decapitated neck in a fountain of red. It spread over the platform like oozing lava. The crowd gave a moan.

Violet had been watching the execution of her lover intently. She gave out an anguished, muffled cry when she saw the head topple and the blood rush out. Her stomach was in a tight knot. Sweat ran off her body. Her throat was dry and she was trembling. "Oh, god! Oh, god! Oh god!" she kept murmuring. It was the most horrific thing she had ever seen. It was nothing like witnessing an execution from a window in the seraglio, though she had been appalled at the cruelty of it even then. Seeing it up close was a thousand times worse. Knowing that she would soon follow, that her separated head would fall into the very same basket, made her shiver.

Cheng's body was tossed into a cart behind the execution platform.

Lieutenant Wong was next. He too conducted himself with military dignity. His was, perhaps, the most unfair sentence. He was not responsible for the guards all getting drunk. He hadn't even come on duty until midnight. He had spent his time making the rounds, kicking sleeping guards into wakefulness. It had been a futile endeavor since, as soon as he left, the guard would fall asleep once again. And there was nothing to say that even an alert guard would have prevented the invasion. Most of the guards were in the front of the fortress by the gate and a two man patrol walked the circumference of the inner wall every hour. They probably would never even have seen Cheng as he swiftly climbed his rope.

Violet closed her eyes as soon as she heard the drum begin its beat. She did not want to witness it again. The 'thump' of the axe striking wood resounded through her nonetheless.

Next was the foolish, little maid, Shushun. She had been crying and sobbing the entire time. When the major barked his command to the soldiers to go get her, she began a high pitched wail that escaped the cruel leather that filled her mouth. She kicked and fought as her naked body was dragged to the execution platform. The soldiers on either side of her, her arms held tightly in their hands, merely lifted her from the ground and carried her along.

When they reached the stairs, she placed her bare foot on the step in a futile bid to keep the men from bringing her up. It delayed her demise by only a few seconds. They brought her to the end of the bench and a soldier tried to tie her ankles together. Her gyrations made it impossible. A fourth soldier mounted the platform to assist him. Her ankles were bound in short order.

The men tilted her naked body and slid it into position. Quickly, the straps were tightened around her and her head was captured. Her hair had been, as had Lijuan's, shorn to the neck and posed no interference with the executioner's axe. The drum began its remorseless beat and then silenced. As the executioner swung the axe above his head, the girl gave out a piteous wail. In a second, it was cut off forever.

Lijuan was next. Violet had watched Shushun's trek to the execution platform with horror. She closed her eyes when the axe fell, but opened them again rapidly after she heard the loud 'thump' that denoted the end of her life. She turned to Lijuan. The poor, little maid was crying and sobbing with abandon. Her face was covered with tears. She looked back at her mistress. Violet wanted terribly to speak to her, to calm her. She tried to tell the near hysterical, young woman with her eyes that it would all be over very shortly. Lijuan seemed to understand her gesture and she gave her mistress an unhappy nod.

The naked, little, pixie-like maid gave the men no trouble. She could not walk and so they did her the favor of carrying her. She stood forlornly at the back of the bench while they tied her ankles together. Tears were streaming down her pretty face. Violet caught her eyes as she was lowered down and slid forward. She was in abject terror. Once the frame was lowered around her neck, her eyes were pointed downwards. The sight of the severed heads in the basket set her off and she began to cry and wail.

The drum spoke its cruel message and then stopped. A moment later, the axe came crashing down. "Thump!"

Now, it was Violet's turn. Her stomach roiled and her heart started to pound. She was slick with sweat. Her throat was dry and her body shuddered with fear. She heard the major's command and she saw the soldiers marching towards her in lock step. She struggled to hold back her tears. Her neck was untied and the men lifted her to her feet.

A calm settled over her as she was led to the platform. She mounted the stairs with her head held high and her back straight. She uttered a prayer, thanking God for relieving her of her miserable life.

While the men tied off her ankles, her naked body trembled, but she looked serenely over the crowd. Her eyes met those of her lord and master. She would be beyond the reach of his cruelties shortly. She emptied herself of her hate for him, forgave everyone who had harmed her, even Robert, the man who had betrayed her.

Hands guided her body into a tilt and she felt the cool surface of the bench on her breasts, belly and thighs. The hands slid her forward until her neck was in place. The frame was lowered over it and she was strapped tightly to the bench. She resisted the urge to squirm. One of the men gathered her long, brown hair and pulled it to the side to ease the executioner's way. He stepped back and the drum began its death rattle.

General Wang's unhappiness with the proceedings had grown steadily as each of his victims was led to their death. He would look down at the naked and bound body of his concubine and wonder to himself, "Why am I doing this?" He had changed his mind about whipping her before she died. What would be the point besides mere cruelty? He would get no pleasure from it under the circumstances and, besides, the crowd could easily see from the deep red lines all over her body and the dark, black and blue wounds, that she had paid dearly for her transgression. Enough was enough. He was afraid that if he saw her being whipped, he would lose his nerve about having her executed.

He thought of the performance she had given him last night. Her voice had been clear and true. It was too bad that at virtually the last minute he had gotten a full appreciation of what an accomplished courtesan she could have been. She had placed so much emotion in the singing of her songs that it had almost broken his heart.

Last night, after her performance, he had gone to his salon and reread her letters to Robert during their long distance courtship. It was all he would have left of her. Her handwriting had a special beauty to it. He could sense her inner self in her words of hope for the future. She clearly was a woman with great gifts to give. She spoke often of her love for music and the piano particularly. It was too bad that, when he had first read the letters about a year ago, he had not bought her one. It would have been a great solace to his sometimes lonely heart to hear her play. It was too late for that now.

By the time he had finally gotten the fortitude to put the letters away, he had drunk more than half of a bottle of scotch. He had the Russian whore brought to his room. He whipped her viciously and then fucked her brutally. Even after having come in her body four times, he was later unable to sleep.

As he looked at the clearly frightened Englishwoman, he thought of the delight he had received from her breasts, the way she ran her hands lightly over his head as he suckled her, the way she leaned her head over in a daze and covered his neck with her hot breath.

When he saw her being raised to her feet and begin her march to death, he thought of the first time that he had fucked her, the way she had looked at him. She had revealed to him the depth of her soul, a soul that he would now never touch. He thought of her soft skin and her warm, welcoming canal, the way she cried out when she came. These were now lost to him forever. "Why has this happened?" he asked himself. "Why am I doing this," he repeated in his mind.

Suddenly, he wanted to call the whole thing off. He tried to rise to his feet, but his body was paralyzed. His hands would not ungrip the arms of the chair he was sitting in. He tried to open his mouth to call out, but his lips would not move.

She ascended the platform regally. When she turned to face him, her battered body seemed aglow. When their eyes met, his body shivered and his stomach quailed. A profound ache came over him as he watched her being lowered to the bench and slid into place. Why couldn't he move, he thought desperately. Was it his pride? Was it his knowledge that no matter what he did, even if he saved her, that she would never be truly his? He realized that he was depriving the earth of a great soul. Would the gods punish him for his despoliation of their gift?

When the frame was locked around her neck, Violet tried to recite a prayer that she had learned as a child. She couldn't get past the first line. She looked down in the basket at the bloody heads. The smell of death was all around her. Bright red blood had pooled thickly on the platform in front of her. It saturated the block on which her neck lay. "Please be quick! Please be quick!" she recited again and again in her mind. Her fear had returned. Her whole body was shivering. "Please be quick!" she begged again.

The executioner looked down at the delicate, pale neck of his final victim. He had watched her stroll calmly across the courtyard to her doom. She was a beautiful, delectable woman, even after all the harm those animals in the dungeon had done to her. He sensed a presence in her of the divine spark. The gods would certainly punish him, he thought. He was doomed.

The only thing he could do for her was to ensure her a quick, painless death. He worried that the blade on his axe might have become dull from the four prior uses. It was difficult to cut through the tough bones of the spine. It was easy for a blade to lose its edge. And then there was her collar. He had asked the major if it could be removed. Its presence reduced his target area appreciably. He feared that the blade would glance off it and he would make a mess of the procedure. The thought of having to hack away at this beautiful body appalled him. His stomach revolted at the thought of causing her horrific pain. The major had told him that the general had refused his request. She would go to her death marked as his concubine, his property.

The drum roll began. His sweaty hands nervously gripped the handle of his axe. He heard the woman moan with fear. When the drum became silent, he swung the axe mightily up into the air. He wanted to give her his hardest blow, to do his best to ease her way into her next life. The axe rose over his head and had just begun its downward arc when he heard someone yell, "*Stop!*"

It was too late. He had no power to counteract the forces which now caused the instrument of death to hurtle towards Violet's pale, beautiful neck. He stretched his arms as far out as he could. He leaned forwards. The axe came rushing down. It made a loud 'Thump!' as it struck.

He looked down. The edge of the axe was buried in the corner of the block. The woman was squirming and writhing; she was sobbing and moaning hysterically. She was alive! The back edge of the axe had brushed across her neck, but its body had buried itself into the corner of the block. Blood streamed from the laceration, but it was not fatal. He looked up quickly. Had he made a mistake? Who was it that called out, "*Stop?*" Did he have to lift his axe and perform the deed all over again while the woman screamed in terror? His axe was buried deep into the block. He would have to put his foot on it and work the deadly instrument free. That could take an eternity.

What he saw was the general standing on his feet. He had never seen that look in his eyes before. It was as if he was in a trance. Woodenly, he stepped down off of the platform and retreated into his fortress.

Major Won had no idea what to do. He had been given no order to stop the execution. It sounded like the general's voice, but it had been strained, almost other worldly. Had the gods intervened? What should he do?

There was one person there who knew precisely what to do. Li Pao ran to the platform and ordered the soldiers to release her. When they hesitated, he screamed his order at them again and struck at them repeatedly with his whippy stick. While one unhooked the frame that held her head in place, another undid the straps that held her body confined. They slid her body back. A stream of blood was flowing down her neck. Her breasts and belly were smeared with the blood of her predecessors. She was writhing and moaning. When Li Pao saw that she was retching, he leapt behind her and swept off her gag. She knelt there for a moment, casting her bile out onto the bloody platform.

He ordered the men to carry her body into the fortress and bring her to her cell in the dungeon. They were to lay her on her pallet and leave her there. He reinstalled her gag first lest her moans and wails titillate the audience. When the soldiers had her in their arms and began to hurry away, his eyes sought out her maids, the two who remained alive.

Jinjing and Ting were in the audience. They had cried and cried, breaking into heavy sobs when Lijuan was led to her death. They had collapsed into piteous wails when they saw their mistress being led to the platform and had fallen into each other's arms when they saw the executioner lift his axe. They had not heard the voice yell, "*Stop!*" After a few moments, they became conscious of an excitement in the crowd. Then there had been cries of relief and astonishment. What had happened?

Jinjing in the lead, the two young women pushed themselves through the crowd. They emerged just in time to see their mistress's bloody body hustled towards the castle in the arms of one of the soldiers. Was she alive or dead?

Li Pao spotted them in the crowd. "*Come with me!*" he ordered.

The two maids had never been in the dungeon, but they had heard tell of its cruelties. They trembled as the eunuch led them down the steps. The guards, Scylla and Charybdis were standing by the inner gate, dumfounded. They had certainly not expected to see the beautiful concubine in one piece again, never mind two pretty maids coming down to take care of her.

Jinjing and Ting gave the two gremlin-like creatures a wide berth. They followed Li Pao to Violet's cell. When they saw the bound woman lying belly down on her pallet, crying hysterically, they rushed towards her.

"*Oh, mistress! Oh mistress!*" they cried. They fell upon her, hugging her. Jinjing looked back at Li Pao as if asking for permission to untie the wildly sobbing woman. He nodded his approval. While the willowy Ting stroked the woman's hair and tried to calm her, Jinjing released the ties to her ankles and wrists. She then unbuckled the gag from the back of her head. Together, the two anxious maids rolled Violet to her back and Jinjing removed the thick, leather gag.

The cell immediately filled with the sound of Violet's piteous, heartfelt sobs.

At first, Violet had not known what had happened. One moment, she was steeled for the feel of the blade of the axe striking her neck, waiting for the blackness to come, or whatever else was in store for her on the other side of the veil of death. Then, she heard the loud 'thump!' of the axe striking wood next to her. When she realized that the axe had missed her and that she was still alive, a wave of agony went through her. Violet had not heard the word, "*Stop!*" yelled out in Chinese. Rather, she had heard it, but did not perceive it. Her mind was so focused on the edge of the blade rushing towards her, that all else had been blocked out.

"Is this some kind of torture!" she asked herself miserably. It had taken all of her emotional strength to prepare herself for death; she had none left. All the cruelty and callousness she had suffered in the last year and a half flooded over her like a backed up drain. She screamed at the top of her lungs, her body cringed in hopelessness. "When will I have suffered enough?" she asked her creator.

She felt her straps being loosened and her body pulled back from the executioner's block. She collapsed to the platform. She felt like her stomach was going to heave up from inside her. She couldn't catch her breath as her belly pulsed and sent its acids up her esophagus. When her gag was removed, she bent over and tried to let her inside's command be obeyed, but nothing would come out. She had a moment of alertness when she saw that she was kneeling in a vast pool of blood. She cried out in misery. Someone shoved her gag back into her mouth and rebuckled it behind her head. Strong hands lifted her up and she felt herself being carried away in someone's arms. When she realized that she was being brought down to the dungeon, she moaned and cried. "No more! No more! Please! Please!" she screamed in English through her gag. When she was laid down on her pallet, she struggled to free her bound hands and ankles. "Please! Pleeeeeeeeease! No more, pleeeeeeeeease!" she begged.

Then, soft, gentle hands were on her. She felt her hands released and then her ankles. Warm arms encompassed her and she thought that she heard a young woman's voice trying to comfort her in Chinese. Her body was turned and her gag was removed again. She uttered a wailing, piteous cry. Two bodies were thrown against her. She looked and saw that it was her maids, Jinjing and Ting. She clutched at them desperately. They were sobbing wildly as was she. She kissed their faces, hugged their bodies to her as hard as she could.

"I'm alive! I'm alive!" she thought happily. A sudden tsunami of passion overwhelmed her. She tore at the clothes of her lovers. They had been smeared with the blood that had gathered on her body. As she ripped at their clothes, they began to assist her, pulling their light green blouses over their heads, drawing their blood stained pants off of their hips and down their legs.

The three women fell together in an impassioned scrum. Lips found lips, hands found breasts and thighs, bellies and lower lips. Ting wrapped her arm around her mistress's shoulders and began giving her mouth a delirious kiss. Jinjing kissed her belly, slid her tongue down between her thighs and captured her love button in a long, lustful suckle. Violet's legs splayed wide. Her arms were wrapped tightly around Ting, reveling in the warmth of a human body. "I'm alive! I'm alive!" she kept repeating in her mind.

Soon the lips and tongue at her quim had her body writhing in almost agonizing delight. She moaned loudly into Ting's mouth and then pulled her up above her until she was straddling her mouth, her hands pressed against the wall. Violet buried her mouth in the young girl's sex, breathing in the succulent aroma of her arousal, letting her tongue delve deeply into her lush divide. She wrapped her arms around the girl's thighs, capturing them tightly.

High pitched moans and squeals emanated from the tangle of womanhood. Scylla and Charybdis peered into the cell with wonderment. They looked at each other, perplexed. What was going on?

Their answer came quickly. Li Pao had been standing at the door watching the lustful acts of life affirmation erupt. He spoke to the men sternly. "*Do nothing until you hear from me. I will be sending down a tray of food. If you so much as lay a finger on any of them, I will have your innards dangling from the fortress gates. Do you understand?*"

Both men nodded their heads in confusion. The concubine was supposed to be dead. What had happened? And then, a shiver of fear passed through them. They had treated the woman horribly. Was she now back in the warlord's favor? Would she tell him what they did to her? Had their time for expiation of all their terrible deeds come at last?

In the cell, Violet was screaming her pleasure into Ting's mushy dilated canal as Jinjing maintained a steady assault on her own. Ting came next, her thighs squeezing tightly against her mistress's cheeks. She felt her mistress's hold on her thighs weaken as she absorbed one powerful throb of her pussy after another. She turned and scrambled next to Jinjing. She pushed the larger, stronger girl aside and buried her tongue in Violet's distended, flush quim. Jinjing, not to be deterred from her expressions of lust, moved up the concubine's torso and began suckling desperately at her breasts. Violet's arm pulled her tight against her. "Oh, god! Oh, god!" she called again and again as Ting delivered long, lustful lashes of her tongue against her clit.

Suddenly, Violet seized hold of Junjing's torso and twisted her to her side and then her back. She mounted the voluptuous maid and pressed her pussy against the younger woman's. She abraded her puss firmly against it, up and down, up and down, sucking at her lips until the maid began to call out her pleasure in response. Ting lay against their sides, pressing her body against them, crying in joy and sorrow.

When the women had exhausted their passions, they lay in each other's arms and cried. Poor Lijuan was dead. The delightful, somewhat shy, elfish young woman, who had never harmed anyone, had had her life cruelly taken from her, from them.

Li Pao had gone up to the kitchen on the second floor and had a maid load up a large tray of delicacies and a large pitcher of rice wine and guided her down to the dungeon. They stood at the door to the cell while the passions of the three women wound down. Their writhing bodies were lit by a lantern overhead, and the shadows of each of their bodies flitted over them, making it difficult to distinguish who was doing what to whom.

Li Pao turned to the maid. She was slight and thin. She looked barely over eighteen. She was trembling both at being in the dungeon, but also at being in the presence of the mighty eunuch. She had only been a maid for two weeks. Her family had sold her to the fortress a few days after her eighteenth birthday so that the other members of the family could be fed. Her face was small and innocent. *"What is your name?"* he asked her harshly.

"My name is Wen, Master," she replied nervously.

"Go in the cell and put down the tray. You will disrobe and present yourself to your new mistress. You will take the place of Lijuan. The others, Jinjing and Ting will show you what to do. Do you understand?"

"Y,yes, Master," the timid girl replied. But she didn't understand at all. She had watched the proceedings in the courtyard from a window near the kitchen. It had been horrifying to watch. The other maids had told her about the beautiful concubine in the dungeon and what was to be her fate. She was shocked and aghast when she saw her being carried from the execution platform all covered with blood. And now she was right in front of her and she was being told to serve her. She had heard tales of what went on in the seraglio. She had been forced to give up her virginity to the head cook a few days after she arrived at the fortress and had been fucked by him regularly since then. She had been brought out back behind the fortress by a few of the soldiers twice. She had never had sex with a woman.

To top it off, the lantern that hung from the beam above them made the blood covered mass of feminine humanity that was still coupling languidly inside the cell seem demonic. She looked up at the tall eunuch. He had beaten her once with his whippy stick and she had heard terrible things about his temper. What choice did she really have? To refuse was unthinkable; to be discharged from the service of the warlord would bring great shame on her family. They would never be able to pay him back the sum he had paid for her 5 year contract, small as it was. They would be thrown off of their small plot of land and forced into penury and starvation.

Wen edged herself into the little cell. The three copulating women paid no mind to her. She put down the tray and began to disrobe. She chucked off her wooden clogs and pulled her blouse up over her head. She had large breasts for her small frame, but not more than a handful to the average man. Her areolas were a light pink and her nipples were dainty. She placed her tiny hands in the waist of her white, cotton pants and, swallowing her tension, pulled them down past her slender hips, then to her knees and then over her small feet. Li Pao had closed the door to the cell and locked it. Wen was terrified. How long would she have to stay down here? She had seen the ugly, brutish looking guards. Would she be required to service them? What was going to happen to her?

At the sound of the heavy, wooden door to the cell slamming shut, Jinjing looked up. She saw the child-like, trembling, naked maid. She looked just like Lijuan only even smaller and more pixie-like. Violet was in the midst of a stunning orgasm. Ting was licking her hardened clit with the flat of her tongue, making rapid strokes. Violet's hands were on her head, lodged firmly in her straight, black hair. Her back was arched, her legs splayed wide. "Ohhhh-hhhhhhhhhhhhhhhh! Ohhhhhhhhhhhhhhhhhh!" she called out. "Ohhhhhhhhhhhhhhhhhhhh!"

Jinjing abandoned Violet's breasts to approach the much smaller girl. She could see that she was trembling with fear. "*Who are you?*" she demanded briskly.

"*I, I'm Wen,*" she replied meekly, a tremor in her voice.

"*And what are you doing here?*" Jinjing asked her voice stern and rebuking. To Wen it looked like she was about to box her ears. She broke into tears.

"*M,master Li Pao told me I'm to b,be Whore Number F,Four's new maid,*" she stuttered. Her face was a mask of agony.

Jinjing looked at her appraisingly. "*And what makes you think you can be so honored to be Whore Number Four's new maid?*" she spat out, her voice accusing.

Wen bordered on the edge of hysteria. "*I,I d,don't know,*" she answered miserably. "*I,I'm s,sorry. It, it wasn't m,my idea.*"

Violet's orgasm had come to a dizzying conclusion. She pulled Ting to her and kissed her mouth. She looked up and saw the naked, little maid standing there, tears flowing down her face.

"*Who?*" she inquired dreamily in Chinese.

Jinjing turned to her. "*This is Wen. Li Pao has told her that she is to be your new maid. She still stinks of the pig pen. She knows nothing about being a maid to a concubine. Lijuan was…Lijuan was…Ohhhhhhhhh!*" she cried. Little Lijuan was gone forever. Jinjing collapsed to the floor.

"*Come, Jinjing, come to I,*" Violet told her. "*I kiss you too.*"

Jinjing came crawling over. She threw herself into her mistress's embrace.

"*Lijuan very good. Lijuan very brave. She not want cry. Me love Lijuan. Me love Jinjing,*" Violet said, tears welling up in her eyes. She kissed the voluptuous maid on the mouth and then turned her head to Ting. "*Me love Ting.*"

The three women embraced.

When they parted, Violet rose on her elbows and looked at the trembling, confused, young peasant girl. She looked strikingly like Lijuan. She could have been her younger sister. Violet reached out her hand. She knew that the eunuch was an old fox. It would be hard to replace Lijuan. The four of them had been together virtually every day for a year and a half. They were a family unit of sorts. Even though the maids were essentially enforcers of their master's will, they formed an envelope within which Violet existed. That envelope had been rent asunder. Only someone as vulnerable and delightful as Lijuan had been could possibly hope to be the force that mended the fabric of their relationship.

The young girl was pretty. Violet extended a hand to her. "*Come kiss I, Wen,*" she said.

The frightened girl hesitated. Was the concubine going to make her kiss her pussy? Would the concubine put her hand in her honeypot? Wen had never even suspected that women might make love with each other until she had heard the tales of life in the seraglio and what the master sometimes made the maids do for the entertainment of his guests. She had been appalled. It was bad enough what the cook did to her and the soldiers, but at least that was what she understood that men and women did sometimes.

Being in the dungeon made the slight girl deathly afraid of what might happen to her should she refuse the concubine's invitation. The overhead lantern made the blood stained women look macabre. It was all too much for her to take. As she approached the supine, naked, blood smeared concubine, she began to sob. She fell to her knees next to her, prepared for the worst. The beautiful, naked woman took her hand and pulled her closer. She rose to a sitting position and put her other hand on Wen's tear stained cheek.

"*No hurt Wen,*" she said softly. "*You see, yes?*"

The beauty and placidity of the older European woman calmed her. She cracked a small smile and nodded her head. "*I brought food and wine,*" she said timidly.

"*Food?*" Violet said excitedly. "*Where?*"

Wen turned and pointed to the floor. "*There,*" she said.

The large tray was full of little, covered dishes. There was a large, porcelain carafe and some matching cups.

Violet pushed herself to her knees and crawled over to the large tray. She was ravenous. She started to flip the lids off of the plates. There was chicken and pork, cooked several different ways, carrots in a sweet sauce, a host of vegetables steamed to perfection. There were crayfish and a fish soup, rice and noodles. And there was wine, a large carafe of wine.

Ignoring protocol, Violet began to pick up the plates and shove portions of the food in her mouth. Jinjing tried to pull her hands away, but Violet ignored her. Jinjing surrendered, for now, obedience to the rules of the seraglio. They didn't seem to make much sense down here.

"*Eat! Eat!*" Violet urged her and Ting as she sampled one plate after another. She stopped to pour herself a cup of wine. She drank it back and moaned with pleasure. "*Eat!*" she repeated.

Ting needed no fourth invitation. She picked up a plate of chicken and thrust a piece in her mouth. Violet poured her a cup of wine and urged her to drink. After hesitating for just a few moments more, Jinjing joined in. The carafe of wine was passed to her and she poured herself a cup.

Wen looked on with amazement and also gratitude that attention had shifted from her. It was not for long. Violet, her mouth stuffed with cabbage sautéed in garlic, proffered her the plate. "*Eat! Eat!*" she said gleefully. Wen had never eaten such food in her life. She looked over the feast greedily and then back at her new mistress. "*Eat!*" The concubine repeated. Wen dove in.

For half an hour, the women gorged at the flavorful food. The rice wine was emptied quickly. Just in the nick of time, the door opened and a new maid brought in another tray of food, this time pastry and desserts, and two more carafes of wine. She tried to leave, but Jinjing and Ting pulled her to the floor. After stripping her, they dragged her to the tray of food and made her eat and drink. Li Pao just closed and locked the door behind her.

Within a short time, all the women were drunk as lords. The rice wine was potent stuff, more like brandy. Jinjing and Ting insisted that Wen crawl onto Violet's lap. Violet stroked and kissed her on the mouth. The she sent her around to kiss all the other maids. One by one they put their mouths on hers. When she came to Ting, the tall, thin, young woman held her head for a moment while she tickled the inside of her mouth with her tongue. Wen placed her hands lightly against the other girl, made a feeble attempt to resist. Ting released her and laughed.

Violet poured them all another cup of wine and held hers up in the air. "*Lijuan!*" she said. They other women, even little Wen, all joined in a chorus answering, "*Lijuan!*" They all threw the fiery liquor back.

For a moment, Violet had a flashback to her youth. She had been a Girl Guide. In the summer, they would sometimes have campfires and toast cheese and sing. She started to laugh. They never sat around nude and drank brandy!

She was filled with the thrill of being alive. She didn't know what tomorrow or even the next hour would bring, but for now there was the pure, unadulterated, thrilling sensation of breathing in air, of feeling her heart pumping, of seeing the laughing, smiling faces of the pretty, naked, Chinese maids.

Violet pulled the inebriated Wen to her. "*Kiss breast,*" she said to her invitingly. She held her breast in her hand, proffering her nipple to the young girl.

Wen hesitated. She had never had more than a thimble full of rice wine before in her life, and that she had stolen from a half empty cup one night when her father had passed out drunk. Everything was spinning around her. The other women seemed so happy and carefree. It was anomalous to the setting of the warlord's fearsome dungeon. She had never, needless to say, kissed a woman's breast before. The concubine, her new mistress, seemed so pleasant and easy-going about it that she timidly complied.

Violet's eyes rolled back as the girl suckled her teat softly. After a few moments, she gently pushed her head back and proffered the other nipple to her. Wen leaned across her body and took it between her sweet lips. Violet let her hand flow down the smooth, silky back of the young girl, reveling in the heat of her skin.

All the other women, even the maid who had brought in the reinforcing carafes of rice wine joined in. Her name was Huifang. One of her cousins was one of Pu Wei's maids and she had often listened jealously to her tales about the antics in the seraglio. She was more than thrilled to be part of it now, even if it was in the dingy dungeon cell. When Wen came to kiss her breasts, she held the girl's head firmly to her, prolonging the girl's kiss. Wen emerged breathless. When she came to Ting, who was last in line, after she finished giving obeisance to the tall, thin maid's teats, Ting grabbed her head again and gave her another kiss. This time, she guided the girl's lips apart and entered her mouth with her exploring tongue. At first, Wen tried to break the contact, but her body soon softened and she moaned lustfully.

Another round of rice wine was poured and Violet gave out another toast. "*Wen!*" she cried out, laughing. All the other women, save Wen, followed suit. Violet took the tipsy maid's cup and brought it to her mouth, tilting it until the young girl had drunk it all up.

This time, when Violet brought the young girl to her lap, she kissed her breasts in turn. Violet suckled the rigid, little nubbins until the girl moaned. Then she kissed her and passed her off to Jinjing, who was seated to her right. Each woman took her turn in tantalizing the girl's breasts. Wen jumped a little when Huifang drifted her hand downwards and caressed her downy covered sex. She took her longest finger and dragged it between the young girl's swollen love lips. When she found her moisture she spread it over the girl's rigid love bud, making her moan again.

When it was Ting's turn, the lustful maid buried her fingers deeply into the girl's receptive canal. She stroked and played with it while she licked and sucked at the impassioned girl's breasts. When the girl's breath became labored and she began rocking on the tender, soft hand that caressed her, Ting passed her back off to the mistress.

Violet placed her hands on the girl's cheeks and brought her lips to hers. She spread the young girl's lips and, for a moment, breathed in her sweet breath. She then slid her tongue inside the girl's mouth. Wen was kneeling in front of her, Violet was raised on her own knees. They kissed long and hard. Wen placed her hands gingerly on Violet's soft thighs. Ting crept up behind her and forced Wen to raise herself on her knees and spread her legs. She recaptured the girl's moist and hot gash and began to stoke it lovingly.

Wen gasped when she felt the woman's hand seize her puss. She then moaned into Violet's mouth.

Sex with the cook or the soldiers had not been like this, she thought woozily. She was having feelings that she had never had before. Her blood seemed hot. Her heart was beating quickly and strongly. She melted as her mistress's tongue pleasured her mouth. She felt a surge in her lust. Her pussy tingled like it never had. She spread her legs wider unconsciously and her hands began to rub back and forth on her mistress's soft, hot thighs. Her pussy seemed to vibrate. A rush of pleasure surged through her. And then it happened. She moaned as her sex began to throb and pulse. She shuddered at each fierce contraction. "Mmmmmmmmmm! Mmmmmmmmmm!" she moaned.

Violet took a firmer hold on her head and pressed her lips down hard. Her tongue wrestled with the young girl's. Ting's free hand was squeezing and massaging the girl's dainty breasts. Wen's hands were balled into tiny fists. She rocked her hips back and forth. "Mmmmmmmmmm! Mmmmmmmmmm!" she called out.

When her orgasm faded, Ting let her hands slide off of Wen's body and Violet hugged her body closely to hers. Wen was crying and hugged her mistress back. She had never known that her body could make her feel like that. It was something her mother had never told her, although she had gotten an inkling when she heard her moaning and sighing sometimes from her parent's pallet in their little hut, followed by the animalistic grunts of her father. Now she knew. It was wonderful! Her mistress's body felt so good against hers.

Another toast was drunk and then Violet dragged her new maid over to the cotton pallet and held her tightly while Huifang showed her what pleasure a woman could bring another with her mouth. She then lay back and let Huifang bring her to completion while Wen kissed her and suckled on her breasts. Ting and Jinjing coupled near them and when they had finished pleasuring each other, they brought Huifang to several wrenching orgasms.

At one point, the door opened and the guards Scylla and Charybdis poked heir heads in. Their curiosity had gotten the better of them. All of the women, save Jinjing, stopped what they were doing and started to shy away from the demonic duo. Jinjing though, did not. She rose to her feet and started to berate the gremlin-like men. "*Out, you bastards! Out! You have no business here! Out I tell you!*"

To emphasize her orders to them, she began to pick up the empty plates and lids and throw them at the men. They shattered against the walls and the door. All of the women joined in, throwing dishes and yelling at the men. They were struck several times and then beat a hasty retreat. When they were gone and the cell door locked once more, the women all cheered Jinjing and laughed heartily. Another round of rice wine was poured and Violet toasted "*Jinjing!*"

Unfortunately for the brave maid, she was sent down to the dungeon about a year later on some minor infraction for a week's sentence. Scylla and Charybdis remembered her act of impertinence very well.

One by one, the women passed off to sleep. The light from the lantern faded and then went out.

军阀 外家

CHAPTER NINE

It was about two o'clock in the afternoon when Li Pao came back down to the dungeon. He opened the door to the cell and, holding his lantern high, took in the sight of the naked, passed out women, the clothes strewn around the room, the empty and smashed dishes, the turned over flasks of rice wine scattered about. The blood from the concubine's neck wound had been smeared all over the other women's bodies, making them look like painted horses. He saw the new maid nestled in the arms of the English whore. He smiled.

Everything had worked out as best as it could. It was too bad that the maid, Lijuan, had to die, but someone had to pay for the crime against his lord, and she had fallen asleep on duty. He had thought the warlord was never going to stop the concubine's execution. When he saw the blade go up, he lost all hope. Then, he heard his master's shout, but he, like everyone else in the crowd, thought it too late. His stomach sickened when he heard the 'thump!' of the axe striking wood. When he saw she was still alive, he gave a prayer of thanks to the gods.

He had known that the warlord would be intrigued when he heard that Whore Number Four had learned to play a Chinese instrument and had learned to speak Chinese. That was why he had brought the maid Lijuan up to tell the warlord her tale. When the beautiful concubine sang to the master those sad, soulful songs, Li had thought that his strategy to save the whore would succeed. As the executions went on, he began to have his doubts. Then, when he saw that the executioner had missed her neck, he went into immediate action lest anyone else get the idea that the execution should go forward anyway.

He knew that the concubine would be overwhelmed with dismal sorrow and the residuals of her terror as a result of her harrowing experience. He looked for and found her surviving maids as soon as he had insured that the concubine was successfully hurried off. When he saw the maid Wen upstairs in the kitchen, he had an inspiration. He knew that the whore would see the likeness to the slain maid Lijuan at once. A little rice wine, some food and dessert and nature would take its course. When he was a eunuch in the Emperor's employ many years ago, a concubine who was condemned to be strangled for one offense or another was reprieved at the last minute, just as the executioner had wrapped the knotted, silk garrote around her pretty throat. She had fucked her maids like a tiger for a week.

It was time now, though, to reassert his authority.

"*Wake up! Wake up!*" he yelled. Jinjing was the first to raise her head. She blinked a couple of times, trying to throw off her lethargy. Li Pao brought his whippy stick down on her back twice, shouting again, "*Wake up! Wake up!*"

Jinjing howled from the pain and scooted to her feet. Her scream alerted the other women to the emergency and the naked women all quickly rose to their feet and gave the eunuch a respectful bow.

"*You, you, you,*" Li Pao shouted, pointing his whippy stick at Jinjing, Ting and Huifang. "*Get dressed! Take trays! Go upstairs!*" To Wen, he shouted, "*Go get broom! Sweep up floor!*" Shards of broken pottery lay all about, a danger to bare and tender feet.

While the other maids dressed, Wen scurried from the cell. The two guards were seated at their station by the inner gate to the dungeon. She begged them piteously for information about where to procure a broom. She was embarrassed at the malformed, malicious men's lascivious glances at her nudity. The men considered for a moment whether to extract some benefit from her before they aided her in her quest, but reconsidered in light of the prior instructions of the eunuch to leave the women alone. Charybdis nodded to a closet. Wen rushed over to it and removed the straw broom and a dustpan. She hustled back to Violet's cell.

In the meantime, the other maids were struggling to dress. Their clothes, all identical, light green blouses and white pants, had become all mixed up. Li lost his patience and began lashing out with his whip, making the girls squeal and cry out, but not making their job any easier. Huifang was finished first and she piled what she could onto one of the large trays and hurriedly escaped the cell.

Jinjing, after she had pulled her blood stained blouse back over her torso, gave the eunuch a forlorn look and then looked back at her mistress.

Violet had backed herself up into the corner of the cell. The women had escaped into a little world of their own for a few hours, a world where whips and beheadings did not exist. It was a rude awakening indeed to have the eunuch rush in and disturb their tranquil sleep so violently. This was the life she thought she had escaped. She had given little thought to her future during their celebration of her victory over death. It was now right in front of her.

Li Pao addressed the anxious Jinjing. *"You go upstairs. The whore will follow later. Tomorrow, next day, maybe. She stays with me for now."*

The maid didn't know whether to be happy or sad. What did he mean that she would stay with him for now? Was he going to whip her? When she saw Li Pao's whip being raised, she did not wait for an answer. She picked up the remaining tray and rushed from the cell. It didn't matter. The mistress would be with them soon!

Ting followed quickly on Jinjing's heels, scooping up an empty carafe and a couple of plates that the other maids forgot in their haste.

Just as Ting fled the cell, Wen reappeared. Without waiting for further instructions, she went right to work. Li Pao gave her a cursory look and brought his gaze back to bear on the naked concubine.

"*Hands in front!*" he ordered her. He was watching her carefully. Her reaction would tell him whether she needed to spend a few more days in the dungeon under the whip or not.

Violet considered the order. How could she return to a life of total subservience after what she had been through? Or did her experience change anything?

If she were to refuse, she would have to be prepared to go all the way, make them beat her until she was dead. Otherwise, there was no sense in it. The last thing she wanted to do was go through a travail of torment only to end up with the same result. And there was the fact that somehow, the fates, God, something or someone wanted her alive. She remembered the night of her magical lovemaking with the soldier. When the alarm had been sounded and he had retrieved his knife, a look had crossed his face as if he were determined to take her life. Then, the look changed, as if he had decided he wanted her to live.

Violet had watched her lover march off proudly to his death. But, as long as she was alive, he was not really dead. He lived on in her. He had redeemed his earlier torment of her on the trip upriver and now represented everything that was good in the world to her. She wanted his memory and the memory of their night of bliss to live on and it would only live on as long as she did. So, until the chance of escape ever presented itself to her, she would obey. And, she knew, to obey meant to serve her lord.

Li watched the calculations going through the concubine's brain. She was a clever one, that was clear. She would make the right choice, and he would have another chance to make her into the concubine that his master needed and deserved.

Violet gingerly put her hands in front of her, wrists crossed. Li had a long, thin, leather strap in his belt and he took it out. He used one end to bind the whore's wrists together. He then pulled her to the middle of the room and looped the other end over the hook that hung from the beam. After taking down the empty lantern, he pulled on the strap until Violet's hands were stretched tautly high above her and tied it off. While Wen swept furiously, he took the straps that had previously bound Violet's wrists and ankles and tied off her feet to recessed iron bars on either side of her, pulling her legs widely apart.

Wen had finished sweeping up the small cell. "*Go, get rid of that and bring back a bucket of hot water,*" Li Pao told her. "*There's a basket out in the hall, bring that in too.*"

Wen brought in the basket and then ran out to find a bucket of hot water. She had to approach the guards again. They always kept a fire going to fight off the dampness of the dungeon and usually had a large teapot simmering. Trying to stay on the good side of the powerful eunuch, they poured the contents of the simmering teapot into the bucket and topped it off with cool water. While the water in the bucket was not hot, it was at least warm. Wen went running back to the cell.

In the meantime, Li Pao had delved into the wicker basket and pulled out some jars of soap and lotion, a hairbrush, a razor and a towel. He also retrieved a small leather ball like the concubines had been given on the day of Me Ling's wedding. He presented it to Violet's mouth.

When the eunuch had strung her up, Violet had prepared herself for another beating. Seeing the eunuch remove the soap and lotions from the basket had given her relief. When he proffered to her the ball of leather covered opium, she balked at receiving it. She had spent most of her time in the seraglio in a drugged haze and the only positive thing about her imprisonment in the dungeon had been her ability to think clearly. Taking the opium now would put her back on the merry-go-round. She looked the eunuch in the eye. She was hardly in a posture to refuse him anything and she knew that his calm demeanor could turn to rage at any moment. Sorrowfully, she opened her mouth and admitted the drugged, leather ball.

Li Pao understood the reticence of the whore to be drugged. He admired that in her. The other concubines were only too happy to subsist in a state of mild euphoria all day. Eventually, he would lower the English whore's dosage somewhat, but for now, she needed to be able to put behind her the experiences of the last two weeks and her near execution. And, she had to relearn her lesson of absolute obedience to her lord. Her coupling with the soldier had been an act of defiance. The opium would melt her defiance away.

When Wen returned with the bucket, Li was studying Violet's tormented body. He could still see the lines of red that he had placed there. Most of them would fade with time, but there were one or two that might persist as faint, white lines. The witch who devised all of the potions given to the concubines would have a remedy for that. The whore had lost weight while a prisoner and she had lost her milk. She would fill out quickly under the guidance of her maids. As to her milk, he had already started Pu Wei off to milk production. He would let the Chinese whore service her master until the end of the next cycle. The master went on his trip to Shanghai in a few weeks. When he went on his next trip after that, he would decide whether it would be the Russian whore's turn or this one's. Who knows, the Russian whore might even be gone by then. He had sensed a slight change in the master's attitude towards her. She would still bring a good price.

Li proceeded to wash the blood and grime off of Violet's body. He had Wen go get a cup so that he could wash her hair. When he was done, he rubbed a soothing lotion all over her and brushed her hair until it was silky and shiny.

The hair on Violet's loins had started to grow back so he crouched down in front of her and gave her pudendum a good shave. When it was nice and smooth again, he covered it with lotion, rubbing it in until he sensed the concubine squirming from arousal.

Violet felt like some mannequin on display as the eunuch cleaned her body. Her legs were spread out wide and her thighs and her arms over head were strained. The pleasant feeling of being washed coincided with a surge of relaxing pleasure from the opium in her mouth. When she felt the eunuch shaving away her pubic hair, she knew what would come next, what always came next. Her slice lubricated in learned anticipation.

Li Pao began by placing his finger of Violet's button of delight and stroking it softly. He waited until it became rigid to slip his finger down the length of her gash and then delve inside her. This was an important lesson for the whore. She had stolen her pussy from her master and now must give it back. At the same time, she would need to relearn the fact that her pussy ruled her and not the other way around. Since General Wang, through him, his eunuch, ruled her pussy, he ruled her.

Violet tried to fight off the sensations of arousal that were rising in her. They emanated from her distended slice and flowed to her thighs and belly and then radiated throughout her whole body. She shook her hips in a vain attempt to ward off the hand that was driving her to pleasure. Her hands strained in their bindings above her and her ankles pulled at their ties. She knew that the eunuch was drawing her back into her life as a whore and she wanted to resist it. She would serve her lord dutifully, she had decided that she wanted to live after all, but she wanted to do it on her own terms, not as a sex addicted slut. Her wishes and wants were, though, of no moment.

In her rising lust, she inadvertently squeezed down on the ball of leather in her mouth and within moments a wave of euphoria swept through her. Her resistance to the eunuch's manipulations of her crevasse collapsed. She gave out a sigh and she felt her knees weaken. Now, her body and mind craved consummation of her lust. She tried to thrust her loins at the man's active, knowledgeable hand. She moaned.

Seeing the concubine submit to her need for pleasure was satisfying to the eunuch. He had spent his life studying women and he knew how to make one into a whore. He slowed his efforts for a few moments, forcing the Englishwoman's drive to completion to slow. She moaned and wriggled her hips. When she had cooled sufficiently, he resumed the stroking and teasing of her cunt. His hand was slick with her discharge, making it easy to thrust several fingers at once into her gaping orifice to simulate her usage by a cock. When she started panting and writing again, he slowed once more. And then again and again. She was groaning with need when he brought her over the top. Her body shook, her hips rocked. Her chest and face had blossomed pink, her breasts had engorged with blood. She moaned and groaned as her pussy shoved all other mental and physical needs aside.

The English whore reveled in the flow of pleasure through her body. She groaned with ecstasy at each thrilling, intense paroxysm of her pussy. The hand kept tantalizing her, bringing her past her first orgasm into a second. Her mind stepped off to oblivion. Her limbs strained at her bindings.

She just wanted to collapse into a ball, but her body was stretched out like a hide to be tanned. Her third climax was almost painful the way it electrified every nerve in her body. "Oh, please stop! Please!" her mind ranted. "Ohhhhhhhhh! Ohhhhhhhhh! Ohhhhhhhhhhhhhhhh!" she exclaimed.

Satisfied that he had proven his point to the whore, Li Pao allowed her lusts to recede. He picked up the towel that he had used to dry her hair and wiped off his hand. It was time to go. The slut had much to think about.

He ordered the diminutive maid to return all of the soaps and other accouterments of toiletry to the basket. He reached into the concubine's mouth and removed the ball of leather only to put a fresh one in.

When all was ready, he had the maid retrieve her discarded clothes and then, taking the basket and the lantern, he left the cell and shut the door, sealing the concubine into darkness once again.

Wen made a move to put on her clothes, but the eunuch stopped her. "*Drop that,*" he told her, "*and come with me.*"

The maid shivered with fear as he led her into the neighboring cell. Li pointed to the floor with his whippy stick and ordered her, "*On knees!*" Within a few moments, he had the child-like, young woman's ankles tied off to the recessed rods in the floor and her hands bound behind her. He had no collar for her, so he looped a strap around her neck and tied it off. He then ran the free end under the rod in the floor by her chin and then a few feet away from her. He pulled on it until her head was bowed and her breasts crushed against her knees. He picked up his whippy stick.

Wen was whining and crying. Her worst fears on coming down to the dungeon were being realized. She was going to be left behind! The men outside would rape her and beat her. Was this a punishment from the gods for her copulating with the women a few hours ago?

Li Pao spoke to the bound and trembling girl. "*I am leaving you here so that you can contemplate the enthusiasm and dedication that you will display in caring for your mistress. You will note that I did not say 'serving your mistress.' You serve only Lord Wang. The English whore is his property. It will be your duty to see she obeys all the rules of the seraglio and is kept passionate at all times so she can be always ready for Lord Wang's use. Do you understand?*"

"*Y,yes, Master,*" Wen eked out. She didn't want all this responsibility. She would rather go back to the kitchen and suffer the rapes of the cook and the soldiers than to have so weighty a task. Why she had been selected, she didn't know. She had watched as two maids lost their heads for breaches of their responsibilities to their lord. She didn't want to end up like them!

"*I'm going to give you five strokes of my whip so that you will have a memory of what will happen to you if you default in your obligations,*" he advised her. "*I will come and get you in the morning.*"

The poor maid started to sob when she heard the sentence imposed on her by the eunuch. She wanted to tell him that she already had a good idea of what would happen to her if she was derelict in her duties. She didn't need five blows from his whip to know that a terrible future would await her. "*P,please…*" she stared to say.

Li Pao had let his whippy stick fly. "Whooosh! Crack!" the flexible cane struck the young girl across her defenseless, tender buttocks.

"Owwwwwwwwwwwwww!" she screamed.

"Whoosh! Crack!" the whip landed again, further up on her posterior. "*Oh! Oh! Oh! Oh!*" the terrified maid exclaimed. "*Oh, p,pleeeeeeeeease! Noooooooo! P,pleeeeeeeeeease!*" she begged.

Li Pao always let the woman beg and plead for mercy to her heart's content on her first real whipping. It helped when she degraded herself totally in her futile attempts to assuage her punishment. Her desire to avoid a repeat was heavily strengthened. On her next one, the slut would be gagged.

Wen's screams intensified at each stroke of the whip until her voice was hoarse. He laid the last one on particularly strong since it was the one she would remember the best. "Whoosh! Crack!"

"Ahhhhhhhhhhoooooowwwwwwwwww!" the high pitched voice screamed.

Li Pao said nothing to her as he prepared to go. She was blubbering loudly. He tied off her bound hands to a rod in the floor behind her to complete her immobility and added a gag and a blindfold to her oppression. He picked up the lantern and left.

* * * * * * * * * * * * * *

General Wang had retreated to his salon on the second floor of the fortress right after he had left the execution grounds. He found the bottle of scotch he had been working on the night before and started into emptying it.

"How could I have been so weak?" he asked himself. "She's just a whore! I could get a hundred whores!" Of course, he could send word down to the dungeon to have her strangled even now. She would be dead and his torment would be over. He would probably have some tough nights, but he would get over it. But how was he going to repair his reputation? He ruled his empire largely through fear. He had now shown the public that he had an Achilles heel. What would the soldiers think? Would he have to fear a palace revolution now? Why were the gods tormenting him this way? Had he lost the mandate of heaven?

He had finished off the bottle long before his eunuch and chief advisor came in about 4 o'clock that afternoon. He had sat in his chair all day, refusing lunch, refusing all visitors. Li Pao had expected as much. It was a hard thing to accept that you had a heart, especially for a ruler like General Wang. What the general didn't see yet was how delicious the English whore's return to subservience would be. And Li doubted that he had done himself any harm in the view of those he ruled. A great ruler did not rule by fear alone. Fear was of preeminent importance, true, but men who were only feared were hated.

The general had shown a human side. Songs would be sung about him and the English whore, poems written. His men would look upon him as one of them. The people would admire the strength of his heart.

Li Pao was a consummate politician. He had believed that the crowd would be horrified at the death of the concubine, especially after the deaths of the two pretty maids. They could only take so much blood and gore. He had felt the growing tension in the crowd as the beautiful concubine had approached the execution platform. He had heard their gasps and moans of pity when they saw her standing behind the bench on which her torso would lay. Her body seemed to shimmer in the light. Her face was serene, but at the same time victorious. It was as if she had defeated death.

He knew that every man who was watching would give his life's blood for an evening with her, just as had Lieutenant Cheng. She was too precious a jewel to squander. From now on, all eyes that cast themselves on the castle would think of her locked away inside, the property of their lord and master. How lucky he was to own her! How wise of him to not let her die!

But what to do with his lord until he could shake himself out of his doldrums and realize that he had achieved a great victory today over the hearts and minds of the people? He had an idea.

He waited until General Wang saw and acknowledged him before speaking. When the warlord cast his glass across the room, shattering it against the wall in a hundred pieces, he considered that as his permission to speak.

"*My Lord,*" he said obsequiously, "*the English whore has been returned to the dungeon.*"

Wang looked at him glaringly.

"*May I have Whore Number One sent to you?*" Li asked. Pu Wei had inherited that title for now after the departure of Me Ling.

The general just grunted. Pu Wei was already out in the corridor. The eunuch would bring her in in a minute. She had been instructed to use all of her powers to seduce and please her lord or suffer terrible consequences.

"*I will bring her to you, Lord, but first, may I speak?*"

Wang looked up at him. "What can be said?" he thought. He nodded nonetheless.

"*I believe that you did the correct thing today, Lord. The Englishwoman is a great possession. It would have be a shame to waste her. Everyone knows that. The people were happy that you spared her.*"

Wang looked up, surprised.

"*Oh, yes, Lord,*" Li Pao continued. "*To have her brought to the edge of death and then saving her with the utterance of one word when all seemed lost was a magnificent gesture. I would have never thought of it, Lord. You are very wise.*"

The warlord's surprise grew even greater.

"*The gods were on your side today, Lord,*" Li went on. "*They guided the executioner's blade away from her neck just in time. It was a stroke of luck only the gods could provide.*"

"Luck?" Wang thought. "Was it luck?"

Li Pao saw his lord's hesitance in believing that. He would need more convincing.

"*Every good has its bad, Lord, and every bad its good. The invasion of your seraglio by that upstart, whose name will never be mentioned again, was bad. But it has brought us all a new appreciation of the value of the English whore. And, I believe, she will be appropriately grateful to you for saving her life. Those are good things. The gods have opened all our eyes.*"

Wang considered this. He was still mystified as to why he couldn't get up and terminate the execution sooner. His whole body had been frozen. It was like a nightmare. If the eunuch was right, the gods must have caused his fugue. Then, at just the right moment, they freed him to shout, "*Stop!*" A fraction of a second later, it would have been of no use. A fraction of a second sooner, it would not have needed a miracle. Maybe the eunuch was right.

"*I rushed here, Lord, because I thought that you would be making plans to visit the temple at Jinzou that you subsidize for a traditional three days of fasting and prayer.*"

To the warlord, this seemed a brilliant idea. The eunuch was turning defeat into victory. And the gods needed to be propitiated. One never knew when they would take your good luck away. He would go in the morning. There were preparations that needed to be made. But first he would fuck Whore Number One!

"*As you say, Li,*" Wang responded heartily. "*I was planning such a visit when you came in. Have my wives get ready, they will go with me. And bring me Whore Number One.*"

"*She is right here in the hall, Lord,*" Li Pao answered him.

* * * * * * * * * * * * * *

Three times during the evening and night, Li Pao came down to the dungeon to check on his charges. As to the maid, he merely opened the door and shined a light on her to see if she was still alive. She moaned and whined though her gag when she heard the door opening. He saw that she had peed. He had expected that she would. He would punish her for that in the morning.

The English whore was more disciplined. He held a bowl under her and commanded her to release her fluids. Once she had filled it, he took the leather ball out of her mouth so that she could drink and then put a fresh one in. He could tell that she was in a great deal of pain from her stretched muscles. To her credit she did not whine or plead for release. She just looked at him forlornly when he introduced the fresh ball of opium to her mouth.

Now, a little after 9 o'clock the next morning, he was coming down to retrieve her. The general had left a little over a half hour ago. It was a six hour drive to the temple, about 150 miles by winding, narrow, crevasse filled roads. The trip would take more like eight if you figured in the time that the small caravan of wives, maids, servants, cooks and bodyguards finished lunch. Tomorrow morning he would begin his three days of fasting and prayer. When that was concluded, he would undoubtedly spend the next day feasting and celebrating. The temple whores were, he understood, quite talented. On the sixth day, he would return. That gave him five days to prepare the English whore for him.

Yesterday he had sent a rider to Changsha, about 75 miles due south to enlist the assistance of an old acquaintance. She would arrive, if she hurried, about 5 o'clock this afternoon. That would give her up to four days with the whore if she needed it. That should be enough.

Violet's shoulders and thighs had gone way past painful by the time that the eunuch came to relieve her of her torments at last. She had spent considerable time, days and days, almost all of two weeks if you added the time all up, kneeling on her cell floor, bound into immobility. That had been an excruciating experience, but at least her body was, more or less, at rest. The position she had been condemned to assume for the last 18 hours had been exactly the opposite. It was stretched to the breaking point. The only solace had been the opium. She had tried not to squeeze the ball in her mouth because she wanted her mind to be clear, but it had such a soothing effect on her strained muscles that she couldn't help herself. The end result was that she spent much of her time in the absolute darkness of her cell in a dizzy, woozy state. It was almost like she was floating in air. The loneliness of her long, dark hours was, however, just the same.

The other difference between the prior position that she had been tied in and this was that while the other closed her body into a scrunched up ball, in this pose her body was as open and exposed as it could be. It was as if her body had exploded. In her wooziness, she sometimes half expected the door to her cell to lift up like a curtain on a stage and find a whole audience out there looking at her.

The psychological message she was meant to receive was clear to her. Before, her lesson had been about obedience, about imprinting on her mind the power that her lord and master had over her, that he controlled every cell of her body. This was more about openness. A new chapter in her life as the general's whore was beginning. While she had been permitted to maintain a secret part of herself from her lord, the part that rebelled against and loathed her existence as his sex slave, she was now to devoid herself of all reticence, all reservations. Nothing was to be hidden. Every fiber of her being, physical and mental, was to be devoted to her lord.

She was not sure she could do it. She loathed the warlord more than anyone else in the world. On the execution platform, when she had but moments to live, she had forgiven him for what he had done to her. That didn't mean that she had to love him.

Violet had a great deal of time to contemplate the problem. While kneeling all scrunched up was not the optimal posture for sleep, it was still possible. In contrast, over the last eighteen hours, though she had fallen asleep many times, each time, just as she was going over the edge, she would experience the sensation that she was falling. Her body and mind would snap back to attention. She would whine and cry for a while, and then somnolence would creep up on her once more. Her mind would darken for a moment and then she would get the sensation that she was falling free like she had slipped off a cliff, and be jarred back into wakefulness.

Despite having spent many, many hours alone and in the dark she had never gotten used to it. Each time that her cell door closed, a feeling of terror welled up in her. She would begin to sweat and her stomach would feel hollow. And then there were the confinements. It was horrible to have your body confined while at the same time experiencing disabling darkness. She had experienced it again and again on the boat trip to Wang's fortress and each time she had been tied down in this cell thereafter. It was unreal to have lost the ability to move your limbs. For some reason, your mind just refused to accept it. Much of the time, you could think of practically nothing else.

It was especially hard to bear when she knew that up above her was a whole world of free people, relative to her anyway. They were walking around, going about their business, blissfully ignorant of the terrible things that were happening to her. It was only she that the universe had selected for this particular torment. If she were anyone else in the world, she would not be here.

Alternatively, if she had been anywhere else in the world that night a year and a half ago when General Wang came into the casino, at that particular time, she wouldn't be here either. Although Robert had not bought her a ticket to return to England as he had represented he would, he did not get the idea of having her kidnapped until he had seen General Wang that night. If they had gone to the Blue Cantina first instead of last, things would have turned out much differently.

Or if the little ball on the roulette table had landed in black instead of red. She had left her choice of rejecting or forgiving Robert up to chance. If it had landed on black, she would have married him. General Wang would have won his bet. All would have been right with the world. But it landed on red. So, it seemed, she could not blame Robert for her presence here. She could not blame General Wang. It was the hand of fate, God, the devil, karma, whatever you want to call it, that brought her to this particular moment, in this particular space, tied into immobility in bitter darkness.

The opium played havoc with her sense of time. She had gotten pretty good at estimating time in her other sojourns in the warlord's dungeon. The drugs skewed that perception. So, when the door to her cell opened the fourth time since she had been tied in this position, she had no idea how long it had been.

When she saw that the eunuch was accompanied by the little maid, Wen, she had hope that her circumstances would change. She didn't know that Wen had spent the same 18 hours bound into immobility right next to her.

Li Pao had gone to the maid's cell first. She whimpered and whined when he entered it. He loosened the tie that held her hands in place behind her and then the strap that held her head pointed downwards. He guided her until she was kneeling straight up. For the moment, he left her gag in and her blindfold on.

"*Slut, you have dirtied yourself,*" Li Pao told her. "*You have pissed all over the floor. You need to be punished for that. I am going to give you three strokes across your breasts. If you flinch or try to avoid the blows, I will give you five more on your rear and leave you here for another day. Do you understand?"*

The near hysterical girl nodded her head and moaned a piteous affirmation. Her body began to shiver and her head lolled back and forth. She was whining already.

"Whoosh! Crack!" the whippy stick landed across the top of her breasts. They shook and bounced from the blow. "Mmmmmmmmmmmmmm! Mmmmmmmmmmmmmm!" the girl cried dolefully. Her shoulders rounded and her torso swayed, but she didn't flinch. Li Pao readied the second blow.

"Whoosh! Crack!" This one landed across the nipples of both of her breasts. She groaned in agony.

Her chest was heaving and she was sobbing heavily as she awaited the final blow. The eunuch held back, letting her suffer in anticipation. After about twenty seconds, she shook her body and gave out an anguished groan. It was almost more than she could take.

Then, "Whoosh! Crack!" The third blow landed exactly between the first two. The pretty, young maid bent her torso over and howled. Her hands twisted in her bonds. She sobbed and sobbed and sobbed. No one had ever treated her like this. She had done nothing wrong, nothing she could help anyway. It had been a long horrible night. She had thought that it would never end and that she would go crazy before she was ever released. She couldn't help peeing. It had been hours and hours and hours and hours. She couldn't hold it in that long. Nobody could.

And then the lesson hit her. She would be judged by the results of her efforts not her good will in trying to bring them about. If she failed in her duties, for whatever reason, she would be punished.

He released the simpering maid from her bonds and made her mop up her mess.

It was a subdued and wary Wen who entered Violet's cell. Violet was startled to see the evidence of her recent beating across her breasts. It was a salutary lesson for Violet as well. The new maid may be tender and cuddly, but she would work to please her master as hard as any of them to maintain Violet's subservience.

Li Pao released Violet's ankles and then lowered her slowly from the beam above her until she was on her knees. The relieved concubine gave out a great sigh. Li Pao had brought with him a covered wicker basket. He opened it to reveal a beautiful, green banner dress with yellow and blue flowers printed on it. He took the leather ball from Violet's mouth and freed her hands. He ordered the maid to lower the dress over Violet's head.

Violet raised her hands so that the smooth, silky garment could be placed on her body. Clothes meant only one thing: she was leaving the dungeon. A wave of relief passed through her. She would get to breath fresh air, lounge in the seraglio, bathe, sleep. She knew that servicing the warlord would not be far behind, but, for now, she put that out of her mind. When the dress had been lowered over her head and her arms put through the arm holes, Li ordered the maid to brush her mistress's hair. Wen did it as gently as she could, freeing the knots that had developed since her last washing. When she was done, she gathered it behind the concubine's head into a loose ponytail.

Li Pao ordered Violet to rise and to put her arms behind her. He tied off her wrists. There were a pair of green and gold brocade slippers in the basket and Wen applied them to Violet's feet. Li Pao placed a blindfold over the concubine's eyes and attached a golden chain to the ring on her black collar. He handed the chain to Wen. Picking up the basket, he ordered the slave, "*Come.*"

Violet stumbled slightly as she felt herself pulled ahead by the collar, but Li Pao maintained a slow enough pace so that she could follow rather easily. The guards, Scylla and Charybdis, looked upon the small parade as it passed. They had been ordered not to bother the women last night. Seeing the bare flesh of the little maid flow past them, they regretted it. As to the concubine, something told them that they would see her again some day.

Wen was ashamed of her nakedness as she led the concubine through the great hall and up the stairs to the upper floors of the fortress. All eyes were on them. They went all the way up to the third floor and the entrance to the seraglio. The guard unlocked the door for them and let them enter.

Violet's heart leapt as she realized that she was passing into the outer area of the seraglio. She felt like she was home. They stopped at a door, and when the entered the room, she could tell by the smell of the perfumed bathwater where they were. Li Pao removed her blindfold and released her bound hands. After removing the chain from her collar, he nodded towards the gleefully awaiting maids, signaling her to join them.

As Li Pao left, Violet jumped into the arms of Jinjing and Ting. They hugged and kissed her excitedly. The bath was all ready, and after undressing her hurriedly, they led her into it.

The water was soothing. Violet felt a wave of relief run through her. Her ordeal was over. As bad as life as General Wang's sex slave was, it was by far better than the life she had been leading for more than two weeks. She was trying not to cry. She sank under the hot, sweet smelling, oily water and let it cover her head and shoulders. It was one of the most wonderful feelings she had ever experienced.

The maids brought her to the shallow end and began to soap her body. Wen was standing there, not knowing what to do. Jinjing ordered her to pour more hot water into the tub. She rushed to the hot water tank and opened the valve that released it. When the tank was empty, she filled it again with cold water so it could be heated by the coal burning fire underneath. She then hopped into the tub.

When Violet saw the little maid in the water, she jumped back into the deep end and lowered herself under the water, rinsing off all of the soap. When she came to the surface, she put her arms around Wen and kissed her. She turned to her other maids and said. "*Wen need bath. Please.*"

Jinjing and Ting looked askance at the new maid for a moment but then gave in. They urged her over to the shallow end and dutifully soaped her up. When Ting saw the traces of Li Pao's whip, she became more sympathetic and caressed Wen's face.

After they had washed Violet's hair, they had her lay down on the mat beside the tub and covered her with a creamy, sweet smelling lotion. Violet reveled in the feeling of their soft hands on her body. She rolled to her back when they had finished with that side of her. The warm gentle touch of the maids soon had her lusts building. When hands touched the inside of her thighs, she spread them. Jinjing and Ting were trying to show Wen what to do. When their mistress spread her legs, revealing her soft, hairless slit, they ordered Wen to pleasure her. Wen looked at them hesitatingly.

Yesterday was the first time that she had even known that you could do this kind of thing. She had screamed with joy when it had been done to her so she knew that it was extremely pleasurable. To have it done to oneself was one thing, to do it to someone else was another. Then she remembered Li Pao's whip and her long night in the dungeon. She didn't want to go through that again. She nodded her assent to her sister maids and brought her torso between the mistress's thighs. She leaned over, paused for a moment to consider the line she was crossing, and then slipped her tongue inside the edge of the glistening gap between the engorging love lips. She lapped its length from bottom to top, stopping only when she reached the little nubbin at its apex.

Jinjing and Ting whispered words of encouragement to her, telling her to let her tongue dawdle on the mistress's clit, to drag her tongue down the widening gap, to insert it deeply within, to take the love button between her lips and suck on it gently. Wen placed her tiny hands on the insides of Violet's pale and tender thighs for support while she licked and suckled and licked at the other maids' commands. She heard the mistress give out a deep, languid moan and she became excited. When her thighs began to twitch and her hips began a slow, lazy rocking motion, Wen's slit began to water. When the mistress's body began to shudder and her moans become staccato and urgent, her own lusts began to rise.

At Jinjing's instructions, she flicked the tip of her tongue again and again atop the mistress's hardened clit. Her mistress's body convulsed and writhed beneath her. Ting had covered the mistress's mouth with her own so that her moans had become muffled, but Wen could hear them grow louder and more urgent. The woman gave out a long, virtually anguished moan and then her body relaxed.

The maids let Violet sleep for about an hour. Ting lay next to her, holding her tight while Jinjing washed Wen's hair. After, they gently shook the relaxed and fulfilled concubine awake. They had her sit on a large cushion where they made up her eyes, plucked her eyebrows, brushed lotion into her hair and did her nails. Jinjing showed Wen how to apply the dark red makeup to Violet's nipples and, after bringing her to her feet, how to outline the long lines of her slit.

Violet felt happy although she felt a twinge of sadness whenever she looked at Wen. She had thought that she had saved Lijuan's life the night of the invasion, but she had only preserved her so that she could be tortured and then cruelly beheaded. She hoped that Lijuan was in a better place now.

When Li Pao came back in, all the women bowed to him. He instructed the maids to get the razor and some soap and he proceeded to shave Violet's loins. When he was done, he placed her legs over his shoulders and mouthed her to completion. Violet's impassioned cries of lust echoed off of the walls of the small, tiled chamber.

Li Pao left again and the maids adorned Violet with a blue and green, silken robe. They tied it around her waist and brought her into the next room. Violet recognized it as the room where they had brought her on the day of her induction as a concubine. She had been fed a sumptuous meal here. There was a 4' by 4' lacquered table in the middle and while Jinjing pulled the chord of the servant's bell, Ting and Wen led Violet to the table and brought her to her knees. Ting showed Wen how to tie off the mistress's wrists loosely behind her back with a soft, silken cord and explained that the concubine was never permitted to feed herself, clean herself or even to touch the sensitive parts of her body.

When the food came, Violet had another feast. This time, seraglio rules were again in force and she allowed the maids to feed her little bits of this and that, and to bring the cup of black tea to her lips. Violet ate until she was sated and then some. Jinjing and Ting had received specific instructions to put some of the flesh back on her bones and they insistently made Violet finish all of the rice and all of the meat. Violet knew better than to resist her maids when they were insistent about something.

After the meal was finished, they brought Violet back to her feet. Jinjing ran back into the bathing room and returned with two leather bracelets connected by an 18" length of chain. She explained carefully and emphatically to Wen that when moving from room to room in the outside hallway, the mistress's hands should always be bound and her legs connected at the ankles by a chain. Normally, the maids would have brought Violet back to the inner seraglio by themselves, but this time they had been instructed to ring when they were finished and Li Pao would come and escort her.

When the eunuch appeared, he led Violet and her maids not to the inner seraglio, but down the hall the other way. He opened a door with a key and ushered the small group inside. The room was outfitted as a bedroom. The walls were painted a soft, pale green and the floor was covered with a dark green rug. A vase of flowers stood upon a polished, mahogany table. The bed was wide and covered with a single, peach colored, silken sheet. Violet looked at the bed with great anticipation. She had had a catnap in the bathing room, but was still exhausted from her ordeals. Li Pao instructed the maids to put their mistress to bed. Wen was to remain as her guardian.

Jinjing and Ting showed Wen how to tie off the mistress's ankles and wrists to each other and, after kissing the recumbent concubine, left the room. Wen, who had not gotten much sleep the night before either, knelt on a cushion by the door and struggled to keep watch over her.

军阀 外家

CHAPTER TEN

It was a little after 5 o'clock that the car from Changsha pulled up to the outer gate of the fortress. Arrangements had already been made for its admittance. While the passengers, two women, one older, around 45 or so, the other young, maybe 20, waited, their baggage was unloaded by Wang's soldiers and word was sent to Li Pao.

The eunuch hurried down to the inner gate and met the women there. He greeted them effusively and escorted them inside the palatial fortress. They were assigned the best of the guest rooms. Their personal luggage was brought there while two large, wooden boxes were brought up to the seraglio. At the outer door, they were handed off to four of the maids who carried them to one of the rooms down the hall.

Li Pao had the guests, after they had gotten settled, escorted to the small dining room on the second floor. While their meal was being prepared, Li and the older woman spoke.

"*Xifang, it is good to see you,*" Li told her. "*It has been many years. I thank you for coming on short notice.*"

Xifang answered him. "*It is good to see you too. After I read your letter I knew that my services were badly needed. In light of our long acquaintance, I could do nothing other than come at once. Is the concubine out of the dungeon?*"

"*Yes, just this morning. She ate some hours ago. She is sleeping in an isolated bedroom just one door down from where you will work. I had the room set up in the manner that I understand you prefer.*"

Xifang was tall and a little broad shouldered for a woman. Her voice was husky, but her mannerisms were effeminate. She had modest sized breasts and long, black hair tinged with grey and tied back behind her head loosely. Her face, made up demurely, was not what you would call pretty. It had a definite grace to it though. Her nose was perhaps a little too long and wide and her face just a little too heavy. She was wearing a green and yellow striped, cotton, shirtwaist dress that went down to her ankles and she had golden rings on several of her fingers. Long silver and gold earrings dangled from her ear lobes.

Her companion remained silent. She was wearing a light pink blouse and a pair of white cotton pants that followed closely the contours of her compact rear and graceful thighs. Her face was pretty. She had green, teardrop eyes and a short, gracefully formed nose. Her lips were plump and had been painted a deep red. Two small golden rings dangled from her ears. She was slender and, compared to her mistress, short, about 5'2". When dinner was finally served, she ate with relish, but always with an eye to her mistress as if to ensure she did not break any rules.

Li Pao and Xifang spoke about old times while they ate and compared notes of long past acquaintances.

"*I heard that you were in Changsha from Hu Chi, who passed through here about a year ago. I hadn't seen him since our days in the Emperor's seraglio.*" Li said.

"*Yes, Hu,*" Xifang replied. "*He was attending the seraglio of a rich merchant in Changsha for several years. When the merchant died, his wife decided to sell off all the concubines to a brothel. I had a letter from him a few months back and he says that he has found work in a seraglio in Nanking.*"

"*Pussy is pussy, eh, Xifang,*" Li Pao joked.

Xifang smiled. "*Yes, pussy is pussy. But to develop a really good pussy, you need to call on me.*"

"*Yes,*" Li Pao agreed. "*I remember your work in the Emperor's seraglio well. I believe that you were serving under Shuang Xue at the time. She put great faith in you. Is the old hag dead?*"

"*Oh, yes,*" Xifang replied after swallowing a long, flat noodle. "*Many years ago. She left me everything, all her recipes, her tools. She was working on a treatise which I have continued. It was started by her mistress. When it is done, it will be the most comprehensive treatment of pussy ever written. While I'm here, if you don't mind, I'd like to inspect the pussies of the other concubines and all of the maids. For the book, of course.*"

"*I will make arrangements for that,*" Li answered. "*You will be especially interested in the pussy of the Russian whore. She has a love bud that's as big as an acorn.*"

Xifang's eyes lit up. "*Truly?*" she asked. "*I would be most happy to examine it. I have a lotion that would make it act like a hair trigger.*"

"*That would be most interesting,*" Li stated. "*Also, while you are here, I would like you to confer with Ying Tai. She is from General Wang's village and prepares all the potions for the concubines.*"

"*I would consider it an honor to compare recipes with her,*" Xifang answered.

After the meal was concluded, Xifang said that she wanted to go see the English concubine right away. "*I'll perform the procedure later tonight, but I want to get her prepared.*"

Li Pao led Xifang and her acolyte up to the room where Violet slept. Xifang was carrying a little, black bag. When they entered the bedroom, Wen jumped up with a start. She bowed obsequiously to the eunuch, hoping that he didn't realize that she had been asleep. Xifang looked over the naked form of the young girl and patted her on the shoulder. She took one of her nipples between her thumb and forefinger, pinching it lightly.

"*She's very cute. May I have use of her while I am here?*" Xifang asked.

"*Certainly,*" Li Pao replied. "*She's at your disposal.*"

Violet was wakened by the voices in her room. She was on her side facing the wall and had to look over her right shoulder to see who it was. She didn't like the looks of the older woman. Something told her that she should be afraid of her.

"*Nui*," Xifang said to her acolyte, "*please untie her legs so that I can examine her.*"

Nui jumped at her mistress's command. She approached the bed and untied the straps around Violet's thighs and ankles and then turned Violet to her back.

Violet was not sure what to make of all this. She saw the steel eyed look that the eunuch was giving her and she knew that she had to be obedient. She knew how much worse her punishment would be if it occurred in front of one of the master's guests, even if she was a woman.

Xifang stepped forward to examine the concubine. Violet had her legs together and the older woman pushed them apart and raised her knees. She motioned for Nui to take hold of them. While the younger woman stood next to her, her hands on Violet's ankles, holding them up and apart, Xifang commenced her inspection. She first spread her hands over Violet's taut belly. Then she took hold of her plump mounds and squeezed them gently, flicking her thumbs at the nipples. Her hands then ran down her sides, over her hips and to the concubine's pale white, soft thighs.

"*Yes, she's very beautiful,*" Xifang commented. "*A bit marked up, although I guess that that could not have been avoided under the circumstances.*"

"No," Li replied.

Violet was frightened and humiliated, but passively let the woman examine her. What else could she do? She resented being treated like a piece of meat on display at the market, but she had no means of stopping the woman, and no inclination to suffer Li Pao's whip. She prayed that there was some benign explanation for the presence of the woman and her apparent assistant. On the other hand, little that had happened to her since becoming General Wang's slave had been benign.

Xifang's hands ran down Violet's pale, soft thighs and over her pudendum. She took one hand and gently spread Violet's love lips apart while she stroked her clit with the thumb of the other. Her eyes watched carefully as the concubine's slice obediently moistened. Once wet, she plunged two fingers into the gap and drew them back and forth slowly. She bent down and inhaled the aroma of Violet's arousal and then took her love bud between her lips and suckled on it softly. Within a short time, Violet gave out a lustful sigh. Satisfied at her latent lusts, the older woman took Violet's outer labial lips between the thumb and forefingers of each hand as if she were measuring them. "*Very nice,*" she commented. "*There should be no problems.*"

Xifang rose from Violet's pussy. "*I need to spend a little time with her now,*" she said to Li. "*Nui will watch over her from here on in. No one should talk to her or see her except myself and Nui until I'm finished in three days.*"

"*Done,*" Li Pao answered.

Violet was having a hard time understanding what the two people were saying. It sounded like Chinese, but it wasn't.

This was because Li and Xifang, when they came in the room, had switched over to the dialect used by the eunuchs in the former Emperor's seraglio. There was often a need to discuss things when the concubines were around that wasn't for their ears. It was a dialect going back about 600 years used by a circle of no more than 150 people at a time.

"*I will need a small amount of clean burning coal and a clean, brass urn to burn it in. Please let the guard at the outside door know that either I or Nui may be coming and going. Most of my time will be spent in the room with the concubine, but I will be*" *taking breaks from time to time. I'll do the operation in about two hours. I have a lotion I need to administer first and it will take that time to set."*

Li Pao nodded. He issued an order to Wen, and the little maid followed him from the room.

Xifang reached into her bag and pulled out a small, bamboo ring and a blindfold. She ordered Violet to sit up. Xifang handed the blindfold to her assistant and she tied it around Violet's eyes. The concubine moaned a protest and pulled at her bound hands behind her. Xifang placed her strong hand on Violet's cheek and pressed in on her jaw, forcing her mouth ajar. She slipped the ring behind Violet's teeth and let Nui buckle it behind her head.

Violet's fear was growing stronger. She had watched Li Pao and Wen leave with deep foreboding. What was the woman going to do to her, she wondered unhappily. What was this all about? At first, she thought that the woman was going to buy her. Panic had risen up in her breast. Then there was a brief conversation between the eunuch and the woman, which Violet did not understand a word of, but it certainly revolved around her. She got the impression, taking into consideration the hands on examination and all, that it was about something that the woman was going to do to her. This seemed even worse: it almost certainly involved her pussy.

She was too frightened to resist the woman. The blindfold went on and the bamboo ring went into her mouth before she really knew what the woman was doing. Her stomach turned over and her heart began to beat hard in her chest.

She was whining from fear when they stood her up from the bed. She felt the young girl's hands untying her wrists. Her blue and gold, silken robe was drawn down her arms and off of her body. When her hands were brought around the front, she made a feeble attempt to resist them being bound again. The woman's hand held her arm tightly, her grip as harsh as any man's. There was no sense in resisting. She knew that it could only make things worse.

When her wrists were bound before her, palm to palm, she felt herself brought back to the bed. The firm hands of the woman forced her to sit on it and then lie on her back.

Xifang looked at the body of the English whore for a moment. She really was delectable. It was understandable why General Wang had fallen for her. There existed a rift between them now based on the woman's sin with the soldier and that rift needed to be repaired. Something needed to be done so that both she and the warlord could have no mistake as to whom her pussy belonged. That was Xifang's job.

Nui placed leather bracelets on Violet's ankles and tied a three foot long strap to the ring in her left one. When Nui was finished, she signaled her mistress and she and Xifang took hold of Violet's ankles and brought them up as close to the squealing woman's chest as they would go. After Nui passed the end of the strap through the ring in Violet's collar, Xifang pulled it through the ring in Violet's left ankle bracelet and tied it off. There was just enough strap left over on Violet's wrists to pull them up to her chest and loop it through her collar ring, tying them off there as well.

Violet was whining with unhappiness. The heels of her feet were resting on her breasts. Her pussy never felt more exposed. She jumped when she felt the woman run her hand over it. Her thumb separated her love lips and slipped inside. She ran it in and out a few times, spreading her moisture.

Satisfied at the concubine's grotesque posture, Xifang went back into her bag. She removed a jar of brownish crème. She opened the jar and took out a large dollop and then spread it over Violet's distended labia. Violet felt a tingle on her flesh as it went on. The woman spread it over her inner flesh as well and just inside her opening with her fingers. She put a small dollop atop her love button. Violet strained at her bonds in weak protest.

Xifang went back to her bag and took out a long, thick facsimile of a cock. She spread the lotion thickly all over it and then poised the tip over Violet's exposed canal. She nudged its blunt head into the hole and began to push it slowly in.

Violet rebelled at the sensation of her pussy being filled with the cool, cock-like object. "Gaaaaaaaaaaaa!" she called out. It was the only sound that she could make. "Gaaaaaaaa! Gaaaaaaaaaaa!" she repeated loudly.

"*There, there, my little English whore,*" the woman said. "*Don't be upset. It's just a wooden cock smeared with some lotion I want to administer to your insides. It will make your pussy feel really good. You'll see. In the meantime,*" she continued, her voice growing harsher and more emphatic, "*no talking. I don't think I have to point out to you the vulnerability of your position.*"

Violet understood about half of what the woman said. She got the gist though. She understood the words for pussy and good. She certainly knew the phrase '*no talking*'. The woman's tone told her the rest. It would be hell if the woman decided to administer a whip to her now. Violet would issue no more protests, but she couldn't help a whine of fear and unhappiness escaping.

The woman ran the fake cock in and out of her pussy a few times until she was satisfied that it could move with ease. She took it out and smeared it again with the lotion. This time she inserted it and left it in place. Violet felt her fingers apply some lotion to the delicate and exposed ring of her rear entrance, making sure to get some inside and around the tissue just past the opening. A moment later, a thick plug covered with the same slime was eased inside her nether hole. Lastly, she dabbed some of the ointment on her nipples and areolas.

Violet could feel the tingle caused by the lotion all over her outer sex, throughout her crevasse, on her nipples and in and on her anal ring. What it was that the woman was giving her, she didn't know, but she didn't like it. It seemed to stimulate her sexual excitement, something she desperately didn't want right now.

Xifang's preparations were almost done. She took out another jar. It held a smoky white liquid. She opened it and poured some of it into a vial, measuring it carefully. She looked back at Violet, as if considering her weight and size, and poured in a little more. Putting the jar down, she edged herself up on the mattress until she was next to the bound woman. Nui took Violet by the hair and pulled her head back, making her ringed mouth available.

Violet knew that she was going to be fed something when her head was pulled back. She had been fearfully expecting it ever since the ring had been installed in her mouth. She waved her tongue around and tried to shake her head. The young women's firm grip on her hair kept her still. Violet moaned as she felt the thick, cool substance pouring on her tongue. She didn't want to swallow it, but there was so much it filled the lower portion of her mouth and started to slide down her throat. The taste was awful, like something that had rotted. She swallowed the rest so that she wouldn't have to taste it any more.

Xifang smiled. The nasty taste was an add on ingredient to her potion. It always worked like a charm. No slut wanted that taste lingering in her mouth.

At Xifang's instruction, Nui released Violet's hair. Xifang produced a thick, leather prong and inserted into the hole that was Violet's mouth. It filled her almost all the way to her throat. It had two leather tabs at the sides with slots in them. The slots fitted nicely over two small buttons attached to the belt that held the ring in place.

The English concubine did not have much time to consider her present circumstances. Within a minute after swallowing the older woman's potion, her mind went all foggy and she entered a dream-like state.

Seeing that the concubine was properly prepared, Xifang put all the lotions and potions back into her black bag and stood up. She didn't have to tell Nui what to do. The young girl stepped over to the door and went to her knees. She would watch over the concubine until her mistress returned.

Li Pao was waiting for Xifang when she entered the hall. He led her to the room that had been made ready. It was about 15' by 20'. There were no windows. A thick, soft matt of woven straw had been spread over the floor. The walls were dark blue. A bronze brazier had been brought in and was filled with coal. Xifang's boxes had been opened. A smaller box made of hard wood and stained a deep brown was sitting on the mat. There was also a large framework set up with straps at certain intervals.

Xifang looked around the room and nodded. "*Perhaps some pillows, two or three large ones would be nice. Nui will be sleeping here with the English whore until we're done.*"

Li nodded politely in affirmation.

"*I have about an hour and a half until I can begin my work. I'd like to see your potion maker now. I'd love to compare notes.*"

* * * * * * * * * * * * *

Over the next hour and a half, Violet struggled to focus her mind to consciousness. Something was going to happen to her and she desperately needed her faculties. The potion that the woman gave her made her mind swim. The only thing she could really focus on was the tingling on her breasts, and in her pussy and rear. It was like tiny little effervescent bubbles were exploding again and again on her tissues. It was particularly disorienting to feel it deep within her coosh. The whole outside of her pussy felt vibrant and alive.

After a while, the potion seemed to be wearing off. The back of her neck began to hurt from the strain of the pull of her legs. Her hips had become sore. She pulled at her bindings and rocked in protest against her cruel positioning. Every time she turned around, it seemed like they came up with some new way to abuse her. Her whole body ached with fear when she tried to speculate what they were going to do to her pussy. Her mind tried to reach out to her maids, to Tatiana who was probably no more than a hundred feet from where she lay. All she wanted to do was to get back to the seraglio and be with her. She would serve the warlord as well as she could. She just wanted some peace from all of the assaults on her body.

Violet jumped when she heard the door opening. From the footsteps, she realized that the older woman had come back. The woman walked up to her and drifted her fingers along Violet's labia. The sensation made Violet jump. "Where did that come from?" she thought nervously. Her love lips had always been sensitive, but not as strongly as this. The hand slid across them once more and Violet moaned into her gag. "Oh, god!" she exclaimed to herself. Now she knew what the old lady was doing with her lotion. She prayed that what the lotion had done to her pussy wasn't permanent.

Violet sighed with relief as her wrists and ankles were released from her neck ring. The woman's strong arms, assisted by the dainty ones of her helper, brought her to her feet. The woman withdrew the cock-like object from her pussy. As it traversed her pussy's walls, a wave of pleasure coursed through her so intense that she felt her knees weaken.

Before she could regain her composure, she felt herself propelled by her arms from the room. They entered the hallway and walked about twenty feet down. Violet heard another door open, they crossed the threshold and the door shut behind them.

The woman brought Violet to her knees. A hand released the leather prong from her mouth and her head was tilted back again. She felt more of that awful tasting potion being poured between her gaping lips. She whined as it slid down towards her throat. She didn't want to be all woozy. She wanted to know what was going on. The hand kept her head leaning back until she swallowed. The gag was placed back in.

She felt like there was something around her, like a frame or something. The women retied her wrists to her neck ring and then pushed her back. Violet felt her back side go over the lip of a platform of some kind and then felt her back on some padded wood. He rear was higher then her body and her pussy extended over the edge of the platform.

Her mind began to reenter a befogged state from the potion. She moaned in unhappiness. Her body felt too weak to resist anything that the women wanted to do to her. Straps went over her chest and belly, fastening her to the padded, wooden plank. Another strap went around her neck, fixing her head firmly in place. She felt her legs being spread and her knees and ankles being strapped to a metal pole on either side of her. Once they were attached, the poles moved until her knees were brought up almost all the way to her belly and then spread widely apart.

Her pussy was now totally exposed and totally subject to the women's depredations. Violet imagined what might be in store for her. She had heard stories of some cultures where they sewed the women up, cut off their outer sexual parts to enforce chastity. She began to whine miserably. Straps went around the crux of her thighs forcing her hips into stasis. She began to pray. "Oh, God, did you spare my life only to force me to submit to worse tortures? Please help me, please!"

Xifang tested Violet's body to make sure that she was held absolutely still. There was one test that she knew was a sure indicator of her ability to move. She coated the wooden prong once more with the brownish cream and introduced it once more to Violet's sex. She brought it in slowly, running it in a little bit and then pulling it back, running it in a little more and then pulling it back, again deeper and then back once more, until it was sunk wholly into Violet's crevasse. The fucking of her pussy was having the expected effects on the woman. She moaned and her head shifted back and forth, her hips and legs strained at their bindings. She tried to arch her back. Even when she began to pant and moan in earnest, she was not able to move a single muscle below the neck.

Violet felt like she was being tortured by the fake penis. She could never remember her insides responding with such intense delight. It was as if she could feel every millimeter of the wooden prick as it traversed her canal. Her whole body except for her cunt wanted it to stop.

She tried to move her hips, close her legs, writhe her torso, anything to deter the instrument from electrifying her insides. Her body was incapable of movement. Her pussy, however, rejoiced every moment that the prick was in motion. She felt her orgasm building quickly. "Mmmmmmmm! Mmmm-mmmmm!" she moaned in protest. Her mind swirled with the sensational effects. It was like her pussy had subsumed her whole body, taken command. When she crested, the shocks of her pussy's contractions reverberated all through her. If she had not been strapped down, she would have been writhing and thrusting her hips madly. She could feel her thighs shuddering, but they had no where to go. She moaned again and again, loudly, "Mmmmmmmmmmmm! Mmmmm-mmmmmm! Mmmmmmmmmmmm!"

Xifang was satisfied now that the woman could not move. She was also satisfied at the effect that her salve was having on her pussy. She was looking forward to the next three days.

Nui had been busy stoking the fire. It would take a good twenty minutes to build up the right amount of heat. That was all right with Xifang. She had something she needed to do.

She crept between Violet's outstretched thighs. She had a ruler and a blue fountain pen. She took her pointer finger and laid it at the top of Violet's outer labia pointing down, and curved it so that it reached into the small entrance to the woman's tunnel. She placed a line on both sides of her outer love lips at the bottom of her finger across from where it intersected with the inner labia. Placing her small finger at the bottom of the woman's vagina in the same manner, she placed a blue mark on both sides at the top. She measured the distance between the two marks, making sure that they were the same on both sides. She put a blue dot in the middle of the two lines on each side and one just above the lower lines and one just below the upper ones. After rechecking each marking for accuracy, she put the ruler and marker away. Then she knelt and waited for the fire to get hotter.

Violet lay in her bonds in utter misery. She could barely put two thoughts together because of the drug the woman had given her. Her pussy still trilled from its coerced contractions. When the woman was poking and prodding her sex, she couldn't for the life of her figure out what the woman was doing except that she knew that it had something to do with her upcoming torture. After the woman was finished, she could sense the woman and the girl in the room, but they were being very quiet. She began to smell something burning. What could it be? Heat was emanating from an object not more than 10 feet away from her left thigh. And then it occurred to her: they were going to torture her pussy with burning fire as an additional punishment for her dalliance with the soldier!

"Oh god!" she screamed in English. "Please don't burn me! Please! I'm sorry! I'm sorry! Please! Please!"

Her words emerged as muffled phrases. She tried vainly to escape her harsh confines. Her most violent attempt caused the poles that were holding her legs aloft to sway slightly. "Pleeeeeeeeease! Don't do this! Pleeeeeease!" she screamed. The sound was a low murmur.

After that, she just collapsed into misery.

Xifang checked the fire and saw that it was ready. She opened the wooden box and withdrew six long pins. They had razor sharp, tapered points and then extended to the circumference of a pencil. There was a rubber coating half way up so they could be handled when they were hot. Xifang set their front thirds into the white hot heat.

Violet had felt the fire getting hotter and hotter. When she heard the woman moving around, she realized that whatever she was going to do to her was coming soon. She resumed her frantic moans and pleas. The drug was starting to wear off and she was fighting to regain full consciousness.

Xifang looked at the cooking needles and figured that they would be ready in a few minutes. They needed to be white hot for her purposes. She looked at the prone concubine and realized that she should probably give her another dose. Not a full one. She wanted the whore to feel what was being done to her. It would make her humiliation and shame so much more intense if she had a clear recollection of it being done. On the other hand, it would hurt like hell and she didn't want the whore to pass out.

Xifang crawled up to Violet's head and knelt next to her. She released the strap that surrounded her throat and pulled the gag free of the ring in her mouth. The concubine's distorted protests and pleas became loud as soon as the gag was removed. "Ouuuuuuu! Oooooou eeeeeeeeeee! Eeeeeeeeeee!" she shouted as her body convulsed against her bonds. Her raillery was ignored.

Nui crawled up the other side and while the young girl pulled Violet's head back to a 90 degree angle, Xifang poured half a dose of her potion into the whore's mouth. She waited until it was fully swallowed before reinserting the gag and binding her throat down once more. When the gag silenced her again, Violet broke out into heavy sobs. In less than a minute, however, her mind had receded to a placid place.

When Xifang went back to the brazier, she saw that the needles were ready. She took out a jar of antiseptic lotion that a European doctor had given her in Changsha a while back, rubbed her hands with it and then smeared it over the concubine's love lips. She then placed a thick glove on her right hand and plucked one of the needles from the fire. With her left hand, she pulled on Violet's left love lip near its top so that it was distended from her pussy. She paused while angling the needle just right and then pressed it firmly and quickly against Violet's labia just at the uppermost of the three blue dots. It pierced it and distended about an inch out the other side.

Violet screamed in pain. If her body had not been tied down, she would have been convulsing. "Ahhhhhhh-hhhhrrrrrrrgh! Ahhhhhhhhhhhhrrrrrrgh!" she called out. There was the smell of seared flesh. Her drugged mind was rudely yanked away from her reverie into terror. "What is she doing? What is she doing?" she thought desperately. "Oh, God, make her stop, please!" she called out from her gagged mouth. Xifang counted to three slowly and then pulled the needle out and set it aside.

The trick was to do it at exactly the right pace. If Xifang tried to do it too quickly, she could mess up the holes, align them improperly. That would destroy the esthetics of the final result. Also, there was just so much pain that an individual could stand at one time. She didn't want to drive the young woman mad.

On the other hand, if she went too slow, the needles in the fire might start to melt. It also prolonged the subject's agony. It was better to get it over as quickly as reasonably possible.

Xifang counted to five slowly and then plucked another needle from the brazier. She held up Violet's left love lip a little further down and pulled it from her purse. The second needle went in perfectly aligned with the first, about an inch apart, right on the middle dot. Violet screamed again. She tried to pull her ankles free, her wrists, her hips, thighs. Nothing would move. "Ahhhhhhhhhgh! Ahhhhhhhrrrrrgh!" she screamed again.

Xifang carefully punched six holes in total into Violet's labia, three on the right and three on the left. The poor woman screamed and cried frantically at each one. There was very little blood. The white hot needle cauterized the wound immediately. Once all the holes were made, Xifang took a little, pencil-thick tool and a jar of salve into her hands. She covered the steel tool with the salve and slid it through each hole, making sure that all of the seared skin was covered. She had a little bag filled with what looked like steel plugs. They too were the width of a pencil. They were wider at the base and had screw threads at the top. She placed one into each hole and then screwed a capped nut onto it. The plug would stay in place being too wide at the top and the bottom to slide out. When all six holes were filled, she sat back and looked at her handiwork. She could hear the concubine still moaning and sobbing from the pain. She would give her another dose of potion in a little while, a double dose. When she awoke, the pain would be just a memory and a dull ache.

* * * * * * * * * * * * *

Violet remained a prisoner of Xifang and her acolyte for three days. Not that she knew how long it had been. She was under the influence of the older woman's powerful potion virtually the whole time. Time lost its meaning. There were no windows with which to measure the passage of the hours. There was no regular routine to her meals or anything else. For all she knew, it could have been a week.

What she did know is that she had never spent so long a period constantly in sexual thrall. Between the older woman and the young girl, Violet was kept on a continuous, finely tuned sexual edge.

It had started some hours after her 'operation'. She still didn't know what it was for. She wasn't allowed to explore her own loins to feel what the woman had done and there was no mirror in the room. Every once in a while, the woman, or the girl, would remove the studs that had been placed in her labia, rub some salve in the empty holes, clean the studs with alcohol and then restore them. Afterwards, whoever had serviced her would, while her legs were conveniently spread, place her mouth on her coosh and begin a new round of sexual ecstasy for her.

During the night of her 'procedure', they mostly used the lotion covered, fake prick to bring her off. She was still ensconced in the frame that she had been strapped to during the maiming of her loins. One of them, Violet never knew who due to the fogging effect of the potion they kept giving her, would spread the tingly lotion over her sexual parts, even the ring of her rear entrance, and then would plunge the faux cock into her pussy coated with it. The feel of the instrument abrading her pussy's walls was exquisite beyond what she had ever experienced. She would cry and beg them to stop, the feeling of intense pleasure overwhelming. Then she would come and her whole body would reverberate with passion.

She only had a vague recollection of being taken out of the frame. One thing, though, she did remember very clearly.

It was during a period of relative lucidity. She was lying on her back on the soft, straw mat. Her blindfold and gag had been removed. Her wrists were still confined to the ring in the front of her black collar. The girl had brought her to the chamber pot to pee and had given her some fruit and some rice to eat. Her pussy lips ached. It was a radiating kind of pain and emanated from each little hole the woman had made. The hurt from each one joined the others in an unpleasant symphony of intense discomfort.

The older woman was kneeling between her thighs inspecting her handiwork. She had just finished applying salve to each hole and restoring the stud that occupied it. Violet was looking up at the woman's refined, but somehow man-like face. Her hands were on Violet's thighs, rubbing them. She was looking back into Violet's eyes as if trying to make a decision. Then, she apparently made it.

She began to remove her dress. The short sleeved garment buttoned up the front. When the buttons were undone, she pulled the blouse portion of it down her wide shoulders. Her two well formed, round breasts were revealed. They were not the firm and uplifted breasts of youth, but they had not yet started to sag and droop. She pulled the dress down to her waist and then stood. Violet realized that the woman was undressing so that she could engage in a sexual assault of her, and she turned her head in dismay. She was too woozy to do much else and her hands were still bound under her chin.

Violet turned back when she heard the skirt fall to the floor and the woman stepping out of it. She wore nothing underneath. Her back was to her, exhibiting her firm, rear cheeks and long, languorous, feminine legs. It was when the woman turned around that Violet got her surprise. She was sporting a long, thick cock in a rampant state of erection.

It was so disconcerting that when the woman, or whatever she was, knelt between her outstretched thighs, Violet tried to move back away from her by digging her heels in the mat. She didn't get far. The woman ran her hands under Violet's thighs and lifted them until her knees were high. The girl, Nui, who was kneeling beside them, found her cock and presented it to Violet's hole. When the tip begged entrance, the older woman pressed her hips forward and let the cock sink slowly within.

The sensation of the all too real prick abrading her still trilling canal was exquisitely pleasurable. Violet forgot, momentarily, about whether she was being assaulted by a man or a woman, and reveled in the ecstasy that the cock was bringing her. Her pussy had never seemed more alive. Its heat made it a far more efficient instrument in raising her lusts than the wooden cock. Violet groaned and shouted her pleasure into the room.

Technically, Xifang was a eunuch. She had no balls. Unlike Li Pao, however, her testes had been removed when she was eighteen, after she had reached puberty. That meant that her cock could do anything other cocks did except fill a honeypot with man juice. She had none.

She had been studying herbal remedies at a school in Beijing when she took a class with the great Shuang Xue. Shuang was renowned for her potions and was often called to the Forbidden Palace to administer to the Emperor's concubines and wives. At the time, Xifang was in every respect a young man. She went by the name Wu.

One day, Shuang asked him to stay after class. Wu was surprised when she asked if he was interested in becoming her apprentice. It was the offer of a lifetime. "*But,*" he said to the middle aged, attractive lady, "*I thought that you took only female apprentices.*"

Shuang laughed. *"Can you keep a secret?"* she asked impishly.

Wu nodded his head.

The woman spread her legs and pulled her dress to her waist. To Wu's amazement she sported a cock! He was dumfounded. Shuang explained that only women were allowed to administer remedies to the females in the Forbidden City. So, in order to ply her trade there, she had had to become a woman. She couldn't very well become a woman if she had testes, the male forces in her body would be too strong. So, her balls were removed. She developed breasts by the use of special potions that her mistress gave her. She grew her hair long, learned to affect feminine mannerisms and became, in all respects but one, a woman.

It had been so for as long as anyone could remember. Her mistress had started life as a man, and hers and hers, for hundreds, maybe thousands of years. One of their specialties had always been bringing passion to the women behind the Emperor's wall. How could you develop hunger for a cock in a concubine without having one?

When the Manchu dynasty was overthrown in 1912 and the Emperor's seraglio disbanded, Xifang, her mistress being retired, developed a kind of private practice in stimulating pussies in seraglios and brothels all over China. She centered her practice in Changsha, and often concubines, and sometimes whores, were sent to her from long distances to spend a few days having their pussies energized.

She had broken the tradition of converting males to half females in adopting as her apprentice the pretty Nui. The handwriting was on the wall as far as her niche profession was concerned. It was only a matter of time until the Christian missionaries and the so called 'modernizers' of China would do away with seraglios entirely. She couldn't justify asking a man to make the sacrifice of having no descendants under these circumstances. On the other hand, she had a storehouse of knowledge both as to herbs and as to pussies, and she wanted to pass it on. She had purchased Nui from a whorehouse in Canton two years ago. She had been impressed with her innate intelligence and all the questions she asked while Xifang was 'treating' a few of the other whores. Once she had fucked her, she decided that she had to have her and accepted her as part of her fee.

Xifang moaned with pleasure as she sawed her cock in and out of Violet's energized pussy. The concubine's hips thrust madly back at her each time Xifang's hips descended to bury her manhood deep inside her hot canal. Xifang leaned down and pressed her breasts against the supine woman's and then took possession of her lips. Violet welcomed her tongue madly, moaning and sighing her lust. When the whore came, her pussy clenched Xifang's prick tightly at the crescendo of each contraction. Xifang kept going, she could go all night. Although she had no sperm, she could still climax. She wanted it to build and build.

She was careful that her loins did not collide with the whore's injured love lips. That would have brought her out of her delirious, lustful trance right away. Her cock, though was relentless nonetheless as it plowed the whore's feverish cunt.

Violet was on the verge of her third climax when Xifang's cock began to throb and jerk within her. She groaned as the pleasure shot through her. Violet exploded an instant later and their mutual moans filled the room.

During the three days, mouths and hands, and Xifang's cock, kept Violet in a trance of arousal. She spent long periods with a hand or a mouth lightly teasing her quim or her nipples, or floating over the energized skin of her belly and thighs, keeping her just on the edge of sexual pleasure. Sometimes she was left alone to sleep fitfully. The lust driving salve was applied every two hours or so, driving Violet wild with sexual excitement. Nui or Xifang would cover the faux cock with the ointment and fuck Violet's pussy or ass with it. Usually, the other woman would have to hold Violet down due to her extreme reactions.

Every few hours, one of the maids would set down by the door outside the room a large bowl of hot water. Xifang or Nui would wash down Violet's sweat covered body with a special soap. Her skin would seem especially vibrant and alive afterwards. The sponge bath was always followed up by an intense orgasm administered by her keepers.

At other times, she would notice that the older woman with the cock had left the room and only the young girl was there to hold her prisoner.

Nui was a slight creature. Her breasts were petit and her hands and mouth small. She was no neophyte at passion, however. She had spent two years in the whorehouse in Canton after being sold off by her family, and another two as Xifang's assistant. She knew what the English concubine was going through, having experienced it personally shortly after Xiafang bought her. Since then, the half woman/half man herbalist kept her pussy well tuned. Several times during the three days, while the English whore slept, Xifang had graced her with her cock.

When Xifang slept, Nui was awake; when Nui slept, Xifang managed the Englishwoman's treatment.

There was one thing that Xifang did not entrust to her diminutive assistant. Every hour or so, she would take hold of the whore's cunt with her hand and administer a thorough massage of all its surfaces outside and in. She carefully and expertly massaged every area, even passing her hand fully within the concubine's canal, and especially concentrating on the area of the roof of her passage just beyond the entrance. This would be greatly to the concubine's benefit, as she would find out soon enough.

Her knowledgeable and experienced fingers pressed in, encouraging the flow of blood, exciting nerve endings, drawing the concubine's life forces towards them. It was a skill handed down through the years. Pussies that she handled in this way were never the same again.

On the morning of the third day, it was time to apply the final touches to Violet's sex. Xifang had just finished giving the whore a grand fucking. Violet laid on the soft mat, her legs splayed widely apart, her energies drained. She had been given a double dose of the herbalist's mind fogging concoction a short while before.

Xifang carefully removed the steel studs from the holes in Violet's outer labia. When that was done, Nui handed her the small wooden box that had contained the piercing needles. Xifang removed from it a thin, silvery, steel cable about 12" long. The ends were capped off with golden studs. She smeared the cable with her healing ointment and then introduced the ends, one by one, into the holes at the bottom of Violet's labia, going inside out. She crossed them and threaded them through the second set of holes inside out again and repeated the procedure for the uppermost holes. When she drew the cable tight, slowly and carefully, Violet's outer labia drew closed, covering up all that was between them.

Nui handed her the next and crowning accouterment. It was a heavy, rectangular, steel plate about ½ inch thick, four inches long and two inches wide. There was a little key hole on its face near the top. On the uppermost side, two holes had been drilled into it that ran through the plate to the bottom. Xifang carefully threaded the ends of the cable into the holes at the top and pushed them through until they emerged from the bottom holes. Then, it was a simple matter to pull the free ends of the cable until the top of the plate rested on Violet's pussy adjacent to the uppermost holes in her labia. As the cable was pulled through, a locking mechanism prevented the cable from being drawn back the other way.

Xifang looked on her handiwork. The shiny, silver plate sat atop Violet's sex. The golden tips of the cable dangled free at the bottom. Where it crossed over her love lips, it glistened in the lantern light of the room. No cock would ever cross the threshold of the English whore's pussy again without the permission of her lord and master or his designee, Li Pao. Only two keys existed. Without a key, it would be impossible to pull the cables out of the shiny steel plate. The only other way to remove the confinements would be with a hacksaw, a task that would take considerable time and effort.

Embossed on the plate in three bright, gold ideograms, running vertically, was the phrase roughly translated as, "Belonging of General Wang.," or, "Possessed by General Wang."

The arrangement of the holes and the placement of the cables had two significant features. At the bottom, a small gap had been left so that any fluids that accumulated in the whore's pussy could leak out. At the top, the clitoris had been left free and there was a gap large enough for a single finger to slip in. At just the right angle, a curled finger could penetrate Violet's pussy and caress the top of her canal. That was the significance of giving special treatment to that area. It would be particular sensitive to a finger's caress and would be capable of bringing the concubine to a high state of arousal, even climax. The point was not to deny the concubine all pleasure from the treasure between her thighs. The purpose was to demonstrate unequivocally both to the whore and to her master who could claim title to her pussy.

Xifang tested the gap at the top by inserting her pointer finger into it. The tip of her finger easily slid into the moist gash. She began to slowly massage the roof of the whore's tunnel. After a few moments, the beauteous concubine gave out a moan of arousal and her legs shifted. Perfect!

Now that Xifang was sure that her handiwork was fit and proper, there was one more thing to do. She unlocked the plate and eased the cables free from it. She unlaced the cable from the first two holes on each side, exposing the entrance to Violet's womb. Nui handed her three, round, silver balls connected by short silvery chains. They were slightly smaller than a ping pong ball. Xifang tested them. Inside each ball, which was slightly bigger than the opening to Violet's tunnel, was another ball, solid and heavier than the first, floating in a mildly viscous fluid. When the ball was shaken, even slightly, the interior ball knocked up against the inner surface of the outer ball, causing it to vibrate.

Ben wa balls had long been a staple of the Emperor's seraglio. They were used to keep the concubines in heat and to help tighten the muscles of their pussies. Also, when using the woman's nether entrance, the balls in her pussy would shake and collide, assisting the whore to reach orgasm. Even the slightest motion of the whore's hips would produce the desired effect. Xifang often had watched as the concubines in the Emperor's seraglio unconsciously rocked their hips back and forth, their bodies receiving a constant flow of pleasure.

Xifang slipped the silvery balls into Violet's vagina. A two inch long length of chain dangled from the front of the last one in so that the series of connected orbs could be easily withdrawn when it came time to penetrate her with a cock.

If Violet had thought that she had spent her time in the seraglio in a sexual haze before, she had not experienced anything yet. The salve that Xifang had been applying, and the careful and expert massage she had given them, was designed to wake up the nerve endings in the whore's tunnel. Once awakened, the use of the salve could be discontinued. Use of the pussy three or four times a week would ensure that the nerve endings remained at alert. If necessary, it could be tuned up every few months or so. Fucking, for Violet, would never be the same.

Once the ben wa balls had been inserted, Xifang laced violet's pussy back up. She locked the free ends of the cable into the plate and pulled it tight. It was time to show the whore what had been done.

Nui set up a mirror that had been kept in one of Xifang's crates against the wall angled slightly upwards. When that was done, the two women brought Violet to a kneeling position, her back slightly tilted away from the mirror. They kept her legs spread wide.

"*Wake up, little whore,*" Xifang said to her. "*I have something to show you.*" She patted Violet's face. "*Wake up, wake up,*" she said sweetly.

Violet had felt the woman doing something with her pussy, but had been too far gone to decipher what it was. She knew that it had something to do with the holes she had placed there. She tried to bring herself to alertness. Her pussy felt strangely tight. It seemed to be filled with something. A heavy weight rested on her love lips. It was all so confusing. She felt the tap of the woman on her face and she brought her eyes into focus. She looked into the mirror. She was aghast at what she saw.

Violet began to cry. Her hands were still joined in front of her and connected to her black, concubine's collar. The two women who had been tormenting her for days knelt at either side of her, holding her arms so that she could stay kneeling up.

"What have they done to me," she thought miserably. She saw the golden ideograms on the plate that hung down over her labia. She recognized the ones that represented general Wang's name. They were the same as on her collar. She guessed what the other one meant.

"Oh, god, what have they done to me?" she repeated. She squirmed in the grasp of her tormentors. "*Please take it out! Please!*" she said plaintively. "*Please take it out!*"

"*No talking, whore, or I'll whip you,*" Xifang told her sternly. "*Take a good look. No more spreading your legs for any man who desires you. This pussy belongs to General Wang.*" Xufang lifted the steel plate so that Violet could see her handiwork underneath. The light glinted off of the silvery threads that closed off her pussy. She drew her finger up the tightly bound lips, making Violet jump. It made her issue another moan. Her eyes were filling up with tears.

Xifang nodded to Nui and, with her help, brought the whore to her feet. They walked her across the room. Violet was startled to feel the vibrations in her tunnel. A wave of desire flooded her and she collapsed in the two women's arms. "What have they done to me?" she asked herself once more. "Ohhhhhhhhh!" she moaned with unhappiness.

Nui and Xifang walked the concubine back and forth across the room several times. When she was erect, the steel plate hung free of her loins, swinging back and forth as she walked, pulling on the cable with each step. Violet felt like her pussy was humming. The constant vibrations made her weak in the knees.

After three trips around the room, the women relented and allowed their charge to collapse on the floor. She rolled into a ball, bringing her knees together, and sobbed.

Xifang let Violet cry. She needed to get it out of her system. It was a frequent reaction to having a pussy bound up. She would get used to it. She would see, and Xifang would demonstrate to her shortly, that she could still get immense pleasure from her treasure. It just couldn't be penetrated by interlopers ever again. And, she would long for the presence of a cock to relieve her constant arousal. When her master fucked her, she would be properly grateful.

After a short while, Nui and Xifang rolled Violet to her back. Xifang had measured out a generous dose of her potion. Nui quickly took hold of Violet's cheeks with her hand and Xifang poured the potion into her mouth. Violet moaned with dismay. Nui clamped her hand over her lips to make sure that she swallowed her medicine.

They waited for about ten minutes for Violet to sink back into her stupefied state. Xifang rolled her back to her belly and raised her hips. She and Nui had remained naked for the most part during Violet's ordeal and Xifang's cock was at the ready. She pressed it against the dainty star between Violet's rear cheeks and slowly, but steadily began to penetrate her there.

Violet moaned with pleasure. The ointment that had been applied to her rear passage made the tissue there as sensitive as her pussy. She felt her pussy clench. When the woman began to fuck her, the balls in her tunnel rocked excitingly back and forth. By the time that Xifang's cock began to dance in her rear, Violet had come three times.

军阀 外家

CHAPTER ELEVEN

It was after midnight of the third day when Xifang finally released Violet to go back to the seraglio. She and Nui had washed her thoroughly, even dipping her long, brown hair in the large bowl of hot water that her been brought by one of the maids and shampooing it. After she was cleaned, Xifang had her lay on her back with her legs spread and unthreaded the cable from her labia. She gave her pussy one long, last, enthralling fuck and then stitched it up again.

Li Pao was at the door when it opened. Standing next to him was one of the maids, a girl named Shu. She was fair of face and had a curvaceous figure. For some reason she did not understand, the eunuch had made her undress and placed a thick, leather collar around her neck. Her hands were bound to it as if in an attitude of prayer. She looked nervously at the concubine as she was led from the room. Her hands were bound behind her and Xifang handed off to the eunuch a golden chain that was attached to her collar. She saw the flash of a glittering object dangling from the concubine's loins and wondered what it was. She didn't have time for a good look, however, because as Violet was led out of the room, she was dragged in.

The little maid shivered with fear when the door closed behind her. She looked up at the naked, older woman. Xifang had used her several times over the last three days in the sumptuous guest bedroom on the second floor. Shu had been shocked beyond all reason when, after the woman disrobed, she saw the thick, long cock. She had made her scream with it.

Nui brought the unhappy maid over to the apparatus where Violet's pussy had been maimed and made her lie down on it. She fastened her legs to the poles and strapped in her waist, chest, neck and thighs.

"*Now, Nui,*" Xifang said, kneeling down next to Shu's supine body, "*after I give her the potion, I want you to apply the lotion to her pussy and rear. Make sure the wooden cock is well covered with it before you slide it in. Then you can start up the fire again. Li Pao has graciously allowed you to practice on this slut. Once you mark off her pussy, I will confirm the measurements. Later, after you have pierced her, we will work through the manipulation exercises that I have shown you. At the end of three days, I want this slut to come any time anyone touches her pussy.*"

Shu had just begun to plead and cry for mercy when Xifang shoved the ring gag into her mouth.

* * * * * * * * * * * * * *

Violet barely noticed it when they entered the communal room of the seraglio. She had proceeded down the hallway in a daze, conscious only of the heavy weight on her loins that swung back and forth and bumping up against her bound labia as she walked. If the eunuch had not supported her arm, she would have fallen to the floor. Li Pao brought her to a halt outside the door to the inner seraglio and, after unlocking it, escorted her in.

Kneeling by the balcony window was one of the chaperones. She was dressed in a plain grey and brown robe. The room was dimly lit by the low light of a single kerosene lantern. The chaperone rose to her feet and greeted Li Pao with a bow.

Wordlessly, the eunuch handed off to the chaperone the chain that led to Violet's collar. She guided Violet to the hallway that led to the concubines' bedrooms. She didn't stop at the room that had been Violet's before all her troubles began, but went on to one at the end of the hall. During Violet's absence, the rice paper partitions of this room had been replaced by regular plaster walls. A heavy, wooden door had been installed. The chaperone took a key from the pocket of her robe and unlocked the shiny, brass deadbolt.

The room was laid out like her previous bedroom. Violet's maids, Jinjing, Ting and Wen had been kneeling on the rug in front of the bed expectantly. They jumped up when the door opened and rushed to receive their mistress. They took her into their arms while the chaperone released the chain from her collar. Violet smiled and kissed them all. They each hugged her tightly and kissed her back. Jinjing released Violet's hands from behind her while Ting removed the bracelets on her ankles. Wen pulled back the silken sheet on the large bed.

A sigh of relief passed over Violet's lips. She was home, or what she now called home. For a moment, it was as if all her travail had been a bad dream. Little Wen even reminded her of Lijuan.

The moment, however, that she moved her hips to sit on the bed, Violet received a stark reminder that it had all been very real. The silver balls in her pussy collided and vibrated, sending her a small shiver of excitement. It reminded her of what the man/woman had done. Jinjing made a noise of alarm when she saw her trussed loins. The room was lit by a small kerosene lamp on a nightstand next to the bed. Ting brought it over and, after Jinjing spread Violet's legs wide, they all, astonished, examined Xifang's cruel handiwork. The chaperone, a small, grey haired lady with a bony face and deep set, black eyes, peered over the foot of the bed. "*I bet that hurt,*" she said. The young women were too absorbed with looking at the heavy plate and the shiny cable beneath it to give any reply comment. Ting ran her fingers over Violet's bound labia. Despite her exhaustion, Violet gave a little jump.

Violet went to place her hand on the thick, heavy plate that hung from her loins to examine it more closely. Jinjing quickly seized her wrist. "*No touch*," she said firmly. Sadly, reminded that the pretty, loving maids served also as her jailers, Violet pulled her arm back. She smiled at Jinjing and stroked her face as if to tell her that she forgave her.

"*Come on, come on*," the old lady said. "*Get her ready for bed.*"

The maids looked back at the woman and nodded.

Li Pao had provided special security arrangements for the wayward concubine. The maids produced a foot long, steel chain. At each end, the chain diverted into a little 'y'. At the end of each 'y' was a leather bracelet.

While Wen watched, Jinjing and Ting rolled the virtually comatose Violet to her belly and drew her arms back. They affixed the bracelets to her ankles and wrists. There were golden locks embedded in them and the ends of the bracelets made loud 'clicks' as each one was closed around a limb.

Ting brought out a narrow, leather belt. Violet was rolled to her side and the belt went around her thighs just above her knees. Before she pulled the belt tight, Ting had to raise the heavy metal plate connected to Violet's loins so that it would not get caught between her thighs. A padlock was run through the buckle, fastening the belt firmly in place. One key fit all the locks. Jinjing handed it to the chaperone. She put it in the pocket of her robe. When she left the room, she locked the door from the outside.

Li Pao was waiting in the communal room, and when the chaperone returned there, she gave the key to him. After he left, the old lady resumed her perch by the balcony window.

Violet, her ankles and wrists hogtied and locked behind her, let the harbingers of sleep creep over her. She was back in the seraglio; life would return to normal. Except for one thing. She was now more heavily embonded to the cruel warlord,

General Wang, than she had ever been before. His ownership of her loins was dramatically and irrefutably demonstrated by the heavy, steel plate that she wore.

But was it really? Her callous master could never erase Violet's memories of the man who had pierced her there with love in his heart. She had promised herself that she would never let his memory die. Soon, tomorrow or the next day or the next, General Wang, her master, her owner, would plunge his remorseless cock inside her. She would moan and sigh with pleasure, she was sure. But it would not be his cock that possessed her. It would be the cock of her lover, his spirit come to inhabit her earthly lover for the night.

Sleep was calling her. The willowy Ting drew off her clothes and crawled into the bed. She stroked Violet's brow tenderly, a tear in her eye. She then pulled the silken top sheet up over the both of them and snuggled up next to her. Wen lay down on the other side of her mistress. They were all asleep within a minute.

Jinjing knelt by the door. She would keep the first watch of the night.